I0607256

I should have left Las Vegas after the first murder. How far would I have gotten in seven days? It's too late to think about that now. I'm what the locals call: all-in.

I approach Dixie Mulholland in her office at the Channel Six television station as if she's expecting my visit. My steps are certain and steady—as practiced. She needs to accept me right away. I've heard being accepted is the same as being unseen. I hope so.

A couple of taps on the open door gets her attention. "Hello, my name is Adam Steel. They told me where I could find you."

Her office is stuffy, pale green, and windowless; a light flickers overhead. With a phone in one hand and a cup of coffee in the other, she studies me across a cluttered desk. "They who?"

"The girl in the lobby."

"Listen, leave your number with her on the way out. I'm late for a meeting—"

"I'm with the Nevada Department of Wildlife."

It's red-hot outside, over a hundred degrees, and my shirt is sticking to my skin. There doesn't seem to be a working A/C vent in the office. Her short blonde hair dances in the breeze of a small circular fan. "The department of what?"

"Wildlife. I'm working with Metro on the Werewolf Killer task force."

She smiles. All at once she's forgotten about her meeting. "Mr. Steel, is it? Come in, what can I do for you?"

Sin City Wolfhound

by

Rick Newberry

This is a work of fiction. Names, characters, places, and incidents are either the product of the author's imagination or are used fictitiously, and any resemblance to actual persons living or dead, business establishments, events, or locales, is entirely coincidental.

Sin City Wolfhound

Contact Information: info@thewildrosepress.com

Cover Art by *Debbie Taylor*

The Wild Rose Press, Inc.
PO Box 708
Adams Basin, NY 14410-0708
Visit us at www.thewildrosepress.com

Publishing History
First Black Rose Edition, 2015
Print ISBN 978-1-5092-0360-4
Digital ISBN 978-1-5092-0361-1

Published in the United States of America

Dedication

For Betty and Sam

Chapter One

I should have left Las Vegas after the first murder.

How far would I have gotten in seven days? It's too late to think about that now. I'm what the locals call: all-in.

I approach Dixie Mulholland in her office at the Channel Six television station as if she's expecting my visit. My steps are certain and steady—as practiced. She needs to accept me right away. I've heard being accepted is the same as being unseen. I hope so.

A couple of taps on the open door gets her attention. "Hello, my name is Adam Steel. They told me where I could find you."

Her office is stuffy, pale green, and windowless; a light flickers overhead. With a phone in one hand and a cup of coffee in the other, she studies me across a cluttered desk. "They who?"

"The girl in the lobby."

"Listen, leave your number with her on the way out. I'm late for a meeting—"

"I'm with the Nevada Department of Wildlife."

It's red-hot outside, over a hundred degrees, and my shirt is sticking to my skin. There doesn't seem to be a working A/C vent in the office. Her short blonde hair dances in the breeze of a small circular fan. "The department of what?"

"Wildlife. I'm working with Metro on the

Werewolf Killer task force."

She smiles. All at once she's forgotten about her meeting. "Mr. Steel, is it? Come in, what can I do for you?"

She puts her coffee cup on the desk and holds out a hand. When we shake, I feel an instant connection. She's attracted to me. I always know right off when someone likes me; it's a natural instinct. In any case, I don't mind her interest—it's mutual. I'm attracted to her scent: the hint of sweat, the trace of excitement on her skin.

My well-rehearsed smile makes an appearance. "I'm new to this type of thing."

"What type of thing is that?"

Lying to someone I've just met, pretending to be someone I'm not, and saying lines I've memorized. "Field investigations. I'm normally stuck behind a desk. I met with Detective Ramirez this morning, and he suggested I talk to you."

"Ramirez sent you?" She slips her cell into her pocket.

"Yes, ma'am, the task force is looking into the possible involvement of coyotes in the attacks. It's a theory, anyway."

She waves to the chair in front of her desk. I sit down, but stay on the edge of the seat. The small room reminds me of a cage. Nothing about it is friendly except for her.

"Do you have any ID?"

"Sure." I check my coat pocket as planned. "Damn, I left my wallet in the car. I could go get it if you want—"

"No, don't bother. Tell me about this coyote theory

first."

I dazzle her with my knowledge of all things canine: where they live, how they hide, and what they eat. I even break down the possible motives a wild animal might have for attacking humans in a crowded city: encroachment by civilization, lack of food, an attraction to pets…

"You think they're after pets?"

"No, not necessarily. But a small pet can sometimes catch a larger animal's attention, and a chase could lead them into a crowded area. If that larger animal felt threatened, it might attack."

"Interesting."

I nod. "It happens more often than you think."

"You know, Metro has never mentioned anything about the involvement of wild animals and, to be honest, the location of some of the attacks, like the one last week on The Strip, makes it kind of hard to believe—"

"The task force is working on so many theories right now; this is just one of them. I was called in sort of last minute." I check over my shoulder to make sure the door is still open. Are reporters always this suspicious, or is it just her? I force another rehearsed smile her way.

She's silent for a moment then picks up the desk phone and dials. "This is Dixie Mulholland at Channel Six. I need to speak to Detective Ramirez, please. He is? Ask him to call me later, would you? Oh, and tell him thanks. He'll know." She hangs up and stares at me with wide eyes. "Coyotes," she says with a nod, "sounds like an interesting theory, and you really do know your stuff. What else can you tell me?"

"Oh, I've only scratched the surface. You know attacks on humans in populated areas are not without precedent."

"I don't mean to be rude," she says as she rises, "but do you mind if we continue this in the coffee shop next door? It's almost noon and I'm starving."

"Sure, no problem." I like the idea. At least if the detective calls back she'll be away from the telephone.

When I stand up and turn for the door, the phone rings.

"I gotta take this, won't be a minute."

I lean against the wall just outside her office. It's called eavesdropping. Finely-tuned hearing is not one of my natural abilities so I listen as hard as I can while shooting a glance down the hall to the exit sign. It's about twenty feet away.

"This is Dixie. No, I can't make the meeting today. Yes, I read the e-mail about the hotel room. Yes, I know it's reserved for VIPs only. I gotta go."

She steps out of her office and smiles. "Ready?"

"I could come back if you're busy. That sounded important."

"Oh, don't worry about it. There's always so much drama around this place it reminds me of a high school play. Apparently, the station has reserved a suite at the New York New York hotel for VIP guests for the fight this weekend. They want to remind us "little people" it's not for our own private use." She laughs and nods toward the exit. "C'mon, are you hungry?"

We talk at length in the coffee shop—well, she does most of the talking sometimes speaking so fast she has to force a breath. That's fine by me. Maybe I'm too hard on myself, but my social skills are rusty at best, especially the ones I haven't rehearsed. So I sip an excellent cappuccino, munch on a sweetly glazed scone, and wait for the opportunity to steer the conversation my way.

"Everyone in the country is watching Vegas right now. I don't know if you know this, but I'm the one who coined the term Werewolf Killer. The networks love it—everyone's using it. And now the police are starting to see the light."

"You mean they really *are* looking for a—"

"A werewolf? No, of course not," she says with a laugh. "What I meant was, the media shouting Werewolf Killer every five minutes has quite an effect on everyone, especially the task force."

"I don't follow."

"Well, why do you think they called you in? The network buzz is so powerful the police are starting to look into any crazy theory, even coyotes. Sorry, no offense."

"None taken. So, is that what you want? To work for a network?"

"Absolutely. I mean I like what I do, and I'm good at it. Sure, I've got my eye on the network. It's the nature of the beast, right?"

"The nature of the beast?"

"Oh, right." She laughs. "Department of Wildlife—beast. Yeah, the network's my goal. Why do you ask?"

This is my chance. "Well, I saw your report on TV yesterday, and it was outstanding. You seem to have a solid connection to the task force, more so than any of the other reporters. You must have a great relationship with Metro. Do they ever tell you things, you know, off the record? Information the public doesn't hear?"

Her smile fades, and she straightens up. "Hey, what's going on? Who are you with and why did you want to see me?"

"I'm with The Department of Wildlife."

"No one feeds me information. I've got my sources just like every other reporter. What are you accusing me of?"

"I'm not accusing you of anything, and I'm sorry it sounded like that. I think you're a great reporter, that's all. No wonder Detective Ramirez wanted me to see you."

It takes her a moment to calm down, and when she does, the excitement in her eyes is gone. "I'm sorry, I have to apologize. It's just that this case has made everyone jumpy, even me. I mean, when I stop and think about going on camera to report another murder night after night, almost like I'm giving the weather…it freaks me out, you know? And then when the networks use our station's feed—and all I can think about is what a great opportunity it is for my career, God, that's a bit twisted isn't it?"

I smile. Her honesty is genuine. She's definitely attracted to me; pheromones are a powerful force. "It sounds like you want this nightmare to end like everyone else."

She nods and takes a sip of tea. "It may do wonders for my career, but it's hell on the nerves." Her eyebrows rise. "So, the task force is seriously looking into coyotes, huh?"

"Yes, or possibly wolves."

"I didn't know there were wolves in Las Vegas. I'm from LA."

"Wolves used to inhabit most of the United States

until they were nearly hunted into extinction. Gray Wolf packs are now common even in parts of California, and, on occasion, they've been sighted in southern Nevada." Googled it.

"Really? You sure do know your stuff." Her enthusiasm returns. "I'm glad Detective Ramirez suggested you talk to me. What about an interview? You have been interviewed before, haven't you?"

"Me? No. Like I said I'm stuck behind a desk all day."

"Nothing to be afraid of. It'll be over before you know it."

That's what I'm afraid of. "I don't think I'm allowed to give an interview unless it's approved by the department first."

"Nonsense. Detective Ramirez will approve it. He sent you to me, right?"

"Right, but I really should check with him first."

"Okay, Mr. Cautious. But I don't want you talking to any other stations." She holds out her hand again. "Deal?"

Before I know what's happening, she suggests we have dinner later tonight. She insists we go "Dutch" which excites me. I love to taste as many different foods as I can. I'm aroused by the way people prepare food using seasonings and spices, textures and colors. I'd never eaten Dutch food before and so I promise to meet her although, for me, promises are difficult to keep.

It's the nature of the beast.

****

Imitation is the sincerest form of flattery. I heard someone say that once and so I say it now, too.

Downtown Las Vegas is a twenty-four-hour magnet, attracting every type of individual you can think of: crowds of gamblers, sight-seers, entertainers, and, of course, people like me, with no place else to go. It's the perfect spot to blend in—to observe and imitate.

There's a small notebook and pencil with me at all times. It's second nature for me to draw anything and everything I find intriguing. Relaxing on a bench on Fremont Street, the pencil and notebook come out automatically and the drawing begins. Without thinking about it, a likeness of Dixie appears. It's in black and white, of course, but the colors are there, in my mind: lightly tanned complexion, pink lips, and bright green eyes.

After hours of browsing through gift shops, wandering in and out of casinos, and observing people, the neon signs spark to life, holding back the night. I relax under the giant canopy covering Fremont—known as The Fremont Street Experience. The light show under the covering goes on for hours; bright colors race by with accompanying music blaring from dozens of speakers. The show is amazing and sparks my senses with wonderful fantasy-like images—a wide-awake dream.

I glance at a sign above a gift shop that reads Time 5:45—Temp 102. My dinner with Dixie awaits and I head down Las Vegas Boulevard (it's not called The Strip this far north) at a quick pace.

We meet as arranged, outside Arnold's, just a few blocks south of Fremont. She pulls up in an outrageously gaudy pink and blue striped Hummer. The colors are amazing and a smile spreads across my face.

"I know it's a bit much," she says, glancing back at

the Hummer, "but I like it. Gets me from point A to point B in style. Where'd you park?"

"Uh…garage on Fourth. Shall we?"

We walk into the restaurant. It's smallish by Vegas standards, nothing showy, but the smells wafting from the kitchen grab my attention.

"Were you finally able to talk to Detective Ramirez?"

"Never got a chance. The case keeps him pretty busy."

Good. "That's too bad."

I keep one eye on Dixie and the other on the patrons around us. Having never been on a date before, I copy what they do: smile, sip water, and flip through the menu. It looks like basic American food to me, no Dutch treats at all. Not wanting to make Dixie feel bad, I don't say anything about it. She orders a glass of white wine. I stick with a cold glass of water.

"Can you imagine?" she says. "Seven murders one after the other. And the way it happens—the victims ripped to shreds, not one bit of evidence left behind. To be honest, I hope it really does turn out to be a coyote or a wolf. I mean, I can't imagine a human being killing like that."

Neither can I.

When the waiter arrives, I order New York Strip with baked potato. She goes with the salmon and rice and another glass of wine. I thoroughly enjoy the meal, despite the odd looks Dixie gives me when I snatch a few bites of salmon from her plate. I hadn't spotted any other people sharing meals so I apologize. She laughs it off. Just like that, it's no big deal.

She says I'm being too gentlemanly by trying to

pay for the dinner.

"No, I said Dutch Treat so let's keep it that way." She pulls out her wallet.

I finally understand what Dutch treat means and feel a little foolish. As we leave, she tucks her hand through my arm, and we stroll outside as natural as can be.

"That was fun," she says. "What about a night cap? There's a place we go to sometimes after work just down the street. We can discuss that interview."

"I'm really sorry, but I have to run."

She stares at me. To break the awkward silence I say thank you, put my arms around her, and give her a quick hug. She hugs back.

I want to stay and try a night cap, whatever that is, but I really do have to run. The familiar tingling in the back of my neck and the wet paste of sweat across my forehead has begun. I want to put my arms around Dixie again; feel her warmth, breathe her in, but it's too late. So I run.

Chapter Two

Dixie popped the DVD into the machine. “Watch this.”

Aunt Rose adjusted her spectacles, leaned forward, and peered at the screen.

Dixie hit “play” on the remote. After reading a brief statement, Sheriff Gale Hendrickson moved away from the podium, doing his best to ignore the reporters. He stopped as a short blonde in a green dress blocked his path.

“Sheriff Hendrickson, Dixie Mulholland, Channel Six News. Can you tell us if the victim has been identified?”

“That information is being withheld pending notification.” The sheriff pressed forward a few more paces. Dixie held her ground. Questions aimed at the sheriff sped over her like low flying darts.

She shouted above them, “Is this the latest victim of the Werewolf Killer?”

Sheriff Hendrickson paused and glared down at her. “Metro does not recognize that term. If you’re asking if this is part of our on-going investigation…I’m afraid that information is also being withheld.”

She turned her back on the sheriff and faced the camera. “Sheriff Hendrickson is neither confirming nor commenting that the woman found earlier this morning—”

Dixie paused the video. "You see that, Aunt Rose? Instead of saying 'neither confirming nor denying' you say 'neither confirming nor *commenting*.' I saw Jenny Cole do that on CBS. That makes it look like the person I'm questioning has something to hide."

"Does the sheriff have something to hide?"

"Beats me."

Dixie hit "play." "Near Calloway Park in Summerlin is the latest victim of the Werewolf Killer. Although I have yet to speak with Detective Marco Ramirez, Metro's lead investigator on the special task force, my sources tell me this morning's homicide victim had indeed been brutally mauled as had the eight previous targets of the Werewolf Killer."

The screen on the television split, shared now by anchorman Peter Hudson in the studio.

"I hate it when they do that," Dixie said over the TV sound, "they make Peter look like he's the one in control, you know?"

"Whoa, Dixie," Hudson's voice boomed, "so you're saying this could be the ninth victim of the Werewolf Killer?"

She hit "pause." "Right, Peter, nine comes after eight. Counting's fun, isn't it? That's what I should have said. Sorry, but I belong behind that anchor desk and you know it."

"Of course you do, sweetie," Aunt Rose said as she pulled the remote from Dixie's hands and turned off the TV.

"The networks are covering this," Dixie said "And who do you think they're watching? A field reporter covering briefings where the police are saying absolutely nothing or that hair sprayed suit Peter

Hudson? You know I'm the one who came up with the term Werewolf Killer—right on the spot, no script, made it up just like that. Now everyone's using it, even the networks."

"Yes, I know, you remind me every time I see you."

"Not only that, I'm the one with the sources."

"Yes, dear, you told me about Marco as well."

"Whoops, I shouldn't have told you his name. Nobody can know about that and I mean nobody. He'll lose his job if anyone finds out." She checked her watch. "Whoa, speaking of losing jobs I gotta go, it's almost seven."

"Sweetie, you know I love you, so take some advice from an old woman. You and Marco broke it off months ago. Don't lead him on."

"You're wrong," Dixie said with a grin, "you're not old."

"I'm serious. You said he's giving you information that could cost him his job. Now, why would he do that?"

"Believe me it was his idea. He thinks the public should know more than they're being told. I didn't ask him for any special favors, and I'm definitely not leading him on. He's just cooperating with the press, that's all."

"Not the press, sweetie, only you. Just be careful." Aunt Rose shuffled close and hugged her niece. "I don't want you or Marco to get in any trouble. I like him."

"I do, too."

"Then why did you stop dating?"

Dixie grabbed her purse and edged toward the door. "It's complicated, but we're still friends. Besides, there could be someone new on the horizon."

"So soon?"

Really? Four months is soon?

"Tell me who this someone new is."

"I met him a couple days ago. He's really nice, a little shy at first, but very friendly. He's tall, adorable, and in great shape—fit, you know? I might bring him by sometime to meet you, but I really gotta go."

"No, you've still got plenty of time, stay and tell me more."

"Sorry, maybe next time."

"Next time, always next time. Why don't you miss work tonight and stay here? There's something I need to tell you—"

"Miss work? Haven't you been listening? The networks are in town. This Werewolf Killer story is what careers are made of."

"Of course I've been listening to you. So, why don't you stay here and we'll talk about your career?"

"You want to talk about my career?"

"Uh, well—why not tell me more about your new friend."

"Sorry, no can do. But as we say in the news business," Dixie opened the front door, turned, and smiled from the porch as the screen door clanged, "details to follow. But I'll give you a teaser: his name is Adam."

****

Steel is my given name. The Alpha named us as we were born: Steel, Mikael, Flynn, Lucy, Ivan, Bane, and Nina. Our mother, pregnant by curse, a rumor among my siblings, died giving birth. That was four years ago—twenty-eight in human years. We are Giant Irish

Wolfhounds, the largest breed of canine in the world. We are also human.

As a human, the first sign of the coming transformation is a tingle in the back of my neck. I recognize this tingle and know I have to get home—the one place I'm safe during the change. So far I've always been able to make it in time. Sure, there have been one or two close calls, but if I can get within a couple of miles, I'm okay.

One word describes the transformation itself: pain. I feel my bones bend, cracking as they reform and adjust for size. There's a searing heat just under my skin, like I'm on fire from the inside out. I can't breathe and it feels like I'm being suffocated by a heavy coat of flesh. It's got to come off. I scratch in full panic mode with one single purpose: to rip every inch of skin from my body. Tufts of gray fur appear under the discarded sheets of skin. My snout elongates and fangs push through my gums. At this point, my vision becomes sharp and focused, but all the colors are now just shades of gray. This is when my human thoughts go dark.

Then, like an unwelcomed guest, pain calls again as I transform back. It drags me out of the canine world, snapping me into human reality. I scratch at the heavy blanket of fur and flesh. My breathing is a series of choked gasps as my bones reform and internal organs adjust.

The pain finally eases and I breathe deep, like coming up for air after nearly drowning. I lay still on the ground for a few moments, naked and afraid. As I emerge from my canine cocoon and rise on two legs, I realize, once again, I've changed into a human being.

The cycle is endless, from human to canine—

canine to human; an unpredictable pattern of change, a pattern over which I have no control.

One look around confirms I made it back home after my dinner with Dixie. The human flesh and torn clothing from my previous incarnation as Adam lie in a pile a few yards away. The only question is how long have I been a canine this time? A day? A week? I never know.

The sun is up, cooking the hard dirt in the backyard and turning my newborn human skin bright pink. I peek through the window into the den where The Alpha usually watches television or works on his computer. The house seems deserted, but I have to be certain. The pack is not particularly fond of me, and I'm in no shape for a confrontation. I'm vulnerable after transforming—hungry, naked, and weak.

I slip around to the front of the house and check the driveway. It's empty, neither The Alpha nor the caretaker are home, a good sign. The front door is always left unlocked, so I let myself in as quietly as possible. The door makes its normal screeching noise, but nobody comes to investigate, an even better sign.

Carl, the caretaker, a wiry old man with graying hair and cloudy blue eyes, always makes sure there are plenty of clothes in the living room for community use. I soon find a pair of jeans, a button-up shirt, socks and shoes. The Alpha may be the leader of the pack, but Carl sees to our basic needs.

Of the entire pack, I'm the only one who loves to venture into the human world; attempting to assimilate, trying to blend. Lucy and Ivan accept their human side to some degree, but the rest of the pack despises walking on two legs. They don't say as much, but I can tell.

I've made it my life's work to study humans: their speech, their mannerisms, even their confusing sense of morality. But it seems the more I learn about human beings, the less I know about being human. And that's what scares me. At least I know something about Adam, I know nothing of Steel.

One night, The Alpha spoke to me in his den, a rare occasion. I tried to explain my fascination with humans. He raised a hand and stopped me. "Hah. Your interest in humans isn't a hunger for knowledge. It's just hunger." He laughed, like it was a joke. I didn't understand at first. Then the murders began, and so did my questions.

Does The Alpha know something about me, about an instinct I'm unwilling to accept? Has he taught me, trained me to do unspeakable things as a wolfhound, things I can't remember when I'm human?

That's when I began to pay particular attention to the nightly news. I watched it from the backyard, through the window over The Alpha's shoulder. He seemed just as interested in news about the Werewolf Killer, and that horrified me. So I formulated my plan to meet Dixie and gain her trust, and her help.

I make my way to the kitchen and open the fridge in search of water, food, anything to fill the crater in my stomach. It's jammed with packages of raw meat and not much else. The smell disgusts me. I grab a bottle of water and drain it in a couple of gulps. There's a loaf of bread on top of the fridge and some peanut butter in a cupboard so I make a sandwich and devour it followed by another bottle of water. It isn't much, but it'll have to do.

Money is the tricky part. The Alpha always has cash tucked away for use by the caretaker. I've learned most of his hiding places, and he's gotten better at concealing it. I check through kitchen cupboards, dresser drawers, and linen closets. There's nothing in the usual places so I decide to try the den; his domain—The Alpha's lair. It always unnerves me to be in his den, only a handful of times, and never uninvited, so I enter like a thief.

Paintings hang on the walls, the only room in the house with any kind of artwork. A bookshelf fills one wall entirely and opposite that, a fireplace with a huge, ornately carved mantel on which sit candle holders, small marble statutes, and glass vases. A grandfather clock in the corner ticks away the time, reminding me I'd better get on with it. I cross the room to the computer desk and rifle through the drawers being rewarded by the discovery of six crisp twenty dollar bills tucked deep inside the center drawer.

A newspaper on the desktop grabs my attention; the headline chills my blood. Plucking up the paper, I check the date against a calendar on the desk. It confirms two nights have passed since my dinner with Dixie. The article terrifies me:

WEREWOLF KILLS AGAIN

"For the second night in a row the so-called Werewolf Killer has claimed a life. The latest victim, found early yesterday morning in Summerlin, follows the previous night's attack near McCarran Airport..."

The grandfather clock gongs and I jump. I toss the newspaper back on the desk as peanut butter churns in my stomach. The sprawling six-bedroom house smells old, a ruin of mold and dust, collecting in my lungs. I want to run outside, but I need to check one more room first. I don't know what I expect to find in the basement, but I'm drawn to it in an almost morbid scene-of-the-crime type curiosity.

The stairwell is not lit, forcing my hands on the wall to feel my way down. At the bottom of the stairs is a hardwood door locked by a deadbolt. I turn the bolt, and ease the door open. The usual stench of feces and urine festers out, making me gag. The room is black, no air conditioning and no windows. Before turning on the light, I try to convince myself to turn around, go back upstairs, and leave. But I can't. I need to see it, to remind myself of how The Alpha treats his pack.

I flip on the light, a bare bulb hung by a chain, and stare at the cages lined up in a row against the far wall. The cages are small, made of wire with slide bolts on the gates. No water bowls, no food, nothing but hard cement and rusty wire.

I switch the light off and turn away. Before the door shuts a noise crawls into my ear. A sniffing, a whimper? My heart double-thumps and I throw the light back on. There's no movement, the basement is quiet, covered in shadows. With a tentative step, I amble forward, using slow cautious steps. I peer into each cage as I sink deeper into the basement. In the far corner, in the cage farthest from the door, I see a form. An outline of fur. It's Lucy. She doesn't move; she can't, the cage is that small.

I lift the latch and open the gate. Her head jerks up and she turns to me, her lips pulling back in a snarl. Even though we're on good terms when we're both human, she's not human now. I can't leave her here. She doesn't deserve this—no one does.

I run back to the door and climb the stairs two at a time, hoping it'll take Lucy a minute or two to wriggle out of the cage and recover her wits before chasing after me. She has no choice; I'm a surprise in her house, it's what canines do. Darting into the kitchen, I tear open the fridge and grab a packet of hamburger. I throw it into the living room at the top of the stairway to the basement. That should slow her down a little.

The sun is set to full burn as I race into the backyard and search through the pile of clothes I'd worn the night I had dinner with Dixie. The sketchbook goes into my back pocket. It'll take me an hour or so to get downtown. Two legs are not as efficient as four.

When I reach Fremont Street, I buy a bottle of cold water and sit in front of a slot machine in an air conditioned casino. Even though sweat drips from my face and my shirt is soaked with perspiration, nobody notices me. It's 111 degrees outside and everybody has their own problems.

I pull the sketchbook from my pocket and start flipping through the pages. My eyes land on the drawing of Dixie, making me smile, like remembering a pleasant dream. The dream soon fades, however, edged out by a nightmare: The Alpha is laughing at me, the private joke falling from his mouth—

It isn't a hunger for knowledge. It's just hunger.

Chapter Three

"Sheriff, Dixie Mulholland, Channel Six news. According to my sources, the victim of last night's attack at McCarran Airport was mauled. If that's the case—"

Sheriff Gale Hendrickson put his hands out, palms up, and shook his head. "Please, everyone just settle down." He pointed directly at Dixie; a flash from a still camera captured the scene. "Once again, I won't address rumors. I don't know where you get your information, Ms. Mulholland, but—"

"My sources also tell me an expert from the Department of Wildlife has been added to the task force. We haven't been told anything about—"

"There you go again. We have not asked the Department of Wildlife for an expert to join the task force. Now, if you'll excuse me, this briefing is over." The sheriff dove into the swarm of reporters and vanished through a side door guarded by two beefy Metro officers.

Detective Marco Ramirez followed him. He scanned the room and threw Dixie a questioning glance before disappearing.

"What the hell is that girl talking about?" the sheriff said, turning to confront him. They were alone in a small alcove just off the main hallway.

Ramirez shook his head. He knew Dixie better than

that. She would never go on air with unsupported information. “I have no idea.”

“The hell you don’t. She’s your girlfriend. You better not be the source she keeps bragging about. So help me, Marco—”

“Whoa, slow down, Sheriff. First of all, I have no idea where she gets her information. Second, we have no experts from the Department of Wildlife on the task force, and third, you know I stopped dating her months ago.” It was the other way around, she’d broken it off, but he kept that detail to himself.

Hendrickson exhaled a long slow breath, his expression turning from a cold stare to a calm gaze. The vein in the middle of his forehead just below the short-cropped silver hair stopped throbbing, flattened, and soon disappeared. “Follow me.”

To avoid the bottleneck of reporters at the elevator, they took the stairs, Ramirez following the sheriff to the third floor and into his office. He closed the door behind him and settled into a plush chair facing the sheriff’s large oak desk.

Pictures of the sheriff posing with various local personalities hung on the wall. All the usual Vegas celebrities—singers, comedians, and magicians—had autographed the portraits along with a line or two of well wishes and good luck for the sheriff. In a place of honor, just behind his desk, hung a large photo of the sheriff posing with the President of The United States. Ramirez often wondered about that particular picture; the sheriff mocked the president’s policies within his inner circle of friends. Well, politics makes for strange bedfellows.

“Sorry I lost my temper, Marco.” Sheriff

Hendrickson lit a cigarette, blue smoke wafting toward the ceiling.

"I thought you kicked the habit."

"It kicked back." He took another puff and stubbed it out. "So arrest me."

"Let you off with a warning this time." Ramirez crossed his legs.

"Marco, I need a favor."

Ramirez let out a slow and even breath. He had trouble playing well with that word. "Are you asking as a friend, or as my boss?"

Hendrickson grinned. "You're the best cop I know, Marco. That's why I put you in charge of this task force. I can trust you."

"I'm a little confused—"

"Hear me out. When I ran for sheriff, you were right behind me all the way. I appreciate that, but never showed my appreciation. You heard there's going to be an opening for deputy chief in a few weeks. I want you to consider it."

Ramirez didn't answer. "You mentioned a favor."

"There's someone I want you to talk to." The sheriff leaned back in his leather chair and locked his steel-gray eyes on Ramirez. "Sonny Russo."

"Say again?"

"He wants to talk, that's all."

"What does that thug want to talk about?"

"C'mon, Marco, the control board gave him a clean bill of health."

"Yeah, and before that he couldn't set foot in Vegas. We used to talk about cleaning up all the low-life filth in this town back in the day when we rode together, remember? And now you want me to talk to this crook? What gives?"

"Nothing. Look, I know how you feel about Russo and his pals. Sure, I used to feel the same way, but you have to admit, we were pretty green and naïve back in the day. He speaks for the owners on The Strip now and that carries a lot of weight in this town." Sheriff Hendrickson stood up, sauntered around his desk, and perched on the edge of it. "The owners are nervous about this situation, and Russo needs to make it look like he's doing something about it. I understand your position, but these are the kinds of things you're going to have to deal with down the road."

"Listen, about that opening for—"

"Hear me out first. Russo didn't want to talk to anyone but you. He has a real interest in the progress of the investigation. I think you'll change your mind about the man once you meet him. Listen, tomorrow I'm doing an interview at your girlfriend's…uh, ex-girlfriend's station. I've been doing so many damn interviews lately so I could really use your help."

"Okay, okay," Ramirez said, hands up in mock surrender. "I give up. When and where?"

"Good, six p.m. tonight at The Grotto."

Ramirez stood and turned for the door.

"Thanks. I'll call Sonny and tell him you're coming."

Sonny? Strange bedfellows, indeed.

****

Two days ago, Dixie and I chatted as we ate dinner. My first date. I often wonder what my life would be like if I were fully human; no transformations, no pain. Now I know. I want it to be just like that night with Dixie: dinner with a friend, good food, conversation. She's definitely gotten under my skin, and I can't wait to see her again.

She's standing in the newsroom with her back to the wall under the big red, white, and blue KLVA banner: *News You Can Trust From People You Can Trust*

I know it's just a slogan, a sign designed by an ad agency for the station, but I tend to look for those kinds of signs. I don't know if I believe in a higher power—a God, or Supreme Being—but I do believe in nature, in instinct, and in the universe. This looks like a clear sign to me, an indication that I'm on the right path: *People You Can Trust*—I like this sign.

"Hello."

"Well, if it isn't the elusive Mr. Steel. Nice of you to drop by."

Dixie seems calm enough, but my natural instincts are on alert. She's upset about something, so I take a guess. "I have to apologize. I'm sorry I had to leave so abruptly after dinner the other night."

"Abruptly? No, not abruptly, you took off so fast I thought you were being chased by Metro. Speaking of which, how are things down at Metro? How's the task force?"

Before I can answer, she darts away from the *People You Can Trust* sign. At first, I think she's going to her office, but she makes a left down the hallway and we wind up in the middle of a big control room filled with people. The lights are dimmed, and my eyes have to adjust to the darkness. Conditioned air rushes in through large vents in the ceiling filling the room with a whooshing sound. I feel like we're surrounded by faceless eyes examining us over computer monitors.

"Well, mister," she whisper-shouts, her eyebrows raised, voice shaky, "what's the deal?"

"The deal?" I whisper too, following her lead. "What do you mean?"

"I spoke to my boss yesterday and told him all about the latest theory the task force is working on, you know, the *coyote theory*. He originally had me scheduled to interview Sheriff Hendrickson tomorrow night, one on one—an exclusive—great exposure. But since I opened my big mouth, he wants me to follow up on the coyote theory instead. He gave the sheriff's interview to Peter Hudson."

"That's okay with you, right?"

"Oh sure, great, fine and dandy."

I swallow, hard. This is leading somewhere and I don't think it's a second date. I once watched a documentary on The Discovery Channel about a volcano on the island of Pago; everybody knew it was going to erupt. Still, some of the locals were so stubborn they refused to evacuate. Right now, I feel like one of those locals. They all perished.

"Detective Ramirez called me this afternoon, and guess what?"

Uh-oh, she's about to blow.

"There *is* no coyote theory. He's never heard of you. I called the Department of Wildlife and guess what else? They've never heard of you either." She pulls her phone out of her pocket. "Did you think I wouldn't check your story out? I'm a reporter—it's what I do. Last chance to tell me the truth before I call the police. Who are you?"

"I'm…uh…"

"Cat got your tongue?"

I glance around the room. "What do you mean by that?"

She hits a few numbers on her phone and brings it to her ear.

I back up a little.

"Running away again?"

"No." I stop and face the molten lava. "I need to tell you something. I wanted to the other night, but…"

"But what?"

"I didn't tell you because…because I've never told anyone who I really am."

"Don't bother. Mr. Steel, I know who you are."

She must be a very good reporter.

"You're a stalker—a fraud—a news groupie."

"What? No, that's not even close." I need to say something, anything that'll make her hang up the phone and listen to me, so I just blurt it out in a voice that turns everyone's attention my way: "I know who the Werewolf Killer is."

She eases the phone down from her ear in one smooth, calm motion. Her eyes bore into mine as she says, "Go on."

"Nine-one-one." A faint tin-can voice rises from the phone clutched in her hand. "What is the nature of your emergency?"

"Hang up the phone first. Please."

Dixie ends the call with the swipe of a shaking finger. Her eyes lock onto mine. "Okay, who's the Werewolf Killer?"

She's nervous, unsure of me and hesitant. But she's a reporter and wants a story—she wants *this* story—and she's not going to let fear stand in her way. I admire her conviction. Now the tricky part: avoiding mine. "I'll tell you everything, but not here."

"Why?"

Because you'd panic and call the police and I'd be locked up. "Because those are my terms. We go someplace private and talk, or I don't talk at all. Period."

Her eyes become cold, icy slits. It takes a few seconds before she says, "You don't know anything. Period." She brings the phone back up and redials.

"Believe me, you'll want to hear what I have to say."

"This is Dixie Mulholland calling from KLVA. There's someone here who's wanted by Metro. His name is Adam Steel."

I bolt out of the control room.

"It's too late," she yells after me. "The police are on their way. If I were you—"

Her voice fades into the background as I hustle down the hallway to the exit. I can't believe she ratted me out to the cops. What happened to PEOPLE YOU CAN TRUST?

Sometimes humans talk in code, they say one thing, but mean another. They tell mis-truths, untruths, and half-truths. They make up names for lying, names like deceptions, white lies, or fibs. In the canine world, that can get you into a lot of trouble. Maybe I shouldn't have lied to Dixie when I first met her. That must have been my human side. I still need her help now more than ever, but next time I'll have to rely on the canine in me to get it.

Chapter Four

Detective Marco Ramirez stepped out of the private elevator into the chilly air of the penthouse suite. Stainless steel doors eased shut behind him. The massive floor to ceiling glass walls offered a postcard view of the Las Vegas valley forty floors below; a dizzying mix of multi-colored neon, endless lines of yellow streetlights, and the sun's orange glow as it dipped behind the Spring Mountains. Ramirez felt queasy and sucked in a lungful of cold air to clear his mind. From this height, the city seemed quiet. A serene, peaceful place where crime was unknown and killers didn't exist, a sinless city.

Classical music drifted through the cavernous room. It was a familiar melody—one he'd heard a thousand times before, but would never be able to name. His steps echoed on the bone-colored tile as he made his way toward a white settee in the center of the room. His fingers ran along the smooth leather.

"Picked it up in Italy," a coarse voice said. "Italy" came out "Itly."

Ramirez turned to face the speaker. His gaze bounced off Sonny Russo and landed on the woman standing beside him. The blonde could have been a model, dressing the part in an iridescent evening gown hugging her body like plastic wrap. Her bare shoulders were tanned, her tanned feet bare.

Russo chuckled. "If you want, I can get you one, too."

"Excuse me?"

"The couch. Gorgeous picked out the color. I woulda preferred brown myself, it hides the stains better, but she said white complemented the room. What the fuck is that, huh?" He turned to the woman and with a finger stroking her naked shoulder said, "Listen, Gorgeous, we guys gotta talk. Why don't you go do your face?"

With that, the woman called Gorgeous slipped out of the room. Ramirez kept his eyes on her until she strolled out of sight.

"So, what about it, Detective…you want one?"

"The couch? No thanks. No place for it. My house is too small, in fact there's hardly enough room for me."

"Hah."

The sound could have been a lot of things, but Ramirez decided "hah" was a laugh.

"That's too bad, Detective. The thing hugs your ass like a pro. Go on, give it a try." Russo motioned toward the settee, then strode around a baby grand piano to a massive bar near a mirrored wall. The mirrors reflected the glass walls opposite, giving the room the illusion of an open rooftop patio. "Whiskey, Detective? Or, maybe you'd prefer a shot a' tequila?"

"Are you profiling me, Mr. Russo?"

"Sonny, please. Everybody calls me Sonny."

"Whiskey's fine."

"Hah."

Another laugh? Ramirez sat on the settee. It felt like Memory Foam wrapped in butter-soft leather, amazing.

"Whiskey it is." Russo filled two tumblers and returned to the settee, holding out a glass for Ramirez. "Tell me about the Werewolf case."

With that, any small talk left the room. This was the first time Ramirez had spoken face to face with Sonny Russo. He knew him by reputation only as the most powerful man in Vegas. It was rumored he had ties to the Russians, Chinese, and Middle East. In fact, Metro had a running joke, if terrorists ever targeted Las Vegas, Russo's casinos would be the only structures left standing.

But the man's unexplained rise to power had come as a surprise to everyone. Five years ago, Sonny Russo ran numbers for the gangs in Chicago. Now, he ran a publically-traded company on the New York Stock Exchange; a legitimate business as far as the Nevada Gaming Commission was concerned. Ramirez wasn't convinced.

"Thanks for the drink. As for the so-called Werewolf Killer, leads come in every day. Our team includes the top experts in all fields of criminology. The FBI is giving us all the support we might need and—"

"Hah."

Maybe it wasn't a laugh, maybe a grunt.

"I'm not wearing a wire, Detective, save all that bullshit for the press. I want to know what's really happening. You must have some idea who the fuck is pulling this shit in my city."

My city? Ramirez took a sip of whiskey.

"That bad, huh? You know..." Russo marched to the window and faced the valley. "I've been looking at a lot of data lately; news reports, spreadsheets, stock prices—you know where this is going, right? Business is off because of that nut job. My people tell me it's off maybe six percent." He spun away from the window and scowled at Ramirez. "Do you know how much money that is, Detective?"

Ramirez shook his head.

"Millions every day…every day, Detective. I got three of the biggest casinos in the world sitting on that road down there and that nut job's sucker punching me."

The music floating across the room filled the silence. Ramirez thought it might have been Tchaikovsky, but he wasn't sure.

Russo attempted a smile. "I assume you know I speak for the rest of the owners? We want this thing to go away. We need to get the numbers up. Sure the Toretta fight this weekend is gonna help, but we want this werewolf asshole caught first."

"I understand—"

"Do you?" Russo's tone changed in a flash. Any discussion that might have been considered cordial jumped out the window, or was it pushed?

Russo pointed a finger at Ramirez. "You know why forty million people come out here every year? Why two million people live here? It's because of my casinos. Without my hotels, this valley is just another piss stop in the desert. Vegas is a playground, one big friggin' playground with twenty-four hour action—lose some cash, chase some tail, then it's back to the salt mines. Only, lately, some of my guests ain't making it back to the mines. They're winding up on a slab. And that, Detective, is bad for business. We need to bring the players back to the playground again."

Said the bully who rules the schoolyard.

"As I said, Mr. Russo, we don't have a suspect yet, but we're following every lead—"

"But you don't got no leads, do you?"

"Mr. Russo, do you have information about this crime?"

"Hah."

Definitely a grunt.

"Look, Detective, I'm not trying to be a prick here. I'm just a concerned citizen."

"I understand, Mr. Russo."

Russo raised an eyebrow. "Do you? You know, shit like this woulda never happened back in the day. Back then this psycho woulda wound up face down in the sand. Fast." He slid into the armchair across from Ramirez. "Now I know this ain't the good old days anymore, but something's gotta be done. What I'm suggesting is a little cooperation, that's all. Share your files with us and maybe my people can help clean this shit up."

A light *tap-tap-tap* sound on the marble floor turned both their heads. Perfume drifted across the room. Both men stood.

Gorgeous was taller in white high heels. "Sweetie, the show starts in an hour."

"Give us a minute, we're almost done here."

She smiled before tap-tapping out of the room. Once more Ramirez bent his neck, following her every move. As she disappeared through the kitchen, he drew in the perfume—an odd mix of cinnamon and roses. He turned back to see Russo's gaze locked on his.

"She's something, huh? Crazy 'bout them Cirque shows. Remember when Vegas used to have real entertainment? Now it's all this circus shit…acrobats in tights, fire and water, what the hell is that, huh? But the suckers can't get enough of that crap."

Ramirez looked at his watch. "Mr. Russo." He moved his head from side to side as he spoke. "You realize what you're suggesting is against the law."

"Hah."

That's it? Hah?

"Look, we're offering to help, that's all. You say you're following leads, that you got experts—experts in what, werewolves?"

"You're talking vigilantism. We don't want—"

"Vigilantes? No, just concerned citizens. It's a legit proposition, just a few honest taxpayers that wanna lend a hand. Give me a call, here's my cell." Russo produced a card and slipped it into Ramirez's hand as he ushered him to the elevator. "After all, there's no crime against helping the law, is there?"

"You do know Metro is just one part of a federal task force working this investigation? The team includes the FBI, Immigration, Homeland Security, state authorities—"

"You know, Detective…" There was no laughter, no grunts, and no "hah." "Like I said, there was a time in this city when nobody would'a pulled this kinda shit—back when the law had balls. Look, I get it, I feel for you guys, I really do. You're hands are cuffed by all the bleeding-heart liberals, you know, search warrants and shit. Well, my people don't gotta worry about that crap. Listen, all we want to know is what you got so far, and where we can help. Call me tomorrow." It sounded like an order as Russo pressed the elevator call button.

Ramirez couldn't help himself. "This is a nice

place you got, Sonny. But don't you think it's kind of isolated, like a prison? Do you ever worry about getting trapped up here, you know, like if the power goes out?"

Russo narrowed his eyes and ran a cold gaze over Ramirez. "Backup generators. Emergency circuits. State of the art. Don't worry about me, Detective. I'm safe here."

As the elevator doors shut and he dropped to earth, Ramirez felt an urge to punch the wall. Instead, he tried, with little success, to forget the scent of cinnamon and roses.

****

Dixie called me a stalker. She's partially correct. I'm a hunter, one of my crossover skills. I can track with the best of them. Not to brag, but my talent in that department is superb. I've found living in a crowded city poses no hindrance at all to my hunting skills. In fact, I've learned to use whatever's available to assist me in tracking my prey.

I wait across the street from the Channel Six Television Station's underground parking garage and bide my time. All at once, I see her pink and blue striped Hummer emerge from the cave-like entrance. With her scent fresh in my mind, I raise my right hand into the air.

"Taxi!" I jump into the back of the Sunshine Cab. "Follow that Hummer."

"Sorry, pal," the driver says. "I gotta radio the destination in. It's the rules."

I hand him two twenties to forget the rules, and he shuts his yap. The hunt is on.

Dixie lives in a cookie-cutter mini-mansion in Summerlin tucked into the foothills at the end of Desert

Inn Road. During the silence of the twenty minute drive in the back of the taxi, I wonder how I'm going to tell her about me. As the various scenarios enter my mind, I escort them out just as quick. Like I said, humans talk in code, but I don't speak the language. I'll have to be subtle so I don't terrify her, but I'll also have to be direct. Tricky. I've heard it said that honesty is the best policy. We'll see.

She parks in the driveway and sits still for a moment. I tell the cab driver to let me out a few houses down from hers. Apparently, he thinks I have to pay a fare on top of the forty I've already given him. I don't have time to argue, so I give him what little money I have left in my pockets. Every day I learn something new; now I understand highway robbery.

Staying low, I inch up the street and use the few hedges along the sidewalk as cover. I don't want to give her a chance to dart into the house before I can get to her. The element of surprise is on my side and right now I need to use every advantage.

She's got her back to the street, fumbling with something in her purse. I approach without making a sound, close enough to touch her.

She spins around and shoves a small black device at me. "Stop right there."

"I just want to talk."

"Talk to this." She waves the device back and forth, at the same time trying to grab the cell phone out of her purse.

"Is that a tape recorder?"

"Yeah, a fifty-thousand volt tape recorder. Step up to the mic." She has to juggle the device and her phone in order to dial a number. She's clumsy and the small mechanism she's so proud of falls to the ground making a zst-zst-zst sound.

I scoop it up and move in closer. She backs up against the Hummer, her eyes shutting tight. I'm trying to be polite and hand back what she dropped, but she acts like I'm holding a loaded gun on her. "What's the matter?"

"Help me." It's barely a whisper. She opens her eyes and fumbles with the cell phone.

I don't want her to be distracted so I pluck it out of her hand.

"Help me!" It's a yell now.

"Would you stop shouting? The whole neighborhood will hear you."

After a deep breath, she screams, "Help me!"

"Let's go inside." I say this while pushing the small device closer to her. It has an immediate effect, and she shuts her mouth. I wave it at her like she did to me. "Inside."

"Be careful with that Taser. If you hurt me—"

"I'm not going to hurt you."

"Careful." She pulls her keys from her purse and backs up the driveway to a small iron gate. She stops and looks up at me. "There are cameras all around my house. If you hurt me, they'll know it was you. You won't get away with this."

"I don't want to get away with anything. I just need to tell you something."

"Okay, go ahead."

"Not here—inside."

She opens the gate, revealing a small courtyard complete with water fountain, and a tiny house to the left.

"Which house is yours?"

She gives me an odd glance. "Which house? What kind of a question is that? That's a casita. You don't know that, do you? And it looks like you don't know what a Taser is, either."

"Sure I do." I've heard about Tasers, of course, but I've never seen one, much less held one in my hand.

She turns and continues through the courtyard to the door of the larger house. With a twist of the key and a push down on the latch, the door opens. We move inside. A small beep-beep-beep sound floats down the hallway.

"What's that noise?"

"That's the alarm," she says, "I'll kill it." She plops her purse down on the floor.

I stay close behind her as we move down a cluttered hallway. Stacks of old newspapers turn the narrow hall into a short obstacle course. I catch a glimpse into the kitchen at the various dishes and cups scattered on the table and countertops. The disorder reminds me of my house. She flips open a small plastic box on the wall. After hitting a few buttons, the beeping stops.

"Okay, we're inside." She can't stop staring at the Taser. "Please don't hurt me."

I toss the Taser and her phone onto the carpeted floor in the living room. I know she wants to retrieve the items, but I block her path. I'm much bigger than she is so keeping her in the hallway presents no problem.

"I'm going to tell you something. I don't expect you to believe me at first, all I ask is that you calm down and hear me out. I'm not going to hurt you."

She nods.

This is it. I need to tell her the truth, and I only hope she doesn't freak out. "Dixie, I have the ability to transform into a wolfhound."

Nothing.

"A canine, Dixie. I can change into a canine."

Nothing.

"I'm half human and half canine."

She isn't reacting and I start to worry. I have to give it to her straight—I hope she can handle it. "I have no recollection of what I do as a canine. For all I know, I may be the Werewolf Killer."

"Okay."

"Okay?" Not only does she not freak out, but her non-reaction to what I've just told her freaks me out. "What do you mean okay? Dixie, I'm a Giant Wolfhound."

"Sure, sure, I can see that."

"No, not now—I'm not a canine now. I'm human now."

"Yeah, of course you are."

"You don't understand."

"Sure, I do. You believe you're a dog. Got it."

I'm getting nowhere. "I meant to tell you the other day, but we hit it off so well I thought…well, I thought I wouldn't have to. I need your help to get information. For obvious reasons, I can't go to the police."

"Oh, don't worry, you won't have to go to them."

The way she says it strikes me odd. I follow her gaze to the plastic alarm box on the wall. After flipping down the cover, I see the words INTRUDER WARNING flashing across a little green screen. That is not a good sign.

A knock on the front door grabs my attention giving Dixie just enough wiggle room to bolt past me. She races down the hall and flings open the door.

"Thank God, you're—"

No one is there.

"Dixie, please close the door."

She turns to me with an expression that awakens something in my memories. I'm sure I've seen it many times before, but not as a human. It's a look that means: bad—as in bad dog.

"Get out of my house." The words shoot from her mouth. She steps outside and backs up to the fountain. I know if I don't leave, she will.

"Listen to me. You know I'm not going to hurt you. I would have already if I wanted to."

She draws in a shaky breath. "Get out."

I traipse down the hall and stand on the threshold. She backs up another step, almost falling into the fountain. "I know what I've told you is a little…out there—"

"Out there?" she says, her voice hard. I can tell she feels more in control of the situation. "No, being abducted by aliens is out there. You turning into a dog is *way* out there. Now, get out of my house. Go on, Fido—outside."

I failed to convince her of anything. In fact, she believes I'm lying to her, or insane, or both. I step outside and give her a wide berth, allowing her enough room to slip back inside. In an instant, the door slams. The noise of the door banging shut reinforces my failure. Not only does Dixie think I'm a bad dog, for the first time in my life I feel like a bad human as well.

I find myself alone in the courtyard. Or so I think.

Chapter Five

The Bentley Mulsanne—onyx paint, freshly waxed, shining alloy rims—powered into the driveway. The soft purr of twelve cylinders revved once then shut down. A man stepped out of the vehicle, tore off his shades, and slammed the door.

"Carl," the man called out. No answer. Even though the yellow van was not in the driveway, the caretaker sometimes parked it around back. The man shouted again, louder this time—an order: "Carl."

Still no answer.

He clicked the key alarm to the Bentley and marched toward the house under an unforgiving late afternoon sun. The house was quiet, dark, and hot. He strode to the kitchen and grabbed a cold bottle of water from the refrigerator. Sweat beaded across his brow, dribbling down the lines of his face in tiny rivers.

A woman approached him in the hallway just outside the door to the den; long waves of maple brown hair, green eyes, and shamelessly naked. She trembled at the sight of him. "Alpha."

The Alpha towered over her, outweighing the girl by at least fifty pounds. He punched her square in the face, sending her to the floor.

"Flynn," he shouted.

A heavy-set man, dark scraggly hair, dull with a face devoid of emotion, plodded down the hall toward him. He, too, seemed apathetic about being nude.

The Alpha pointed down at the girl. "How the hell did she get out? Never mind. Put Lucy back in her cage and then come to the den."

Flynn lifted Lucy's limp body with little effort and hauled her away.

"And where's Carl?" The Alpha shouted after him.

"Take pack for run," Flynn said as he continued down the hall, carrying the girl over his shoulder. "They go for run. I stay, like you ask. I watch house. Steel come in."

The Alpha rushed into the den and headed straight for the computer desk, planting himself on the padded chair. He searched in the center drawer. The money was gone. Besides setting Lucy free and stealing some cash, The Alpha wondered what else Steel had done.

He snatched the newspaper from the top of the desk, the headline grabbing his attention: WEREWOLF KILLS AGAIN. The color photo depicted a scowling Sheriff Hendrickson at a news conference pointing his finger at a reporter in front of him. The caption read: Local television reporter Dixie Mulholland surprises Sheriff Hendrickson with inside information.

"Alpha." Flynn stood at the threshold to the den, waiting, shifting from foot to foot.

"Come in."

Flynn's lips broke into a full smile as he raced into the room and hurried to The Alpha's side. He waited in silence, his body trembling. He rocked back and forth, his hands in constant motion running through his hair and scratching at his face and chest.

"So you watched the house as I asked?"

"Oh yes, I watch like you say."

"Good boy. I'm sure you did a very good job."

Flynn puffed up his chest and beamed.

"Tell me what you saw."

The heavy man furrowed his brow and stared at the floor as if searching for something. All at once, he raised his head and smiled. He used his hands as he spoke, big sweeping gestures, pointing, waving and signaling like an animated traffic cop. "Steel come inside. He change. He eat and come here, here in this room. He go to basement and open Lucy cage. He run away. Lucy change, she eat. I watch all this—I see with my eyes."

The Alpha put a finger to his mouth and tapped at his lips, an unconscious habit as he thought, staring blankly out the window. "Flynn," he said after a minute, "I have a special job, just for you. A very special job. Do you understand?"

"Oh yes." Flynn pranced and spread his arms like a bird about to take off.

"Good boy. Now go put some clothes on and hurry back."

"Yes, I hurry." Flynn dashed out of the room, heavy footsteps clomping down the hallway.

The Alpha knew he'd have to give Flynn very precise instructions, maybe repeat them once or twice for clarity. Flynn was slower than the rest, never quite taking to his human side, but once he understood what he had to do, he'd get it done.

Flynn rushed back into the den. He wore khaki shorts, tennis shoes with no socks, and a pink t-shirt which read: I (heart) You. The t-shirt stretched across his large frame, covering only half of his stomach.

The Alpha closed his eyes and shook his head.

"Tell me, Flynn, where is Steel now—right this very moment?"

"I go find." Flynn turned for the door.

"No, Flynn! Stay. Look with your mind. Where is Steel? Do you remember how?"

Flynn closed his eyes and shoved his hands into his pockets. He scrunched his eyelids tight, and took large gulping breaths.

"That's right, Flynn. Find your brother. Find him with your mind. Take your time."

"I find Steel." Flynn opened his eyes and grinned at The Alpha. "Steel in the mountains." He pointed to the west. "There. He is in—"

"You don't have to tell me exactly where he is. I'll drive you and you tell me if we're getting close to him, like a game, okay?"

Flynn hopped on one foot, then the other. "Like a game."

"First, I want you to change your clothes. Wait. I'll go with you and pick out something…different. Then we'll drive in the car and find Steel."

"Yes, oh yes. Get clothes and go see Steel. Like a game."

"Good boy." The Alpha patted Flynn on the head. "But listen to me carefully, okay?"

"Oh yes."

"You're not going to just see Steel. I want you to kill Steel. Do you understand?"

"Oh yes." Flynn nodded and pranced. "Get clothes and kill Steel."

"Make him dead. Do you understand? Make Steel dead."

"Oh yes."

The Alpha patted Flynn on the cheek. "That's my good boy. Hah."

****

"We've got a situation in Las Vegas, Nevada." Admiral Garrison settled back in his chair, the plush red leather crunching beneath his considerable weight.

Colonel Jon Dayton took a sip of coffee from the cup he'd been offered upon entering the admiral's office. Major Jean Ransom, Admiral Garrison's personal assistant, anticipated Dayton's needs. He appreciated her psychic abilities, and it made perfect sense: mind reading was an ideal skillset for her work at UNPAD; it also proved quite entertaining after hours.

"Once again, it's called telepathy, Colonel, not so much mind reading anymore," Major Ransom said, smiling as she spoke. "And I'm glad you find it so entertaining."

"Major." Admiral Garrison kept his comments direct and to the point, as did most officers in the Senior Service. "If you're quite finished with your one-way conversation, please shut the door on the way out."

Major Ransom gazed at Dayton, smiled again, and closed the door.

Dayton faced the admiral and shifted in his seat as he cleared his throat. "Las Vegas?"

"Werewolves. We've held back on this one, hoping it would have been sorted out by now, but we can't sit on our hands any longer. There's been a series of murders, each victim savagely mauled. The federal task force they've assembled to investigate is at sixes and sevens." The admiral opened a manila file and spread glossy crime scene photos across his desk. "Gruesome business. The forensic evidence is a bit muddled."

Dayton winced at the photos. "Werewolves?"

"Vicious attacks, each one taking place at night; no witnesses and not one solid clue. The press is calling this the work of the Werewolf Killer."

"The press? Admiral, are we investigating because of the media?"

"Certainly not, we're investigating because of the council. The director rang me just an hour ago and wants this top priority. Remember last year, the assignment in New York? The council wants this handled as promptly as that affair."

"It was New Jersey, actually. Vampires. It turned out to be a couple of teenagers on meth."

"Yes, well I think it's a bit more complicated this time, but that's the nature of the job then, isn't it? Look, Colonel, I know your view on our work here. You find it difficult to accept the need for our unique type of expertise—"

"Sir, with all due respect, I've never found anything that comes close to requiring our type of expertise."

"Still, the mandate is clear: to investigate every threat, no matter how curious. In truth, I wanted you on staff because of your misgivings, not in spite of them. I understand the importance for a skeptic on our team. It keeps us honest."

"Sir, I can't pretend to believe in what I've never seen."

"Then perhaps this case will change your view. Take a good look at the photographs and tell me what you see."

"Bite marks, hundreds of them on each victim, suggesting large canine teeth in a classic scissor pattern." Dayton glanced up. "Were the missing body parts recovered?"

"No."

Dayton picked up each photo, examining them more closely. "Claw marks, deep and jagged. In each victim, the neck is eviscerated. These poor bastards were torn to shreds. You said the forensic evidence was muddled. What did you mean by that?"

"This is where it gets a bit dicey. The police have collected evidence at each crime scene—DNA, hair, blood—but they haven't been able to classify it."

"No match in their database?"

"No match of any kind. The DNA in particular is an entirely new strain, never before encountered. They've tested their equipment, recalibrated, and re-examined. They've sent samples to the top forensic labs in the world: FBI, Geneva, Scotland Yard—that's when we got involved. Our lab is stymied as well. It's as if we're dealing with something so unique, so exotic: an unknown entity."

Dayton raised his eyebrows and deadpanned, "A werewolf."

"Exactly what you're being sent to find out—quietly, of course."

"Of course, sir."

"Your flight leaves Northolt early tomorrow morning. Here's the file." Admiral Garrison scooped up the photos and tucked them into a small attaché case. He slapped the top of the case with a meaty paw. "You'll find contact names, background information, all the usual, as well as a complete primer on werewolves."

"A primer on werewolves? Where does one even

find something like that?"

"Assembled in-house, of course. I suggest you use tonight wisely and study up." He pushed the case across the desk, past a green-shaded lamp, and around an engraved plaque: Admiral Reginald T. Garrison, United Nations Paranormal Activities Division.

Major Ransom waited near the door to her office, just down the hall from the admiral's. A smile played on her lips as Dayton approached. "Werewolves in Las Vegas, Colonel? Such an interesting assignment."

"One shouldn't eavesdrop on top secret meetings, Major."

"Eavesdrop? How pedestrian." She put a hand on his arm and led him into her office. "I envy you, you know."

His gaze wandered across her office to a bookshelf filled with supernatural volumes, both fictional and research. He glanced at her desk where a book lay open to an illustration of a large wolf's head. "A woman with true paranormal skills envies me?"

"Traveling the world in search of all things…different. Zombies, vampires—and now werewolves. It's got to be exciting work."

Dayton rolled his eyes. "Oh it is, Major." He traced his finger along the shape of her ear. "And every time there's a reasonable explanation for it. The zombies in Peru turned out to be a tribe of cannibals. The ghost in Australia was a well-orchestrated hoax. And the aliens in France? Let's not even discuss that plumb assignment." He kissed her lightly on the cheek. "C'mon Jean, you've read the reports; you know what I'm talking about. Believe me, there's nothing exciting about any of it, nor paranormal."

"And this werewolf?"

He frowned. "You know the bloody Yanks; probably just another sociopath—an average, run-of-the-mill serial killer on the loose."

"The admiral's interest seems piqued."

He lowered his voice. "If you ask me, the old man is a little too keen on the whole operation, as if he *wants* to find a monster in the wardrobe. Tell me I'm wrong."

"He wants to make a difference, to be prepared just in case. That's why he brought you on board: the best of the best."

"Sure, at fighting real enemies, not tabloid fiction."

"How can you be so negative? This is a well-funded division of the United Nations. The council sees a need for our services and so do I."

"Don't worry, Major. I'll go to Las Vegas and do my best to find out what's really going on. Beyond that…"

"Are you thinking of cashing it in?"

He leaned into her. "Suppose you tell me what I'm thinking? That is, after all, your area of expertise."

Major Ransom grinned. She closed the door and kissed the corner of his mouth. "Colonel Dayton, you should be ashamed of those thoughts."

"Oh I am, Major." He slipped his arms around her waist. "Dreadfully ashamed, yet, surprisingly undeterred."

She put her lips to his ear. "The admiral *did* suggest you use your night wisely."

He pulled back and grinned. "Do you really think I'm the best of the best?"

"Shut up and kiss me."

Chapter Six

"Flynn." It's all I can mutter before he pounces on me.

My brother is a large and powerful canine, but as a human he's clumsy and slow—almost uncoordinated. This fact doesn't seem to bother him, nor does it make the fight any easier. He knocks me to the ground with little effort, pinning me under his weight. My ribs ache, and it's hard to breathe. He lets out a snarl and leans in.

I put my hands around his throat and squeeze. He does the same to me. His eyes are blank, empty slits. He grunts like an animal, bares his teeth, and tries to bite at my arms. I feel raw energy coursing through his body, like a feral beast out of control. He lunges closer, snapping at my face. I choke harder, but it has no effect, if anything, it only enrages him. Even though he's in human form, he's not just fighting like a canine he's got the mentality of one, too. Giant Irish Wolfhounds don't back down.

I move my head, dodging his teeth as slobber splatters around me. With one kick to his groin, I shove his neck forward and send him flying over me. There's a loud bang as his head crashes into Dixie's front door. His body goes limp.

Her door is my line in the sand. I don't know what Flynn wants, but I'm not going to let him look for it inside.

He's dazed, but soon recovers, jumping back on top of me. My fist connects with his nose and he yelps. I throw a right and hit his jaw. He growls and flails his arms, using them like giant clubs against my attack. I manage to throw a fist past his blockade, rewarded by a painful bite on my wrist.

He's pummeling me now, using his fists like meaty paws. My head shakes from side to side with each punch. I throw my arms up and cover my face, but it does little good. Everything moves in slow motion. This fight is over.

Before I black out, I look behind him—past his vacant eyes—and see a vision.

There's an angel dressed in white hovering over us. The angel is not smiling, in fact, she seems angry that we're fighting in her presence. I know we're upsetting the angel, but there's nothing I can do about it—I'm too busy being killed. The angel raises her arms and a lightning bolt flashes out of her fingertips.

Everything turns bright white, then goes black.

"Wake up."

My eyelids rise like a curtain. Objects drag into focus as my consciousness comes back on line.

"Wake up." The angel's lips move and I hear the words a split second later, like a film that's out of sync. I'm in Dixie's house, sitting in the hallway just inside the front door.

"Where's Flynn?" My throat is sore and my voice cracks. "Where's the other man?"

"I tased him."

"You tased him? Where is he now?"

Dixie speaks in a quiet voice. "I heard a bang on my door and looked out the window. That man was killing you, so I used the Taser and dragged you inside." She closes her eyes and wobbles a little, looking like she wants to find a landing spot on the ground. "Then he…"

I help her down, feeling her fear in the form of tiny tremors under her skin. I'm sure it's not me she's afraid of anymore—she's found a new fear.

"Where did he go after you tased him?" Again, she's silent. "Where did Flynn go?"

"Who the hell is Flynn?"

"The other man. The one I was fighting with outside."

"He…uh…" She turns her head and stares at me, right through me, with cold, unseeing eyes. "He…ran away. He…uh…he."

I stand up, slower than planned, but finally manage to find my balance. With one glance out the window at the pile of skin and blood in the courtyard, I know what Dixie saw, and what she's trying to say. She struggles for words—trying to explain what, for her, is impossible to describe. She witnessed the transformation.

I watch her face when I say, "He changed into a canine."

There it is: the reaction I wanted when I first told her about me. She winces, shakes her head, and trembles. Her eyes find mine. She tries to stand using the wall for support, but only manages to stumble back down to the floor. I offer her my hand, but she goes out of her way to avoid me. After a couple of false tries, she finally gets up under her own power.

"Dixie, it's important. Where did he go?"

"I dragged you inside—I don't know why—and I

locked the door. He was killing you." Her voice is shaky, her brow twisted. "Why was he trying to kill you?"

"Dixie, listen to me, it's important." My head aches, but I force the words out, "Where did the other man go?"

"Everything you said is true. I looked out the window and…he changed into a dog—a really big dog. I think he's still outside." Her breathing is heavy and forced.

I take another quick glimpse through the window. There's no sign of him.

"He turned into a dog. How could he do that? No one can do that."

I try to speak in a calm reassuring voice, but it's difficult. Her fear has rubbed off on me. "I want you to think very carefully, please. Where did he go after he changed?"

"I think he ran around the house, to the backyard."

Right on cue, I hear frenzied scratching at the back door. Dixie turns toward the living room, but I grab her arm. "Where're you going?"

"To call the police."

"He'll be inside before you dial. Get your keys. We gotta get out of here." She's still confused and stands frozen in place. I shout at her, "Get—your—keys."

I tear the front door open and we bolt outside, running across the courtyard. She slows down, staring at the pile of flesh and clothes on the ground. I have to put my hand on her back, pushing her past Flynn's human remains.

The thump-thump-thump of padded paws, sounding like a race horse in the stretch, terrifies me.

Flynn must have caught our scent. He rounds the corner of the house and charges at us.

Dixie hops inside the Hummer. Whether she's forgotten about me, or decides to subject me to another beating and sure death, I don't know. The Hummer door remains locked.

****

Colonel Jon Dayton's military jet landed at Nellis Air Force Base at eight-forty PM local time. He'd spent the last ten hours in a seat designed to transport a man much smaller than his six-foot-four frame. His legs were numb, and his neck begged for mercy. Despite the physical discomfort, the ten hour flight had given him more than enough time to study the information in the attaché case Admiral Garrison gave him in London.

The struggle to pry himself from the cockpit was rewarded by a blast of 100 degree heat outside the aircraft, quite a change from the drizzly conditions he'd left behind. He climbed down to the tarmac and stamped his feet on the hard surface.

Dayton glanced back at the modified Tornado F3 and saluted the pilot.

A sedan eased forward, stopping near the wing of the European jet. The driver got out, giving Dayton a friendly nod and a wave. "Colonel, Paul Cuthbert at your service. Welcome to America."

"Mr. Cuthbert—"

"Cutty." The driver was lively, a young man's spirit in a thirty-something body. The long strands of bright red hair accentuated his friendly nature. "Everybody calls me Cutty. You can put your flight suit in the trunk, Colonel."

Dayton pulled down the zipper of his suit. The t-shirt and jeans he wore underneath were damp with perspiration. He tossed the helmet and suit into the trunk.

Cutty gave Dayton a toothy grin. "Ready?"

"Absolutely, Mr. Cutty. I'm at your disposal."

"Hey, love the accent, but it's just Cutty. Next stop: The world famous Las Vegas Strip. Ever been?"

"First time."

Cutty held the door open for him, and he slid into the backseat of the black sedan.

Dayton expected a quiet ride to the city. He knew Cutty, parenthetically a member of UNPAD, had been told nothing about the details of the mission. The man's orders were simple: keep a low profile and assist when ordered. Apparently, Cutty had his own definition of "low profile."

"I hope the flight didn't drive you crazy. Ten hours of sitting in that tiny seat. Man, I've been there before; like wearing a straightjacket in a phone booth, am I right? Wow, it's hot. Why can't the UN afford to get the damned air conditioning fixed in this car? I mean, world peace, global warming—all worthy causes—but you got to have A/C in the desert. I mean it's a no-brainer, right?"

Dayton quietly suffered Cutty's chatter, but soon agreed with him about the heat as sweat snaked down his face and breathing became a labored chore. He felt like the guest of honor in the back of a hearse. "This is ridiculous," he chimed in, "is it always this hot?"

"I know, right? I mean, with all the money the UN's got, how about a little maintenance budget for us worker bees?"

"What do you recommend? Window up or down?"

"Pick your poison: hot air furnace or sauna."

Dayton slid the window halfway down, deciding on a little of both, and tried to relax. He surveyed the neon glow of hotels on The Strip as darkness began to blanket the valley.

"Won't be too much longer, Colonel. About a half hour down the 15 to Trop. I got you a sweet deal at the MGM—practically had to sell my soul to get it, too. Big fight weekend coming up and everything's sold out. Anyway, the air is so cold there you'll wish you brought a coat." Cutty's laugh was true and honest, almost an onomatopoeic effect of "yuk-yuk-yuk."

"Good," said Dayton. "I want to rest-up and get started first thing tomorrow."

"Yes sir, Colonel. Pick you up before the rooster's awake. Yuk-yuk-yuk."

Blessed A/C enveloped him as he entered the lobby of the MGM Grand Hotel and Casino. He was finally able to breathe without a struggle. Cutty handed him the plastic room key and a standard issue suitcase containing suit and tie, casual wear, and sundries.

He soon settled into a comfortable suite on the fifteenth floor of the massive complex. His window faced the Statute of Liberty across the boulevard welcoming the huddled masses to the New York New York Hotel and Casino. He shut the curtain and flipped on the TV.

The bathroom was spotless, like a surgical suite prepped for use. He undressed, started the shower, and stood under a cool stream of water for several minutes. After cranking off the faucet, he heard a baritone voice in the bedroom; a TV newsman demanding attention.

"The latest on the Werewolf Killer, as well as my

exclusive interview with Sheriff Gale Hendrickson, next on Six At Ten."

Dayton returned to the bedroom, a towel wrapped around his waist and another thrown across his shoulders. He plopped down on the bed and faced the flat screen panel on the wall.

"Now, news you can trust from people you can trust, this is Six At Ten with Peter Hudson." The jingle that followed was heavy on drums, a little xylophone thrown in for good measure, and finished with a flourish of snare and bass.

"Good evening." The station logo under the stoic figure behind the anchor desk read Peter Hudson—Six At Ten, while the graphic behind him and to the right depicted the black silhouette of a snarling wolf's head, reminding Dayton of the book on Major Ransom's desk. "We start our newscast tonight with my exclusive interview of Sheriff Gale Hendrickson. The topic? The Werewolf Killer. The interview was taped earlier today and will be shown in segments throughout tonight's broadcast."

The image changed from Peter Hudson at the anchor desk to a close up of a man in uniform. The background was stark, black, and forbidding. The uniformed man sat in a stiff-backed chair under the glare of harsh spotlights.

"Sheriff Hendrickson, thank you for being here." Peter Hudson gave just the hint of a smile. It didn't quite reach his eyes.

Sheriff Hendrickson nodded. "My pleasure, Pete."

"Sheriff, I'd like to start by asking you about the progress in the so-called Werewolf Killer investigation. What's the latest on the case?"

The sheriff nodded. "Well Pete, as you know, Metro does not recognize that particular term. I believe that name was fabricated by someone in the media, and I, for one, think sensationalizing this crime is wrong. I think you know what I'm talking about."

"I understand, sir, and I couldn't agree more. Now, can you tell our viewers about any progress you've made in the investigation?"

"Of course, first and foremost, our hearts go out to the victims and their families; that goes without saying. This investigation is our top priority. Metro is using all available resources and examining every bit of evidence. We've been joined by experts in all fields of criminology, on both a local and national level."

"I'm glad you brought that up. Now, according to sources close to the investigation, we hear an expert from the Department of Wildlife has been—"

"Let me stop you right there." A vein in the middle of the sheriff's forehead pulsed. "We have not asked for help from the Department of Wildlife. Again, that is a rumor, and rumors do not help the investigation. I can tell you this: we're dealing with a very sick individual, plain and simple. This crime will be solved, and the person responsible will be brought to justice."

"What can you tell me about the current morale of your officers?"

"Our morale remains high. My office is confident in the work of the task force. Tonight, my men are working with extreme diligence to protect the community, and we feel very confident in our ability to do just that. All patrols have been doubled, additional units added, and every lead is being thoroughly investigated."

"Sheriff," Hudson paused, drew in a deep breath, and looked directly into the camera, "are we any closer to an arrest?"

The sheriff took a moment before answering. "What I can say is this: to the individual responsible for these crimes, it's only a matter of time before you are apprehended. However, it is in your power to do the right thing, right now. Turn yourself in to any police officer, any sub-station across the valley, and avoid a confrontation with my officers. That confrontation will not end well for you. When you surrender, you'll be treated fairly and with due process. This I can promise with no hesitation."

Hudson stared again into the camera. "Sheriff Hendrickson, what people want to know tonight is: are the streets of Las Vegas safe?"

The camera zoomed in on the sheriff's face. The extreme close-up shot revealed the purple vein pulsating in the middle of his brow.

The scene switched back to Peter Hudson live at the anchor desk. "That, of course, was Sheriff Gale Hendrickson in an exclusive interview taped earlier today at the Channel Six studios. When we return, more of my exclusive interview with Sheriff Hendrickson. You won't want to miss it."

Dayton turned off the TV and grabbed the small attaché case. Putting aside the grizzly crime scene photos and mountain of information on werewolves, he found the yellow notepaper with contact names. He scanned the list and stopped at Detective Marco Ramirez, lead investigator of the task force.

He placed the list on the writing desk and lay on the bed. Even though it was relatively early, Dayton knew the only sure remedy for jet lag was a full night's sleep. He'd contact the detective in the morning. Until then, a pleasant dream involving a certain Major Jean Ransom would be nice.

Chapter Seven

Flynn races around the corner of Dixie's house at full speed, running straight for me. I bang against the side window of the Hummer and finally hear the lock mechanism click. Flynn crashes against the door, slamming it shut with me inside.

Dixie turns the ignition. The engine whines until she lets go of the key. She throws it into reverse, launching us backward into the middle of the street. Before the Hummer stops, she grinds the gears, and we drive away on screaming tires. Flynn tries to keep up, but his image fades in the rearview mirror.

"Thanks for letting me in the car. I didn't think you would."

She doesn't answer. Her eyes are fixed on the road. The wide pavement is firm and smooth. We streak past well-spaced houses on oversized desert landscaped lots. The street is deserted, everyone either at work or indoors.

"Flynn's always had a mean streak, but he's never attacked me like that—"

"Why the hell was he at my house?"

"I can only guess he was commanded to kill me."

"Commanded? Like sit, roll over—kill?"

"Exactly. We obey The Alpha, whatever he commands us to do. The Alpha is our Supreme Ruler. We *must* do what he says."

She peeks in the rearview and eases up on the accelerator. "What in the hell are you talking about? I don't understand." She brakes hard, pops a tire over the curb, and throws open her door.

"Where're you going?"

"To be sick." She barely gets the words out.

I feel bad for her. I want to put my hand on her back and tell her everything will be all right, but I don't. I'm tired of lying.

She slams the door shut and faces me. I feel twice as bad, but not for her. Her eyes are wide, examining me—judging—like I'm some sort of problem to be solved. Or worse, like I'm some kind of monster.

It's time to try and make her understand. "Dixie, listen to me. I was born a Giant Irish Wolfhound with the ability to transform into a human being, as you see me now."

"And that other guy? The one you called Flynn?"

"He's my brother."

"Your brother? Another dog?"

"We prefer canine."

"Don't get all superior on me."

I don't know if she understands what I'm telling her, my instincts are numb. It's time for the truth, no rehearsed lines; no practiced speeches. "I've watched you on TV. In your reports, you used the term Werewolf Killer, as if you knew there was something more to these murders than anyone else suspected. Like there was something the public wasn't being told. I assumed you had a connection on the task force. When I asked you about it, you said you didn't, but I don't think you were telling me the truth."

She scowls. "The truth? Oh, that's good;

everything you've told me has been a lie."

"I had to fabricate a few truths to gain your trust."

"Stop right there." Her scowl turns into a grimace. "You used me for…for what? What do you want from me? Why don't you go to the police?"

"I can't go to them. I don't know anyone on the police force, not like I know you."

"You don't know me. You think you do just like everyone else in this city. I'm on TV, it's my job, but you don't know me."

"Look, if I went to the police and started asking questions about the Werewolf Killer they might suspect something. They might lock me up, and if I transformed in jail, well that wouldn't be so good. So I decided to come to you for help. I need to find out who the Werewolf Killer is, even if it turns out…even if it turns out to be me. And you can help, on their level."

"Their level? But I'm not a police officer I'm just—"

"Human. You can help me as a human. You know people. You have connections. You have abilities I could never hope to have. Please, I'm begging you."

Her expression changes. She grunts. "You're a dog, and you're begging."

"What do you mean by that?"

A loud thud grabs our attention. Flynn has caught up to us and paws at the rear window, smearing slobber on the glass. He jumps forward and snarls through Dixie's window. She screams and hits the gas.

"We're a mile away from my home," she shouts over the roar of the engine, "how in the hell did he find us?"

"He's a hunter. A good one."

"He's more than that; he's a killer. You said you don't kill on command, right?"

How can I answer that when I'm just not sure? "I must be wired different."

"Then I've got news for you: you're not the Werewolf Killer." She jerks a thumb over her shoulder. "He is."

Something I'd already considered. With Flynn's lack of conscience and total contempt for all things human, he'd make a perfect killing machine. But Flynn never acts on his own; he never does anything without clear instructions. His commands come from The Alpha. From here on out, I must assume I am, indeed, wired differently from the rest of the pack and take matters into my own hands.

She has to stop at the exit gate. It creaks open in slow motion. She presses the gas pedal and kisses the gate on the way out then speeds up.

I buckle my seat belt. "Drive me home."

"No way, we're going straight to the police."

"I need to get to The Alpha. I'm sure he's behind the killings. I have to stop him now, while I'm human."

Her tone changes. She surveys the rearview mirror and eases off the accelerator. She seems a little more confident, more in control of the situation. "Tell me about this Alpha person."

"He's hard to explain. I don't know much about him, but I'm certain of one thing: he ordered Flynn to kill me."

"Why would he order your brother to kill you, or kill eleven other people for that matter?"

"I don't know."

"Don't you think you should find out before you

confront him?"

"I can't take that chance. I don't want eleven to become twelve." After a few quick turns, we head east on Charleston Boulevard. She stops at a red light. "Please drive me home."

It takes her a few moments to answer. "Okay, but I need to make a call first."

"No. Don't call the police."

"No, no police, I promise. I'm going to call a friend of mine. He'll meet us there."

"Who? What friend?"

"He's with the station."

"No, Dixie. You can't report—"

Flynn paws at the car again. He caught up to us faster than even I would have thought possible.

Dixie mashes down the gas pedal. "What dog can run that fast?"

"Flynn can, and he won't stop." I weigh the options. There aren't any. "Let me out, I've got to face him."

"Are you crazy? He'll tear you apart."

Maybe. "Stop the car."

I rip open the door and scramble onto the sidewalk before the Hummer stops moving.

"Get outta here." My last round with Flynn exhausted me, but chasing us had to weaken him as well. It might be an even fight this time. Dixie speeds away.

Flynn is on me at once. His jaws snap and drool splatters in all directions. He knocks me to the ground and goes for my throat. I roll away and kick at his soft underbelly. He yelps. With my back on the ground and my hands around his throat, I feel his resolve—he means to end me.

I use my knee to jab him in the ribs. He's dazed, giving me a chance to kick him into the street. The screech of tires and deadening thud happens in a split second. Flynn tumbles out in front of Dixie's Hummer.

I drag his body off the road, smearing the pavement with a trail of blood. Vehicles slow down, drivers craning their necks to sneak a peek.

It takes all my strength to climb back into the Hummer.

"Is he dead?"

I lean back in the seat and nod.

"I doubled back, and he was just there. I hit the brakes, but—"

"Don't feel bad."

"I don't. I couldn't very well let anything happen to you." She opens the center console, slams it shut, and riffles through her purse. "Damn. I left my phone back home."

"What do you mean 'let anything happen to me'?"

"You're a once in a lifetime story, Adam."

"This is more than a story."

"You're right. You, my friend, are a worldwide exclusive. Let's go back to my house and I'll call the station—"

"You don't get it. The Alpha needs to be stopped before someone else is murdered, maybe tonight."

She sits still, a worried look crossing her face. "But your brother, Flynn, he was the Werewolf Killer, right?" Her brow furrows. "And he's dead."

Once again, is honesty the best policy? "There are five more siblings in my pack."

****

Colonel Jon Dayton made himself comfortable in Detective Ramirez's chair, strumming the top of the desk while twirling a black pen embossed with gold letters: LVMPD. The flurry of activity in the task force bull-pen energized him. Metro officers answered phone calls, jotting down information as fast as they could; police cadets scampered by with sticky notes, relaying them between desks.

One desk in particular, manned by an animated lieutenant, seemed the hub of it all. The lieutenant directed the movements of the cadets like an orchestra conductor, pointing, waving, and shouting out orders: "Hand up at station six, see what he needs." "Bring that note over here." "C'mon, keep it moving people, hustle up now." The sound of telephones ringing, cell phones buzzing and keyboards clicking lent an electronic soundtrack to the movements of the conductor.

Dayton liked the vibe; the behind-the-scenes investigative work few people ever see. As far as John Q Public knew from watching countless action films and television dramas, heavily armed SWAT teams and high speed chases solved crimes. Sometimes, maybe. In the real world, Dayton knew information took criminals down; the hard-working people in rooms like this caught the bad guys.

"Cadet," the lieutenant shouted, "take this to the map, hustle up now."

The cadet took a slip of paper and darted across the room to a large map of the Las Vegas Valley. He handed the note to a sergeant who read the information and thrust a pin into the map. The sergeant gave the note back to the cadet and said, "Take this to station six. Let's go, move it." Perspiration streaked down the cadet's face as he ran across the room to station six and handed the note to an officer. The officer studied the note for a few seconds, then picked up a phone, dismissing the cadet with a wave of his hand. The cadet ran back to the lieutenant's desk and stood by for new orders.

Dayton panned his gaze across the other cadets—dozens of them—performing similar duties, scurrying from one desk to the next, carrying bits of paper containing tips, leads, possible sightings, confessions, intelligence, follow-ups, and complaints. There was excitement in their movement, optimism so palpable it was contagious; a clear belief the very scrap of paper they carried might be the one bit of crucial information that would lead to the arrest of the Werewolf Killer. Here, in this room, lay the hope of a troubled city.

The over-sized map held hundreds of pins; a tapestry of yellow, green, black, blue, and red. Dayton knew from experience the red pins were the most significant, tending to indicate major incidents. In this case murder. He counted the red pins: eleven.

"Colonel Dayton," Detective Ramirez approached the desk. "This is Special Agent In Charge Ed Miller of the FBI."

Dayton and Miller shook hands. "Sorry I missed you this morning, Agent Miller. Detective Ramirez filled me in on the particulars. It's quite an undertaking."

"Interesting choice of words. I didn't know the NSA had a dog in this fight."

"I'm awfully sorry, but that information is classified at this time." Earlier, Dayton flipped through his collection of IDs, choosing to pose as a member of the National Security Agency, a cover he'd used before while in the states—the secretive nature of the organization itself precluded questions.

"An NSA agent from across the pond?" Agent Miller said. "Have we run out of home-grown patriots?"

Dayton smiled, then deadpanned, "How perceptive of you, Agent Miller—so unlike the FBI. In that case, I suppose I'd better come clean: I'm really a United Nations intelligence officer sent here with orders to track down a werewolf."

Both Detective Ramirez and Agent Miller grinned, then chuckled.

Ramirez pulled his cell phone out of his pocket. "Excuse me, I'm gonna try Dixie again."

"Still not answering?" Miller said.

Dayton chimed in, "Is there a problem, Detective?"

"A friend of mine, Dixie Mulholland. She's a reporter with a local television station, and I haven't been able to reach her all day. Probably nothing, but it's not like her to not return my phone calls."

"Ah, yes," Dayton said, "The Werewolf Killer reporter."

Ramirez smiled. "She'd shake your hand if she heard you say that." He kept his ear to the phone for a few moments, then tucked it back into his pocket. "Still not picking up. I'm sure she'll call back."

Dayton excused himself and strolled to the big map, hurried cadets weaving their way around him. He studied the array of pins trying to visualize some type of pattern, design, or shape. The colorful markers were scattered across the map like a Magic Eye 3D image from the 90's. But just like those infuriating illusions,

Dayton could not bring a clear picture into focus.

It seemed the only way of solving this crime would be to know where the next attack was going to take place, like knowing for certain where lightning would strike.

Chapter Eight

Dixie drove east on the 215. She kept her gaze cemented on the road, guiding the Hummer between the white lines, and the speedometer closer to eighty than seventy. The highway was fairly crowded in the early evening, but she had no trouble powering around slower traffic with ease. Although her eyes concentrated straight ahead, and Adam had told her what exits to take, her mind zig-zagged in all directions.

Was the world ready for Adam Steel? What were the ramifications of a story like this? She had to consider the bigger picture: the scientific, religious, even political consequences had to be weighed before going public with such an earth-shattering story. Was it even her place to bother about such issues?

This was the biggest discovery of all time, but the even bigger question kept gnawing at her: Was *she* ready to tell the story?

She drew in a deep lungful of chilly conditioned air and concentrated on silencing the doubts. This was a once in a lifetime opportunity, what every reporter dreamed of: a worldwide exclusive with living proof sitting right next to her. In the long run that meant, no more fighting for air time, no management approvals for her stories, and a free pass to the all-boys club. This was her ticket to the big show—the networks.

And it wasn't as if she chased Adam down and

forced him to tell her the truth. The story came to her, like a story that insisted on telling itself.

She grunted and whispered, "Look what followed *me* home."

"What was that?" Adam said.

Yes, she was up for it. She was ready to tell the world about Adam Steel.

"Adam," she said in an easy, off the cuff manner—after all she didn't want to spook him; he trusted her, but who knew how long that trust would last? "When did you know you were able to turn into a dog?"

"Canine," he said, stepping over her last word. "And I'm not getting all *superior* on you. Call me a snob, but I prefer canine. I'm not a house pet; I'm a Giant Irish Wolfhound. And, you've got it wrong. I don't turn into a canine. I am a canine who transforms into a human. It's something that's happened to me all my life. Canine, human—human, canine—back and forth."

"Do you have any control over it?"

"None. It happens when it happens. Sure, I get a little advanced notice, like the night we had dinner. I knew it was about to happen. That's why I had to run away."

"That was two days ago. Is that common, two days on, two days off?"

"No. Sometimes I remain in human form for weeks, sometimes for just a few days. Like I said, I have no control over it."

"How does it feel? You know, how does it feel being a dog?"

"Canine. I don't know. I have no recollection of what I do as a canine, and that scares the hell out of me." He pounded on the dash. "If I knew, if I had any clear memories at all—"

"Calm down, Adam. Tell me why you think this change happens to you."

"It happens to all my brothers and sisters, and we don't know for sure. There's talk about a curse—they're just rumors really."

"You mean like a spell, or whammy, or something?"

With a shrug of his shoulders, he said, "I guess."

"You guess? You must have some idea why this happens—"

"I don't, okay?"

"All right, all right, don't get mad. I'm just trying to wrap my head around this, that's all." She shook her head and furrowed her brow. "It's just that…that—"

"What are you trying to say?"

"You just seem so *normal*. You speak perfect English, look like a typical man, and you carry on a good conversation. If I didn't know, I would never be able to tell. How do you pull it off?"

"I've worked hard at it all my life. I listen to people and try to imitate them. I've even sat in on a few open lectures at UNLV. But to be honest, there's no substitute for watching old movies on TV. Television is the best instructor. And, let's face it, without TV I would never have met you."

She smiled. "You said your family lives in Las Vegas. Were you born here?"

Adam turned to her with a cold stare. "You're interviewing me, aren't you?"

Dixie swerved onto the I-15 at the last minute, cutting off a smaller vehicle in the process. "Whoa, almost missed the exit."

"Answer me. This is an interview, isn't it?"

"I'm just asking a few questions. I mean, it isn't every day that you meet a…whatever it is you are."

"I'm a canine…and you're a reporter."

"C'mon. It's my job to ask questions, and you came to me because of my job, remember? We can't very well change our stripes, can we?"

"What does that mean?"

"We are what we are. I report the news, and you, my friend, are definitely news. What do you expect me to do with that, huh?"

"I came to you for help, to find out what's going on." He lowered his head. "I had to find out if I was the Werewolf Killer. But this isn't on me anymore, Flynn convinced me of that. This is about that psychotic old man, The Alpha, who thinks he has the power to make us do anything he wants, terrible things. Well, it ends today."

"And then what? After it's over, I mean. Are you going to disappear into the background? Fade from the radar and find a safe place to hide?"

He nodded. "Sounds good to me."

Dixie choked the steering wheel. "But the whole world needs to know about you and your kind—"

"My kind?" His voice rose a few decibels. "So they can examine *my kind*; study *my kind?* I'm not a lab rat to be tested and analyzed."

"I never called you a lab rat."

"You know what they'll do—they'll dissect me."

"Don't be ridiculous."

"Am I? Listen, you said yourself you couldn't tell there was anything different about me. And there isn't.

I'm just someone who happens to live in two different worlds, and I choose being human over being canine, that's all. I love being free, exploring new things, and meeting new people. I enjoy art, and movies, and eating good food; I love seeing the world in color, and reading and drawing—"

"You draw? Can I see them?"

"Would you stop being a reporter for just a minute? You don't know how lucky you are to be human. I swear, you and *your* kind take it all for granted." The drone of the Hummer's tires begged for him to speak up, to shout, but instead he lowered his voice, "Please promise you'll keep my secret, that you'll find a way to change your stripes."

"I can't promise that."

"Then I'll lose everything."

"Hold on, this is the exit." She whipped off the freeway and drove through a red light. "Where do I go? How do I get to your house?"

"Keep in the right lane, the turnoff is coming up. Right there." He pointed. "Turn here."

She turned the wheel, and they skidded onto a rundown road with no street sign. They sped past shrubs and cactus, blurred images of a barren desert.

"Slow down," Adam said. "The road leads up that hill."

"What road?"

"Turn right just past the sign."

"What sign?"

****

Claremont Estates—1965

The sign is weathered: faded paint, sunbaked, and cracked. The only reason I see it is because I know where it is, having passed it hundreds of times before. Like I said, I look for signs from the universe—I hate this sign.

Claremont Drive is a gravel road winding up a small hill just south of Las Vegas. The dozen or so ranch-style homes on the hill were built in the late sixties; oversized lots offering perfect views of The Strip. Unfortunately, the sixty-plus years of desert sun have cooked the structures into uninhabited ruins. Built before post-tension requirements, most of the foundations are cracked and unstable. The homes are now abandoned, condemned by the city, and keeping with the tradition of Las Vegas, scheduled for demolition.

Pine trees, cactus, and shrubs cover the hillside. Miles of chain link fence jigsaw back and forth defining the ancient property lines of Claremont Estates.

At the top of the hill is 7711, a six-bedroom maze of rotting plywood and patches of stucco. Peeling, sun damaged paint gives the house a faded mix of rusty browns and muted tans. The ever present chain link fence defines a huge backyard consisting of nothing more than caliche and sand.

A dog house, the size of an enormous oven, sits in the middle of the backyard. That's my house. I avoid it like the plague and prefer to lay in the shade of a pine tree near the house, away from the backyard. I've never made a drawing of this place in my sketchbook—my drawings are for things I want to remember.

Dixie parks the Hummer at the bottom of the hill, and I jump out. She rolls down her window and wipes a hand across her brow.

"I wish I had my phone," she says. "I'd feel better

if I knew the cavalry was on the way."

"I'm glad you don't. I don't want any more people in danger because of my family. Give me some time, then drive to Metro and tell them what's going on as best you can."

"What do you mean as best I can?"

"I mean don't tell them about me. They're more apt to believe you if you say it was an anonymous tip. Hopefully, it'll be over by the time they get here. And don't go back to your home tonight, not until it's safe."

Her brow wrinkles. "Why wouldn't my home be safe?"

"Flynn has been there, and that means The Alpha knows where you live. He's a very powerful man. Don't underestimate him."

"But you said he only has power over your pack, and only when you're dogs, right?"

"Listen to me, Dixie, my family is extremely dangerous. We're not puppies, doggies, or pooches; we don't fetch and we don't play Frisbee. We're Giant Irish Wolfhounds, and we were trained by The Alpha. And once again, we prefer to be called *canines,* not dogs."

"All right already, I'm sorry."

A dry, hot wind blows across the hill whipping up dust devils. "I'm the one who should apologize. I'm taking everything out on you, and I shouldn't. There's something about this place that stresses me out."

"You think?"

I smile at her. "Thank you, Dixie Mulholland."

"For what?"

"I came to you for help, and you have helped, more than you know. Without you, I wouldn't be here right now; Flynn would have made sure of that. Now, go tell Detective Ramirez everything, almost everything. That should give me enough time to deal with The Alpha."

"But—"

"Go." I turn and jog up the road. The tires of the Hummer chomp on the gravel as it pulls away. All of a sudden it grinds to a halt.

"Adam…be careful."

Maybe she told me to be careful because that's what humans say when they're afraid and don't know what else to say, but it doesn't matter; I believe her. I feel recharged, encouraged by the knowledge I've found someone—a human—who knows me, the real me, and she's okay with that. Of course, I know she's using me to further her career, but that doesn't bother me so much anymore. I know from experience stripes are hard to change.

She's on my side. I've never had that before—ever.

I watch the Hummer disappear around a corner, knowing Dixie won't be speeding back to help me, not this time.

Trudging up Claremont Drive is a hike. I stay low and use the overgrown brush along the side of the road as cover. By the time I reach my house, the sun starts to fade behind the Spring Mountains in the west. With only an hour or so of daylight, I've got to act fast; as a human, I have poor night vision and an even worse sense of smell. I wouldn't stand a chance getting into the house undetected at night.

There's no movement in front of the house so I edge toward the mouth of the driveway. The shade under a pine tree gives me much needed cover from prying eyes. I lean against the tree and scan the area.

Our yellow van is parked in the driveway. That means the caretaker is home. The van is covered by a mist of dust and some joker has written “wash me” on the back window. I smile, remembering the joker was Ivan, my brother. Ivan makes me laugh, and we might have been friends under any normal circumstances. But my family is anything but normal. Ivan ran away from home a few weeks ago.

Next to the van is The Alpha’s expensive black sedan. The difference between the two vehicles is striking. The Alpha’s way of making a statement I guess, reminding us of how wealthy he is next to our beat-up, overcrowded cattle car.

I don’t know how or where The Alpha gets his money, but he makes no excuse for it, not to us. The den, his lair, is the nicest room in the house. He drives a luxury vehicle, and wears very expensive clothes. I have no idea why he would choose to mastermind a series of murders. He may be a sociopath, but with the rumors of a curse on my family, I hope that’s all it is.

I guess to anyone who doesn’t know him, The Alpha would appear to be just an old man: short gray hair, tall and stocky, good health, but all and all harmless. As canines, we see a different man: our lives are controlled by him. Everything we do as canines, every action, emotion, and movement is by his command. He is our god.

My senses are on high alert as I follow the path up the driveway to the front door. I turn the knob and try to lift it as I open it so it doesn’t rub and squeak against the surrounding woodwork like it usually does. So far, so good. I shut the door, but only enough to keep out the light. It’s still open just a crack.

My siblings usually nap at this time, if they're all in canine form, something I have no way of knowing. They tend to gather as a pack in one of the bedrooms in the east wing, the coolest part of the house. I take cautious, careful steps through the living room.

Thoughts of how I'm going to kill The Alpha play out in my mind on the long trek down the hallway. If I catch him off guard, I'll sneak up and choke him. If he sees me coming, I'll sucker punch him, then choke him. Either way, choking sounds like the best method. It's quiet.

My mind is so involved in the details of murder I don't notice someone behind me. I become aware of that little detail just before something crashes down on my head. I fall to the floor, limp, seeing shades of red and black. My eyelids are heavy, and my head feels wet. I have just enough strength to roll onto my back and see Bane standing over me holding a rather large rock in his hand. I always thought Bane and I were on good terms.

The Alpha rushes out of his den and stares down at me. He grins and gives Bane a nod. "Lock him in the basement."

Chapter Nine

It's dark, blackout shades—midnight in the desert—scary movie-type dark. My head pounds like a kid using it for a birthday bouncy house. I know where I am even without being able to see: in my home, down in the basement, locked in a cage.

The cage is small, flat, and square complete with rusty wire and sharp edges. It's so small I can't even move my hand to feel the bump that's sprouted on top of my head. Maybe that's a good thing depending on the size of the bump. I've been bent and folded into the cage, and my legs start to cramp. By wriggling my feet, I check the gate to see if it's latched closed. It doesn't budge, but it makes a clanging noise.

"Adam." The voice is soothing, calm, and familiar. "Adam, are you awake?"

"Lucy?"

"Thank God, I thought you might be dead. What are you doing here?" she says, like in one of those old gangster movies I watch where the cons ask: What are you in for?

"I came to kill The Alpha."

Upbeat and enthusiastic she says, "Good for you." After a while and a little more subdued, she asks, "So what happened?"

"Bane hit me with a rock. How about you, what are you in for?"

"'Cause The Alpha's a bastard. He knocked me out with a punch. I woke up just in time to see Flynn lock me up. Can you believe it? Flynn."

There was a time when Flynn and Lucy were close; we all were—we're family. When we were pups, we played together every day, wrestling and exploring the world. Life was fun and always full of adventure. Then the transformations began, we were two years old—fourteen in human years, and some of us—Lucy, Ivan, and I—were fascinated by everything: walking on two legs, learning to speak, seeing the world in *color*! We loved every second of it. The others, not so much. From their expressions, I realized they found it humiliating, practically degrading. All they worried about were the two legs they gave up and didn't even consider everything they'd gained becoming human.

Of course, I don't have any clear recollections of those happy times, but it's funny; I can recall the puppy days more than anything about my last transformation. It's like my mind blocks out what I do as an adult canine.

I haven't spoken to Lucy in a long time, and I'm dying to find out what she knows. "Have you heard about The Werewolf Killings?"

"Sure," Lucy says, her voice light and innocent. "Mikael talks about it a lot."

Mikael: as much opposed to the human world as I embrace it. He groans and moans, puts up a big show whenever he transforms. He's always borne me ill will for being first born, as if it were my choice—luck of the draw.

The first born has a natural responsibility to the pack: to watch over them, keep them away from harm, and lead the way. But as soon as the transformations began, I turned my back on the pack. I still feel guilty about neglecting my duties, but I had no choice. I no longer consider myself part of that world—I am human.

Mikael labeled me a traitor, insisting the only true self we have is canine. I neither agree nor argue with him. I could care less what he thinks; if he wants to spend his life on all fours, so be it. I don't.

"The Alpha is using us," I say. "He's turned us into human-killers."

"Not me," Lucy says in a hurry. "I've never killed a human."

"How do you know?"

"Don't you think I'd remember a thing like that?"

"How? Can you remember what you do as a Wolfhound?" This is called a rhetorical question: one that needs no answer.

"Yup, as a matter of fact I do."

Did I hear her right? "How is that even possible?"

"Don't know, just do. I remember everything—running outside at night, chasing rabbits and cats, barking at the moon—everything. Don't you?"

"No. Do any of the others remember?"

"Ivan does, and maybe Mikael. He doesn't talk to me much. I guess we're all different."

The cramps in my legs squeeze without mercy, but that's not what makes me cry out. It's the sudden realization of what Lucy's just said: we're all different.

Lucy and Ivan remember things they do as canines; Flynn transformed easily at Dixie's house, in fact, he initiated the change. Mikael is just plain mean, a natural born killer. And me? I want nothing more than to live as a free human being.

We're all different.

I always assumed my experiences—uncontrolled transformations, relying on instinct, and not remembering what I do as a canine—were true for all of us. Maybe I was wrong to throw myself completely into the human world when there are still so many things yet to learn about being a canine. And I can think of no better teacher than Lucy.

"Can you transform at will?"

"Sure," she says. "Most of us can, except for you. And Ivan—he can't. I've tried to teach him, but he says he can't stand the taste. Go figure. A strong, healthy hound like Ivan, and he doesn't like the taste of it. Oh well, to each their own."

"What are you talking about? The taste of what?"

Lucy giggles. "Meat, silly. The key to controlling the change is to eat plenty of meat—red and raw, yum. A good steady diet of that and you can pretty much change whenever you want. I guess Ivan is what they call a veginarian."

"Vegetarian."

"Right. Not only that: the more red meat you eat, the less pain there is when you change. That's why Flynn is a little…uh…bulky? He hates the pain, so he eats meat all the time. That way he changes super-fast with no pain at all. He's really good at it."

I debate whether to tell her Flynn is dead, but decide against it. I need to keep her talking—I need to learn more. "And that's all there is to it?"

"Well, there's a little more to it than that, but not much."

"Like what?"

"Like you've got to have an attitude about the

whole thing; not just wanting to change, but really, *really* wanting it—decide what you want and stick to it." She giggles. "The humans have a funny word for it: stick-to-itiveness. I heard that on TV. That's a really funny word, isn't it?"

Lucy is not as dedicated to her human side as I am. I read books, figure things out. She's more of a free spirit and plays it by ear. I love that about her. "It's hyphenated."

"Hyphenated?"

"Words that are stuck together with dashes."

She giggles again. "*Stuck*-to-itiveness."

It's clear why The Alpha imprisoned her. She would no more kill a human than I would. It's not in her nature.

She laughs, a deep throaty sound. "Hey, how about Vegi-tanarian. I just hyphenated veterinarian and vegetarian."

I love her innocence, but I need to keep her on track. "Does Mikael kill humans?"

"Sure, he brags about it. So does Nina. Mikael says something big is coming, and we're on the front lines. He says it's coming soon."

"What is it?"

"He calls it The Convergence. I think that's one word."

The pain in my legs vanishes; there's no feeling in them at all. They're numb. "Yes, it is, but what does it mean? What's The Convergence?"

"I don't know exactly, but Mikael talks to Bane and Flynn about it all the time. He says other packs from all over the country are coming to Las Vegas."

"Other packs? Like us?"

There's silence. Then in a small worried voice, Lucy says, "I wouldn't want to be a human when they get here."

"When is this going to happen?"

"Soon. I heard Mikael talk about a big fight weekend. You know, that guy Salmonella making his comeback fight?"

"You mean Sam Toretta. Salmonella is bacteria."

She giggles. "I hate boxing anyway."

"And The Alpha is in charge of The Convergence?"

"No, silly. The Alpha is in charge of our pack. Mikael says each pack has an Alpha. And they're all coming here."

"Then who's doing this? Who's in charge of The Convergence?"

Before she can say another word, the door to the basement creaks open.

****

"Sir, I've got good news and bad, which would you prefer?" Colonel Jon Dayton gripped the cell phone as he sat at the writing table in his suite, the A/C on full blast. The curtains were drawn allowing in only muted rays of sun, giving the room a cave-like ambiance. A half folded newspaper lay on the desk.

"Your choice, Colonel," Admiral Garrison growled. "The council is anxious. They want answers, and they want them now."

"Oh? Has something changed our status?"

"Without question. It seems a pattern has evolved. The same types of attacks have occurred in New York, Baltimore, and Dallas. Not in the numbers seen in Las Vegas, to be sure, but enough to rattle the council."

Dayton took a few seconds to digest the information. "Is it an outbreak?"

"Let's don't get ahead of ourselves, not just yet. What have you got for me first?"

"Well sir, the local authorities seem to be doing everything they can to find the perpetrator. The bad news is: I don't think they ever will. You see, they're using standard law enforcement practices, absolutely useless in this particular case."

"My God, Colonel. What you're suggesting..." The Admiral's voice trailed off.

"Yes sir, I believe this is an actual event. I won't go so far as to say we've found ourselves a real live werewolf but, then again, it might be something more lethal, even more cunning."

Admiral Garrison grunted. "Stand by, Colonel. I'm going to patch the council in." After a series of clicks, the admiral said, "Go ahead, Colonel Dayton, you're on speaker."

"Good afternoon or evening, as the case may be. As I've just informed the admiral, what we seem to have here is terribly clever, in an almost human sort of way. There's no predictability to the attacks, no common denominator in the victims. It's as if he's challenging us to stop him, like playing a game with us."

A woman's voice said, "A very deadly game."

"Yes, but that's the human side of it."

"I don't follow, Colonel. The human side?"

"Yes, ma'am. Call it the logical, thinking side of the beast. The other side is more visceral, more creature than man. The attacks are so violent in nature; it's simply not possible for a human to kill in this manner.

The photos will bear that out."

"Yes, we've seen the photos. So what you're saying is this creature is half human, half beast, is that a fair assumption?"

The air conditioning unit clicked off sending the room into a deadly silence. Dayton moved to the thermostat and requested colder air. "That's my initial take. You see, a serial killer will inevitably leave clues, evidence, make mistakes, that sort of thing. There's none of that in this case. Quite the opposite. The attacks are quick, violent, and clean."

"Admiral," the woman's voice said, "switch us off the line. We'll get back to you shortly."

Admiral Garrison sucked in a large breath. "Colonel, you said you had some good news."

"Well, sir, call it a hunch, but Detective Ramirez, the local officer in charge of the investigation, can't seem to find his girlfriend."

"Excuse me? It sounded like you said—"

"Yes, sir. She's a reporter for one of the television stations here in Vegas. Her name is Dixie Mulholland, and she's been covering the case exclusively. She's gone missing. It just strikes me as a bit odd—not likely for a reporter to keep a low profile under these circumstances."

"Of course, Colonel, you're closer to the investigation than I am, but I don't see what one has to do with the other."

"Sir, Miss Mulholland is the reporter who first called our friend the Werewolf Killer. She's always seemed one step ahead of her colleagues. I have a strong suspicion the girl found something, or something found her."

"It sounds a bit farfetched. And, I don't want to make any assumptions, Colonel, but—"

"Unfortunately, it's all I've been able to find that might be considered anything close to a lead. In the meantime, sir, can we get the DNA from the other attacks looked at, compared to what we have here in Las Vegas?"

"It's already been done. It's a match."

Dayton felt cold fingers walk down his spine.

"Is there anything else you need, Colonel?"

He'd anticipated the question. The answer, however, would take some salesmanship. "My gut tells me the missing reporter has somehow gotten herself into the thick of it, but it's only a guess. I need someone here that can help look into that aspect of the case without being too obvious. Someone with the ability to get inside her head, so to speak."

"Major Ransom."

Dayton smiled. "An excellent choice, sir."

"As a matter of fact Major Ransom is already in the States. I sent her to Dallas just yesterday to help with initial inquiries. And you're right, if, as you suspect, this reporter is involved but can't be located, Major Ransom is the most obvious choice. Tell our man Cuthbert to make the arrangements, and I'll inform the major." A quick chortle. "That is, if she doesn't already know."

"Perfect." Dayton smiled.

A click echoed across the line followed by the woman's voice, "Colonel Dayton. The council has decided to broaden the scope of the investigation."

"And that would be?"

"It seems, due to the additional attacks, the

parameter of the mission has been upgraded. Your orders are now quite singular in nature: to capture the creature…alive."

The air conditioning clicked off again. Silence crowded the suite.

"Colonel, are you still there? You have carte blanch. Anything you need. Admiral, keep us informed." Click.

"Sir, this is the first event that has ever seemed, well, real to me. As I said, it may not be a werewolf, but it does appear to be something new, something undiscovered. I don't know if capturing it would be a wise—"

"It is not a request, Colonel." The line went dead.

Dayton placed the phone down and leaned back in his chair. This changed everything.

He picked up the newspaper, peering at the front page picture of Sheriff Hendrickson pointing a menacing finger at the short blonde reporter blocking his way.

"Where are you, Miss Mulholland, and what do you know?"

Chapter Ten

Light washes in from the open door of the basement as footsteps echo on the hard cement. My heart thumps in my ears, cadenced to the same rhythm as the steps. Neither Lucy, myself, nor our unknown visitor say a word. I can only lift my head about a half an inch before it hits the top of the cage.

A whisper cuts through the silence, "Adam, are you in here?"

"Dixie? Is that you?"

The latch to the gate of my cage slides open. My legs neither hurt, nor do they move—they're just numb. "Pull me out."

"Why can't you crawl out?"

"My legs don't work, they're cramped up."

Lucy joins the conversation. "Hurry up, grab his feet and yank him out of there."

"Whoa, who the hell is that?" I hear Dixie shuffle back a few paces, no doubt startled by Lucy.

"That's my sister. Open her cage, too." Nothing happens. "Hurry, Dixie, please."

"Why is she locked up?"

It's apparent to me now that clear sides are evolving: good and bad canines; good and bad humans. "Don't be afraid, she won't hurt you, she's on our side."

Lucy's gate opens and shuffling and scraping

sounds echo through the basement as she backs out of her cage. It's a struggle for her, even with full use of her limbs; there's no way I'm ever getting out without help.

"C'mon, help me grab his legs." Lucy takes charge—she's like that.

They drag me out of the cage feet first. The back of my shirt snags on a piece of wire. It claws into my back making me yelp. They keep pulling and haul me out as the buttons of my shirt pop off. I roll over onto my back and stare up at my rescuers. They eyeball each other like gunfighters in an old western.

Dixie's inspection of my sister starts at Lucy's gray eyes, runs the length of her naked body, coming to rest on her dirty white feet. I can only imagine the kind of judgements Dixie's making about my family. I slip out of my torn shirt and hand it to Lucy. "Here, put this on."

"Why?"

"Please, do it."

Formal introductions will have to wait. I'm desperate to escape the basement, frustrated about being locked up in the first place, and angry at my frail human legs. "Help me get up; we gotta get out of here."

Without hesitation, Lucy grabs my left arm, Dixie my right, and together they manage to hoist me up. My legs are twisted and hopeless, looking like they belong on a rag doll. Painful tingles shoot down them, feeling like little rivers of lava. It's not the worst pain I've ever felt, but it's close.

With my arms draped over their shoulders, they manage to lug me to the base of the stairs. Glancing up at the steep climb ahead, my heart sinks. No way can they haul me all the way to the top. "You two get out of here. You'll have to leave me behind."

Lucy grabs my belt with one hand and reaches under my arm with the other. She puts her foot on the bottom step. "Well?" She stares at Dixie.

Dixie stares right back—challenge accepted. They drag me upstairs like I'm a piece of furniture. By the time we reach the landing at the top of the stairs, I'm in agony. With considerable effort, I'm able to wiggle my toes.

I turn to Dixie. "Why'd you come back for me?"

"I never left. I followed you up the hill. When you went inside, I parked off the road and waited. For Christ's sake, what was Sonny Russo doing here?"

"Who?"

"The casino owner?" Dixie stares at me like I'm supposed to know who she's talking about. "He walked right out of your house, got in a car, and tore off down the street. A few minutes later, another man came outside with two huge dogs. He put them in the back of a van and took off. I didn't know if you were, er, I mean, I've never seen you as a dog."

"Canine." I correct her, then give Lucy a quick, self-conscious look. It's always been an unwritten rule with my pack—The Alpha has drilled it into us—never tell humans our secret.

Lucy scowls. "The human followed you home?"

"Anyway," Dixie says, "I waited a few more minutes and decided to come inside and look around, must be the reporter in me."

"And she's a reporter?" Lucy whispers. "I swear, Adam, you're so human." It isn't meant as a compliment.

"Lucy, please listen to me. I'm still alive because of this human. She's a friend, and she's helping me put an end to this Werewolf Killer business. It's got to stop, especially with The Convergence coming."

"What the hell's The Convergence?" Dixie asks.

"And how are you gonna stop it?" Lucy says. "Please, by all means, tell the reporter."

"By stopping The Alpha. You know he's behind it, and he's using Mikael and the rest of us as his weapon of choice."

Lucy gets in my face. "He's not using me, and not you, or Ivan."

"Okay, but he's still turned the rest of the pack into cold-blooded killers. Bane and Nina don't deserve to be used that way."

"Or Flynn," she adds.

Dixie and I exchange an awkward glance. I want to tell Lucy about Flynn, but the words still won't come. It would break her heart. Instead, I rub a hand across my chest. "I need another shirt."

Lucy grabs a dark t-shirt from a pile in the living room and tosses it at my face. "Here. By all means, cover yourself. The human might be offended."

"The human isn't used to our ways."

"I'm right here," Dixie says.

My instincts have been dulled by the cramps in my legs. But as the pain eases up, I begin to sense things. All of the sudden, I'm aware of someone else in the house with us, listening to us bicker. Dixie helps me into my new shirt.

Lucy sneers. "Aw, look at the human dressing her pet."

A low growl sounds in a darkened corner of the

kitchen.

Lucy jerks her head to the right. "Shhh—someone else is here."

Dixie digs her fingers into my back.

"It's Bane," Lucy says. She turns to Dixie. "Get him out of here," then to me, "I'll take care of Bane." She swallows hard and takes off the shirt I'd given her. Then she tears a strip of flesh from her arm revealing matted fur underneath. She does it so fast and without any ceremony, almost as if she's slipping out of a blouse.

"No, let me stay and help." It's pure swagger, of course. There's no way my legs are in any shape for a fight and she knows it. Still, I can't imagine leaving her alone with Bane. He's not quite as big as Flynn, but he's quick and strong—a good fighter.

"Go!" she says, tearing off more sheets of flesh. Her transformation is seamless, rapid, and apparently without pain. In an instant, it's complete. I'm in awe of her skill.

Dixie is trembling and wraps her arms around me. She spins us toward the front door. My legs move, not very well, but enough to allow her to guide me out of the house. I'd be face down on the ground without any support so I hang on tight.

It's a clumsy dash into the early evening and across the street to her waiting Hummer. Snarling and yapping sounds echo from the house behind us. Neither of us dare look back as a high-pitched yip flies over our heads, a sound signaling distress.

Dixie opens the passenger door and shoves me into the Hummer. She jumps in behind the wheel, and we skid away from the house only a few yards ahead of a wild-eyed Bane in frantic pursuit. Ribbons of red drip from his gray beard.

My heart sinks. "Lucy."

****

Sonny Russo held the Cohiba Esplendido Cuban in one hand and a tumbler of McCallan single malt whiskey in the other. The hotels lining Las Vegas Boulevard had already fired up their enormous neon welcome mats even though a good hour of daylight remained. Russo surveyed The Strip and grinned. The tourists, forty floors below, had no idea their movements were being watched, examined like so many ants, by the richest man in Vegas.

So far, so good. He'd done exactly what she asked, and she'd fixed everything as promised. His record had been expunged, his past associations were disassociated, and the gaming control board gave him a clean bill of health. He didn't know how she'd done it, and he didn't care. What he did know was now he was a new man, someone to be admired and respected.

Gorgeous slapped the drink out of his hand, the crystal shattering into tiny shards across the marble floor. "What the hell are you doing?"

Her constant smile, the one he'd once mistaken as sweet, almost innocent, no longer fooled him. It was nothing more than a mask, a façade as fake as the Eiffel Tower down the street. Hidden behind the smile was the secret she never revealed, at least not to him—a dark, impenetrable secret.

"I'm sorry. I didn't hear you come in. It's been a helluva day."

"Has it, sweetie? Why don't you tell me all about it?"

He hesitated. Did she know what had happened? Did she know Flynn was dead? Or that he hadn't killed Steel or Lucy? He decided to take a chance and keep those details to himself.

"Sonny, is there something troubling you? You know you can tell me anything. In fact, I insist."

"No, Gorgeous, not at all."

"C'mon, sweetie, you can tell me. You're my right hand man."

He sighed. "Well, now that you bring it up—I been thinking. You been good to me, Gorgeous, real good."

"That's right, I have been." Her smile remained fixed, unchanged. "You've taken care of my wolfhounds, and I've taken very good care of you."

"Yeah, that's right. Everything's been swell, and I can't thank you enough for doing all this for me. But now—" Was this the right time?

"Keep going, Sonny."

"Well, now that them dogs are starting to, you know, kill people—a lot of people—I figure—"

"You figure what, sweetie? You knew why I wanted my pack. You knew this was coming. Well, here it is. The time has come."

"Yeah, don't get me wrong, I knew. But now that it's really happening, well I figure maybe we should slow down a little. You know, look at the bigger picture."

"The bigger picture?" Her constant grin wavered. "You can see the bigger picture? Well then, by all means, explain it to me."

Sweat formed a slick across his brow. "Oh, now listen, I'm not telling you your business or nothing, I just figured, you know, with all the stuff I done for you,

you know—buying up all them houses on that hill, and practically raising that pack of dogs—I figure maybe it's time we just take it easy a little bit. Maybe we can settle up and make things square."

"Square?"

"Yeah, you know, I got lots of money, and maybe I can just kind of step aside, you know, buy my way out of our little agreement. What'd ya say, Gorgeous?" None of it came out the way he'd rehearsed. He was supposed to be more in control of the situation. She was supposed to be more willing to listen.

Instead, she paced a slow circle around Russo, reminding him of a shark. He held his ground. No, that wasn't quite right—he could not move; his feet were as heavy as bricks. His breath grew shallow, the fine coat of sweat covering his entire face. He'd made a mistake in saying anything; he should have kept his mouth shut.

"Money?" Gorgeous spat out the word as if she'd swallowed a bug.

Was there hope? Could she be paid to leave him alone? "Yeah, that's right, anything you need; anything at all."

"But, sweetie, the only thing I need is for you to keep your promise. Of course my wolfhounds have killed; you've done a wonderful job training them."

Russo began to shake, little tremors at first. His throat was dry, his voice hoarse. "Things are getting a little out of control, aren't they? I mean, we got a good thing going here with the business. I appreciate everything you done for me, I really do, but I think it's time we stop and think about what—"

"Shhh." She placed a chilly finger on his lips. "You've been wonderful, Sonny. You've taken care of all the mundane little details." Did the smile grow? Only just, and just for a moment. "And in return, I took you into my confidence. I allowed you to witness the miracle birth of my human wolfhounds. We've had a wonderful time watching them learn how to kill, haven't we? But don't worry, my sweet, it will all soon be over. The end will soon begin."

"But that's just it, Gorgeous. Everything's going so good for us. Why end it?"

Another touch of the icy finger. "Sonny, I don't think you're listening to me, and that doesn't make me happy at all."

"No, of course not." Had he crossed a line? Was it too late to step back? Yes, it was, he couldn't move at all.

"I'm not being unreasonable, am I? I mean, I told you everything—well, almost everything. I told you there would be blood. I never lied to you, not once—not once—and this is how you repay me?"

"I'm sorry."

"Why are you shaking so? Is it because Steel is out of control, and Lucy and Ivan refuse to participate? Not to mention my poor, darling Flynn lying dead in the street. And as for Detective Ramirez—well that was a waste of time, wasn't it? No matter, I have someone else in mind for that role. Maybe you're right; I made the wrong choice with the detective, maybe I made the wrong choice with you."

"No." But the word fell flat, choked off by the pain that exploded across his hand. He jerked his eyes down to see his left hand holding the cherry of the cigar on the back of his right. He couldn't pull it away. His skin sizzled.

"Like I said, you're my right hand man, Sonny." Her voice remained soft and relaxed. "And what happens when the right hand doesn't know what the left hand is doing? It could be painful."

"Stop, please, I'm begging you."

"Begging? I like that. Now why don't you tell me the truth?"

Russo forced the words out. "Steel's been talking to that smart ass reporter. I used Flynn to find out where they were and we went to take care of her, but there was an accident."

Gorgeous glanced down at Russo's hands. "Yes, accidents happen, don't they? Why don't you go and run that under some water?"

The cigar fell out of his hand. He raced to the kitchen, turned on the water, and thrust his hand under the tap. The water was boiling hot. Try as he might, he could not pull his hand away from the steaming torture.

Gorgeous drew close, whispering in his ear, "Oh my, now look what you've done. Another accident."

"Please," Russo said, "I'll do whatever you want."

The water chilled at once sending waves of instant relief.

"Yes, you will. And this is what I want: kill Steel, Ivan, and Lucy, they're useless to me. Bring Mikael, Bane, and Nina here, I need to instruct them. And find that reporter. She's dangerous, more than even she knows. And never think for one minute you are free to leave. Oh, and Sonny? For God's sakes, stop smoking cigars. They're so bad for you."

"Yes." Russo couldn't get the word out fast enough. He stared at the raw blisters on the back of his hand. It felt like Hell.

"No, sweetie," Gorgeous said as she vanished into a blue mist, her voice still resonating, "this is nothing like Hell. You'll see."

Chapter Eleven

"Lucy—is that your sister's name?" Dixie asks me as she guides the Hummer down the hill, the tires fighting for traction on the loose gravel.

I learned so much from Lucy in the little time we spoke. It isn't fair she's gone. "I should have stayed and helped her."

"How?" Dixie answers at once. "You can barely stand. You would've both been—"

She doesn't finish the sentence. She doesn't have to.

"You don't know anything happened to her," Dixie says. "She looked like she could take care of herself pretty well. I'll bet she's just fine."

It would be easy to agree, to be optimistic, but I can't. The murderous look in Bane's eyes as he chased us across the street told me everything. But it's no good thinking about what might have happened, so I change the subject. "Who is Sonny Russo?"

Dixie gives me a sideways glance. "You're kidding, right? Only the richest man in Vegas. He owns The Grotto, The Sky Dome, and the SRS Casino. He pretty much runs all the action on The Strip."

"And you said he's the one who came out of my house?" My legs continue to tingle so I rub them, trying to improve the circulation.

"Absolutely, no question. I've been trying to get an

interview with him forever, but it's hopeless. He never speaks to the press."

"And he drove away in a black sedan? The one parked in my driveway?"

"That's right, why?"

"That car belongs to The Alpha."

Dixie jerks the steering wheel to the right, and we skid to a stop. "What? That's impossible. There's no way he'd live in that run down house. He may not have more money than God, but they belong to the same country club. Why would Russo waste his time with a bunch of…er…I mean, I don't know why he'd want to have anything to do with…uh…oh shit, you know what I mean. No, Russo can't be your Alpha."

She's probably right; it makes no sense at all. The Alpha lives like a king in his air-conditioned den surrounded by art and luxury. But the rest of the pack lives in squalor in a house that should be, and probably is, condemned. Those of us who can't stand the taste of raw meat go hungry. We're told nothing of who—or what—we are. If Russo has as much money and power as Dixie says, it doesn't show in the way he treats us. "You're right. This Russo guy can't be The Alpha. I must have been mistaken."

"But I saw what I saw. Russo came out of your house and drove away in that black sedan. Look, maybe he knows The Alpha. Maybe they've got some kind of arrangement or something."

"Like what? Why don't you come over, Mr. Russo, and watch my dogs?"

"Canines," Dixie corrects in a heartbeat.

That makes me smile. "Yes, canines." I stamp my feet, testing the strength in my legs. "I don't know what's going on, but—"

The Hummer shakes as Bane jumps at it. He paws and scratches the driver's door in a frantic effort to get inside. Dixie screams.

I shout, "Drive!"

She hits the gas, kicking up a flurry of dust and rocks. Bane chases after us for a few yards, his powerful paws digging into the gravel.

"Get to the freeway. He'll give up."

"Give up? He's followed us all the way down the hill. How fast can he run anyway?"

"About thirty miles an hour tops." A little faster downhill, but there's no use in bothering Dixie with that little bit of information.

We fly across the small access road, turn left onto the freeway entrance, and merge into traffic. She cuts across to the fast lane, holding the steering wheel in a white-knuckle death grip. Her eyes stay fixed on the road ahead, never glancing at the rearview mirror, as if not looking might keep Bane from appearing. We're flying by the cars on the highway.

"I think we're okay." The speedometer reads ninety miles an hour. "I think you can slow down now."

"I'll slow down when we're safe."

"This is the exact opposite of safe." I wanted to add a chuckle, instead it's a yelp. Pain grips my body and I shudder.

"What's wrong?"

"No, not now." I bend forward and put my hands on my head feeling the sticky paste of sweat on my forehead.

"Are you okay?" She says, shooting me a quick glance. "Is it your legs?"

"No, not my legs. Listen to me, and please don't be afraid." But that was a silly thing to say, already her eyes are widening. Sucking in a long, shaky breath, my voice is weak. "I can't stop it; it's coming."

"What is?" She stares at the rearview mirror.

"The transformation. I'm changing."

Dixie swerves out of her lane almost sideswiping a tractor-trailer. A symphony of horns sound and she forces the Hummer back into the fast lane.

"You've gotta help me. I can't go back home. That's what I always do when I change."

"You're changing now? Right now?"

Sucking in a breath through tight lips, I shout out, "Yes. And we can't go to the police—not like this. You need to take me someplace—someplace where I can't run off."

"Run off? Can you hold it?"

"It's not like I have to pee."

"No, right. I mean can you wait a little longer?"

"I can try." It feels like sharp, spiky needles scraping at the inside of my skin. As a young pup, I used to try and delay the change. A personal challenge to see if the process could be controlled, more than that, to see if I could prevent the pain. I'd learned a few tricks: deep breathing, tensing muscles, meditating on all things human. But I never stopped the transformation outright. It always came. "The best I can do is ten, maybe twenty minutes." Of pure agony.

"Okay, okay," Dixie says, "let me wrap my head around this." She's quiet for a few miles. "We can't go to Metro, and you said my home isn't safe. We need a place to lay low for a while."

A groan races out of my mouth.

"Try to relax, I'm just thinking out loud. Okay, I got it." She speeds up, as if that's possible, and the passing scenery blurs. After a few miles, she says, "Adam?" She hesitates, as if waiting for permission to speak.

"What is it?"

"Do you think, I mean—?"

"What is it Dixie?"

"Do you think you'll hurt me? You know, I mean, when you change?"

"No, I would never hurt you." I'm being as honest as I can. "By the way, do you have another Taser in the car?"

"No. Wait, what?"

****

Major Ransom arrived at McCarran International two hours and ten minutes after leaving Dallas. She looked fresh, wide-eyed, and relaxed. With not one strand of black hair out of place, she walked up the ramp and into the waiting hug of Colonel Jon Dayton.

"The admiral phoned. He told me you needed my help. The next thing I knew, I was on a jet headed to Vegas."

"Thanks to our excellent travel agent here. Major Jean Ransom, meet Paul Cuthbert. His assistance has proved invaluable, quite a resourceful lad."

"Thank you, sir. Please, ma'am, everybody calls me Cutty. Good to meet you, Major." He ran his fingers through his red locks and held out a hand. "I hope you didn't mind commercial travel. In any case, you won't notice the temperature until we're out of the terminal. It's a little less shocking that way, right Colonel?"

"Absolutely. I would not recommend a tarmac

arrival, it's brutal."

"Still," Cutty said, "it's six o'clock and you missed the better part of the heat—"

"Gentlemen, please." Ransom held out her carry-on for any taker. "I've been to Las Vegas before. I'm well aware of the climate, and I'll take desert heat over London rain any time. Shall we proceed?"

They headed through the terminal and down the elevator to VIP parking. Cutty opened the back door of the sedan for Major Ransom. Dayton slipped into the backseat next to her. When they were settled in, Cutty guided the sedan through the maze of roads leading to the 215. All windows were halfway down letting the hot air whip through the cabin. They soon headed north on the I-15 toward downtown Las Vegas.

"Okay, Colonel," Ransom said, "you've managed to get me here, now tell me why."

Dayton shook his head and nodded at their driver. Cutty had not been cleared for operational intelligence, his role being logistics only.

Major Ransom smiled, her dimples catching Dayton's eye. "I said: tell me why I'm here. You know how to tell me, don't you? Or have you forgotten?"

He formed the words in his mind, but Major Ransom needed only his thoughts.

I think we have an actual event. Whatever we're after is not human. There's a reporter named Dixie Mulholland who's gone missing. I think she knows not only what we're looking for, but where it may be. It's just a hunch, but I'm almost certain she's the key to finding this Werewolf Killer. I'm hoping we can use your talents to find Miss Mulholland.

"Working on hunches now, Jon?" Ransom smiled

again.

It's the best I've got to work with right now. The only thing, really. This Werewolf Killer leaves no clues and strikes at random.

"I'm going to need a starting point," Ransom said. "I need to meet someone who's close to her."

"Hey, this is the weirdest conversation I've ever listened in on," Cutty said, his eyes sharing time between the road and the rearview mirror. "I guess I'm going to have to brush up a little on my snooping skills."

She's friends with the lead detective on the case, Detective Marco Ramirez, although he has no idea where she is either.

"And what makes you think she knows anything?"

She's a local television reporter and has been working this story from day one. Her name is practically synonymous with the term Werewolf Killer. She hasn't been seen for twenty-four hours. For me, that's more than coincidence. Detective Ramirez is concerned. He hasn't said as much, but I can sense it.

"Be careful, Colonel, you're venturing into…what did you call it? My area of expertise?"

Dayton laughed. "You're rubbing off on me."

"I hope so." She gave him a grin. "And thank you."

"For what?"

"You know what. For inviting me to join you on this adventure."

"Adventure? I hope that's all it turns out to be."

Cutty exited the I-15 and merged smoothly onto Tropicana Boulevard. "Welcome back to the bright lights of Vegas, Major—whoa! Hang on." He swerved to the right and allowed a speeding SUV to zoom by on his left. The larger vehicle blared its horn and clipped Cutty's side view mirror. It sped up and ran through a red light, turning left into the New York New York Hotel parking garage. "Traffic can get a little dicey around here on Friday nights. Sorry about that. You two okay back there?"

"We're fine," Major Ransom said.

Cutty continued east in the left lane, across Las Vegas Boulevard, and turned into the MGM Hotel guest arrival area. He set the brake and swiveled around to face his passengers. "What's the matter, sir, lost your voice?"

"His voice is just fine, Mr. Cutty," Major Ransom said, taking hold of Dayton's hand and picking up on his thoughts. "In fact, I'd say everything is working just fine."

"Collect us tomorrow morning, Cutty," Dayton said as he reached across the major's lap, opening her door.

Cutty stepped out of the vehicle and popped open the trunk. He jogged to the back of the sedan, grabbed Major Ransom's suitcase, and met her at the door. "Yes sir, I'll be here at seven." He handed a plastic room key to Ransom.

Dayton allowed his eyes to linger on the major as she stepped out of the car. "We'll be ready at nine."

Chapter Twelve

Dixie keeps a steady course, northbound on the I-15 toward downtown Las Vegas. I know the gears in her head are spinning faster than the Hummer's tires. I trust her to figure it all out; I have no choice now—the change is coming.

She makes a quick exit onto Tropicana and dives into the far left lane heading east. Traffic crawls ahead, the normal early evening gridlock at The Strip. The pain slithering under my skin moves faster than that. I know she doesn't need me yapping, but I can't help it. "Speed up and go past them."

She edges a little closer to the median divide and slides past the line of bumper to bumper cars. A dark sedan threatens to keep her from making the green left turn arrow just ahead. She leans on the horn and barrels past the sedan, kissing the smaller car's side view mirror in the process. The arrow goes from yellow to red, but she makes the turn anyway, a maneuver rewarded by honking horns, screeching tires, and a few creative hand gestures.

"Good girl."

She raps on the steering wheel. "What the hell, I'm gonna lose my job anyway, what's a traffic ticket on top of that?"

"You're not gonna lose your job. You've got the story of a lifetime, remember? Me."

"I thought that door was closed?"

I don't answer. She's sticking her neck out for me. By my count, she's even saved my life three times already. I can't stand the idea of revealing my secret, but I owe her at least that much.

She turns into the self-park lot and drives up the ramp to level three, the tires screaming on the smooth concrete surface. "It's such a dog eat dog world out there—sorry—I mean, the news business is so competitive. If I slack off, even a little, some cupcake is gonna slide right in and take my place." She snaps her fingers. "Just like that."

"Cupcake?"

"Yeah, some cute little number from LA or Phoenix."

"A number?"

"Would you cut it out? You know what I mean." She dives into a free parking stall, turns off the engine, and faces me. "I've been out of touch with the station for a whole day. That's a lifetime in the news business. They probably think I've jumped ship."

The pain has me in its grip. I see her mouth moving, but the words fade in and out.

"C'mon, let's get you inside. The quicker we get a room, the quicker we can figure this thing out. It'll be all right. I promise to keep you out of the headlines for as long as I can, okay? That's the best I can do."

"Thank you."

She races around the Hummer and opens my door. I stumble out on shaky legs and fall into her arms.

"You don't look so good."

"Thanks again."

The journey across the parking lot to the elevator

takes its toll on me. I want to scratch my skin off, to be free of the human cocoon that holds me prisoner and be done with it. Instead, I force myself to calm down and breathe—to focus on my senses and the changes occurring: colors fading into muted shades of gray, metal wheels grinding on the roller coaster tracks above, and the smell of rain in the air.

"We need to call the police is what we need to do."

The word comes shooting out of my mouth, "No." I grab her shoulders and squeeze tight. "You're friend in Metro…call him. Tell him about the house on Claremont. Tell him you saw a murder, that'll get him there."

The elevator doors open, and we stagger inside. I grasp the handrails, slump forward, and moan. At least it's not a howl…not yet.

"C'mon," Dixie says, "just a few more minutes and everything will be all right. You'll be safe. Hold on."

"Promise me you'll call Detective Ramirez."

"No," she says. "He'll ask too many questions I won't be able to answer. I'll call 911 with an anonymous tip instead. That'll be better, trust me. Please hang on, we're almost there."

My breathing turns into rhythmic panting. I growl and scratch at my arm.

"Stop that." She grabs my hand and holds it in hers. "Don't you scratch anything off, do you hear me?"

The wait in line at hotel registration is torture. Dixie holds both my hands while whispering words of encouragement, "You're doing great. Hang on. We're almost there."

She flashes her KLVA ID card to the registration

clerk and explains we're here to get the reserved suite ready ahead of the VIP guests for the big fight. She also apologizes for her co-worker's sudden bout with asthma.

The bright-eyed clerk makes a pouty-face. "Oh, sorry to hear that, Ms. Mulholland. You know, my uncle had asthma. Your friend's got it pretty bad, though." The clerk leans forward, as if he's a doctor examining my face. "Of course, it could be allergies, you know—it's that time of year. Look at his eyes; they're all red and watery. Or it could be the flu—his face is clammy. He might have a temperature. I don't like the way he looks at all."

Summoning what little strength I have left, I manage a shaky grin, glance at the clerk's name tag, and say, "Listen, Jesus, shut your hole and give us a room."

The clerk straightens up. "Of course. My apologies." He types on his keyboard, hands Dixie a plastic key-card, and scowls at me. "It's pronounced *hay-soos*."

"I'm so sorry," Dixie says as we move away from reception and walk to the elevators. "I'm sure he'll be okay in a little while." Then she whispers in my ear, "Jesus, Adam, keep it together for a few more minutes. We're almost there."

"Don't you mean hay-soos?" I stumble along with her help. She puts her hand behind my back and shoves me into the elevator. "Are canines allowed here?"

"Yes. Listen to me—are you listening? Once I get you settled in the room, I have to call the police from a pay phone down here in the lobby so they can't trace it. Are you gonna be all right by yourself?"

I manage another awkward smile as the elevator doors slide shut. “Dixie.” I paw at her shoulder. “Dixie, when I…when I change, be strong…you’ve got to use a commanding voice. Take charge.” The pain makes me howl at last. I can’t hold it back.

“Shut up, Adam!”

“That’s good. But remember my name,” my body convulses, “Steel.”

We tumble out of the elevator. She supports my weight down the long hallway to the room. She slips the key card into the lock, opens the door, and flips on the light. I brush past her and fall into the bathroom.

The pain takes over. I leave the door open just a crack on instinct. My last lucid act as a human is to turn on the shower; the canine can no longer wait.

****

The size of the wolfhound that emerged from the restroom took Dixie’s breath away—she felt light-headed, frightened, and excited all at once. The words, “What have I done?” fell out of her mouth.

The beast stood at the threshold, his coarse gray hair leaving puddles on the carpet. When he spotted Dixie, his yellow eyes narrowed, his top lip curling up in a snarl. The animal’s beard was streaked with blood.

Dixie backed up against the nightstand, her heart pounding. She stood as far from the wolfhound as possible. The suite that at first seemed quite large now felt like a closet. The nightstand held her in place. She raised her hands in a weak attempt to keep the animal at bay.

“Adam…Adam, stay.”

A low growl, deep and guttural, crawled out of the canine’s throat. Inching forward on massive paws, the wolfhound's head lowered, its shoulder blades rising and falling with each silent step. The hackles on the back of its neck bristled as the animal's tongue lapped at its bloody chops.

Dixie's heart banged inside her chest. The desperate man who promised not to hurt her—the very man she'd helped into this room—had left the building.

"Adam, stop or you'll be sorry." The words fell flat, an empty threat. The wolfhound advanced to the middle of the room. Her path to the door was now blocked.

What was it he'd told her? To be firm; to be in command. He also told her to use his name. She stuck a hand out like a traffic cop. "Steel, stop!"

The wolfhound paused in mid stride, its eyes softening, and the hair on the back of its neck smoothing. Dixie relaxed at once. The word had power—a special word—the last word he'd spoken to her before transforming: Steel. At once she believed, no, more than that, she was convinced some trace of Adam resided in the giant creature.

"Good boy, Steel," she said, testing the boundaries of her new found power. "We're going to have to trust each other." The hand she still held up as a stop sign trembled, betraying the authority she desperately needed to convey. "Mutual trust. You trust me to take care of you, and I trust you not to hurt me."

The animal shook itself dry, throwing water in all directions. She put her hands up against the spray that flew onto the walls, the ceiling, and carpet.

Steel found a patch of dry carpet near the window and lay down, putting his head on top of his paws. He watched her—always—from this resting position; the low growl sounding every time she moved.

The confidence she felt only moments ago faded with each growl. Was there power in the word Steel? Was there trust? She'd heard animals could sense fear. "I'm not afraid of you, you know." But the words were hollow. If animals truly could sense fear, no amount of saying otherwise would do any good. "All right, I'm scared to death of you." It made her feel better to put it out there. After all, he'd been honest with her; it was the least she could do in return.

Steel opened his mouth revealing enormous, knife-like teeth. His huge tongue curled up in a lazy yawn accompanied by a high pitched "ee-yow." It was adorable. In that moment of the yawn, her fear of the wolfhound eased just enough for her to realize the truth: Steel meant her no harm. After all, he'd asked for her help—of course he'd been Adam at the time—and if he meant to hurt her he would have done it by now.

"Just give me a minute to stop shaking. By the way, staring at me isn't helping." She closed her eyes and took some deep breaths, a technique she often used to help organize her thoughts before going on air.

The sound of running water in the restroom reminded her. "I've got to straighten up the bathroom. We don't want housekeeping to freak out, do we? I don't know how long we're going to be here, and I like fresh towels, don't you? Do you understand anything I'm saying? I'm going into the bathroom and do my best to make it presentable, okay?"

All at once Dixie flinched at the thought of the task ahead. She imagined the flesh, blood, and whatever else he'd left behind during the transformation. Cleaning had never been one of her top ten activities, but in this case a little tidiness might prevent some uncomfortable questions. With a deep breath, she ran her fingers through her hair. Steel growled.

"It's okay," she said in a high-pitched, cooing voice—the kind of voice that worked so well on babies and young children. "You're okay, I'm okay, everything is okay—okay?"

Steel barked at the voice.

"Fine." The voice apparently did not work on massive wolfhounds. "I'm going to the bathroom now and clean up." But she couldn't move; her shoes felt like they were made of Velcro, stuck to the carpet.

Steel sneezed.

"Bless you," she said, then smiled at the words directed to the animal. She blessed him out of habit—she did the same with strangers, co-workers, anyone at all within earshot of a sneeze. She didn't know why. To be polite? Was it really the correct thing to say when someone sneezed? What if they didn't want to be blessed? What if they were atheists? Was Steel an atheist? Did he believe in God, a higher power—heaven?

Hell, I'm stalling.

She eased her right foot forward, checking the Wolfhound for any reaction to the movement. There was none except for the incessant low, rumbling growl. "You're gonna have to stop doing that, it's annoying." Left foot forward—growl. "Good boy, stay." It took well over a minute, at this slow and careful pace, to cover the fifteen feet to the restroom. Steel commented on her every advance, but he did not move.

She stopped just short of the restroom, long enough to give the door to the hallway a quick glance. The thought of running out and abandoning him played in her mind for a moment, but vanished as Steel sneezed.

"Bless you again."

She entered the restroom. Steam filled the confines of the windowless room, coating the mirror, fixtures, and walls in a fine mist of condensation. The air was thick and hard to breathe. A pile of tattered clothes covered in spatters of red lay in the corner. A rust-colored trail led across the floor to the shower.

Dixie reached around the shower curtain and turned the faucet off. Small spots of blood blended with the steam on the walls giving them the appearance of water colored roses. The lack of any substantial human remains lifted her spirits at first. Then, in one sudden and disgusting realization she knew why Steel's mouth was covered in blood: he'd consumed the leftovers.

"Yuck."

With a well-soaked washcloth, she set to the task. It took several minutes to wipe the blood from the floor and walls, but the condensation made the job easier than it might otherwise have been. After wringing the cloth out in the sink several times and using a towel to dry the area, she gave the room a final inspection. She picked up the pile of clothes and something fell out, dropping hard on the tiled floor, a small notebook.

She flipped it open and saw a penciled drawing of a face—a likeness of her. "What the hell is this?" She flipped through pages of drawings, sketches, and simple outlines. All were quite good. She tucked the notebook into her back pocket and jammed the rest of the blood spotted clothes, towels, and washcloth into a small wastebasket, putting his shoes on top and shoving it all down as hard as she could. Hopefully, housekeeping would toss it out and not get too curious about the contents.

"Marco would be proud," she said, satisfied with her work. She turned off the light and shut the door.

"Well," Dixie said in a soothing tone, "you certainly do like to draw, Mr. Steel." She put the notebook on the writing table next to the phone. "I guess we don't have to worry about getting you anything to eat for a while." A grimace. "And thanks for that, my appetite's gone, too. But right now food is the least of our worries.

"Pay attention, Steel. I'm going downstairs for about ten minutes. I've got to make that phone call to the police—remember the one we talked about? We don't want it traced back to this room, so can I trust you to behave while I'm gone? Do you even know what I'm saying?" She waited for an answer, then shook her head at the absurdity of waiting for an answer. "I'll be right back, ten minutes, tops. No barking, promise?" She put her hand on the door knob. Steel stood up, his ears erect, tail waving from side to side as if caught in a light breeze. "No, you have to stay here. Stay." She opened the door and slipped out.

After easing the door closed, she raced down the hall, her shoes clomping on the thick carpet. The light above the elevator doors lit and a soft "ding" echoed. A muffled bark sounded from down the hall. Dixie jumped into the elevator, hoping she would only be gone for the ten minutes she'd promised.

On the way down, she visualized the worst case scenario of leaving Steel alone in the hotel suite: someone complaining about a noisy dog, hotel security being called, the security officer opening the door with his pass key and being eaten alive.

The elevator doors slid opened. The noise of the casino assaulted her ears.

It took her a minute or two to find a pay phone. "Nine-one-one, what is your emergency?"

"I witnessed a murder on Claremont Street. Please hurry. It's the house on top of the hill. I think the killer is still in the house."

"What is your name?" *Click.* She ended the call.

Dixie raced back to the elevator and returned to the room in less time than planned. She opened the door with caution, stuck her head in, and smiled. "It's me, I'm back."

Steel stood up and glared at her for a moment. She closed the door and double locked it. He sniffed the air then lay down again on the carpet by the window.

She moved to the bed and lay on top of the covers. With two pillows under her head, she rolled onto her side and stared at the wolfhound. He stared back.

"It'll be okay, Steel. You'll see, I promise."

His eyelids started to close in a slow, measured rhythm, his breathing unhurried and peaceful. Little by little his giant muscles relaxed, and his eyes shut tight. Dixie watched him sleep, curled up on the floor, and wondered what dreams, if any, might play out in his mind.

The more she thought about his dreams, the sooner hers came.

Chapter Thirteen

The hand had, at various times, waved to friends, opened doors, and caressed lovers. It had performed the myriad of functions hands do—when still connected to their wrists, their arms, and their bodies. This particular hand was an orphan, severed at the wrist, and lying in the middle of an enormous backyard on the top of a hill south of Vegas: 7711 Claremont Drive.

The slender fingers were curved, dried and brittle from days of baking in the sun, and adorned with painted nails—turquoise—a diamond wedding ring, and a cut on the inside of the thumb. There were punctures near the wrist, jagged and uneven, where raw strands of dried tendons, muscle, and flesh were exposed. Due to its positioning—propped up at an angle, like a hand reaching up from the ground—the forefinger pointed toward a doghouse just a few feet away. But, of course, its days of pointing, of being able to help tell a story were over: except to those who knew what to look for.

Detective Marco Ramirez crouched down and stared at the hand lying next to exhibit marker thirty-seven. Craning his neck to get a better view of the wedding ring, he made a notation in his book, a notebook now filled with comments, diagrams, and symbols. He noted the turquoise nails and the cut on the thumb.

The entire crime scene was bathed in artificial

light, an eerie, otherworldly illumination, hard on the eyes. The generators for the portable lights circling the backyard were supposed to be the newer, quieter models. However, the constant noise and smell of diesel sent a shooting pain through Ramirez's head. He rubbed his temples, mulling over the impossible task ahead.

Scores of numbered yellow cones cluttered the backyard as crime scene investigators, detectives, analysts, and photographers tip-toed around them. Each cone marked the location of evidence—human remains—littering the backyard. A canvas of suffering almost beyond the scope of documentation.

But there was no choice: the tedious work continued. Video cameras captured real time images, while artists and illustrators drew diagrams, mapping the area with the assistance of measuring wheels, distance lasers, and computer aided design tablets. Each piece of evidence was photographed several times, as it was found, with the numbered evidence cone in the background, and with a ruler nearby to indicate scale. The object was then carefully collected and placed in a bag or box, depending on size. Samples of dirt, in proximity to the collected evidence, was scooped up into separate bags as well.

The body parts were reminiscent of the multi-vehicle accidents Ramirez had investigated when he worked uniform. But the comparison stopped there. None of the highway carnage he'd witnessed came close to this. The poor souls here were not victims of an accident, nobody made an error in judgment, and there was no mechanical failure. They were here because of one reason: they'd been murdered, dismembered, and their remains strewn about the property like so much garbage. At the very least, the act was unthinkable. Another word crossed his mind: unforgiveable.

From the moment the task force arrived at the scene discoveries were made in rapid succession: a basement in the house with several empty cages; a room filled with piles of new and used clothing; bones and dried blood throughout the residence. But the most disturbing discovery of all: a man sitting on a ragged yellow couch in the living room.

The wiry old man with clouding blue eyes sat as if frozen, shaking and chattering under his breath in a language nobody understood. Ramirez had no idea if he were a victim or suspect, and wasn't about to gamble on which.

"I want him taken to UMC," Ramirez told a uniformed lieutenant, "and be alert, this guy could be the key to everything." He turned to FBI Agent Miller. "We need to find out what language he's speaking. It sounds Russian, or Czech to me, but I'm no expert. Let's get one."

"We've got the best on the way from Langley," Miller said.

"Good." Ramirez turned again, barking at the lieutenant, "I want heavy protection on this guy. Stay with the paramedics all the way to UMC. Screen everyone who treats him or even comes close: nurses, technicians—everyone. Keep a record. Check all IDs. I want a tight perimeter, and no press. Is that understood?"

The lieutenant nodded and helped the old man to his feet.

As Ramirez and Miller stepped outside, a

helicopter churned overhead.

"Jesus Christ, that better be ours," Ramirez said shielding his eyes against the blinding search light. He turned to a uniformed officer. "I don't want press helicopters anywhere near this site. Is Claremont still blocked off at the bottom of the hill?"

"I think so, sir."

"Find out."

The old man, helped by two paramedics and followed closely by the lieutenant, stepped outside. Ramirez moved back to make room for them on the narrow walkway leading down to a Clark County Fire and Rescue vehicle. The driveway was empty; a couple of forensics experts busily collected the oil stains left behind.

The old man kept chattering in the unknown language as he passed Ramirez. It sounded like the same few words, repeated over and over, as if it were a chant, or a prayer.

Before being tucked into the back of the vehicle, the old man paused, turned back to face the house, and parted his lips in what could have been a smile. A chill ran through Ramirez.

The incessant noise of the generators and diesel fumes drove Ramirez away from the house and down to the street as the rescue vehicle departed. Three patrol cars, their blue and red lights washing over the hillside, followed close behind.

Ramirez stopped on the sidewalk, his mind stumbling on the old man's smile, on the cages in the basement. He closed his eyes and bent his head down; someday, what happened here would be explained, a crime of this magnitude demanded an explanation.

Agent Miller approached Ramirez. "How many bodies? Do we know yet?"

"No idea," Ramirez said. "The coroner has to piece it all together—like a human jigsaw puzzle—and give us a count. Could take days to get that number. Most of the smaller pieces were buried, in individual graves, like they were being put aside."

"I agree, not buried very well."

"No, I don't think they were being hidden. It's more like they were being held back—saved for later. They had very little bite marks, not like the rest we found."

Miller rubbed his forehead. "Saved for what?"

Ramirez shrugged and let the word escape. "Leftovers."

"Cannibalism? You think those bite marks are human?"

Ramirez shook his head. "No. I think our guy was feeding his dogs."

"Dogs?"

"The cages in the basement—the paw prints in the backyard. Dixie seemed to think we had a Department of Wildlife guy on our team. Looks like we need one now." He stared at Miller, giving the man a smile accompanied by a frown. "I hate to admit it, but I think Dixie must be psychic."

"Really?" Miller said. "Then why didn't she know about this place?"

Ramirez turned and walked away from Miller without answering. He climbed the walkway back to the house. Maybe she did.

****

Colonel Dayton pulled on the cord and drew back

the heavy black shades covering the windows. The morning sun bathed the suite in blinding light. He took a moment, allowing his eyes time to adjust, then focused on the New York New York Hotel and Casino located just across the street.

"A werewolf killer is running loose on the streets of Vegas, and the tourists are all out looking for the cheapest breakfast buffet they can find. Kind of ironic, don't you think? Since they're sort of on the menu themselves."

"That's a bit crass, isn't it, Jon?" Major Ransom slipped out of the restroom, running both hands down the sides of her dark pants. "The authorities are doing what they can. There's basically a policeman on every corner. This has to be the safest city in the world."

"Really?" Dayton picked up the remote control and switched to a news channel.

"…another murder last night in Sin City. That brings the total number of victims attributed to the so-called Werewolf Killer to twelve. The local task force has not issued a statement about last night's attack, but a press conference is scheduled for—"

He turned off the television and sat on the edge of the bed, his shoulders slumped.

Ransom joined him and put a hand on the back of his neck. "Don't blame yourself. Two million people live in this valley, and we're looking for one—just one."

"We weren't looking last night, were we?"

"Don't, Jon—"

He stood up and stepped back to the window. "There's a killer out there somewhere. The kind the admiral has hoped existed for years."

"What are you saying?"

"Don't you know? Can't you read my mind?"

"I can, but I want you to say it out loud so you can hear how silly it sounds."

"Silly? Don't you think the home office is giddy with delight? We've got ourselves a real live werewolf." Dayton lowered his voice, doing his best to mimic Admiral Garrison: "We knew it, we knew it all along. There are things out there, things that can't be explained. Now you know the truth. Now you know—"

"Stop it. Admiral Garrison would never gloat like that. He's a truly dedicated man. It's not his fault. Do you think he's happy about it?"

Dayton turned to her. "I'm sorry. It's just, now that it's real, I feel so useless. I mean, we're actually trying to find a werewolf. And you're right, it does sound silly when I say it out loud, but there you have it."

"At least we know what we're looking for. That gives us an edge, doesn't it?"

He didn't answer.

"You're frightened."

"Damn right. Aren't you?"

"Of course, I am," she said. "Terrified, actually."

He helped her up. "You are?"

"Yes. That was the worst impression of the admiral I've ever heard. It scared the hell out of me."

They laughed.

"C'mon, Major," Dayton said as he grabbed his room key. "Let's go in search of a cheap buffet breakfast."

"Yes, sir." Ransom smiled. "Then let's find ourselves a werewolf." She stopped in the middle of the room. "Wait." She stepped back toward the window and gazed across the street.

"What is it?"

"Hush." Major Ransom closed her eyes, placing her palms on the glass.

Dayton came up behind her and whispered, "What's wrong?"

"I don't know. There's something—very close. I don't know what it is, but the feeling is quite strong." She opened her eyes and turned to him. "It's gone now."

"Just like that? What was it?"

"Jumbled images: a red leash—panic. I can't explain it, but it was very real."

"C'mon, you need food; we both do."

They rode the elevator to the lobby in silence. When they stepped out, the noise of slot machines, gamblers, and piped-in music assaulted their ears. The backs of their hands rubbed against each other, then came together.

"No," Major Ransom said, stopping and gripping his hand tighter.

"No, what?"

"We're not going to tell Detective Ramirez who we are."

"You're going to have to stop reading my thoughts. I was just mulling it over. After all, there's no precedence for this situation. We've always investigated, what we thought was, unexplained activity. We've never really found anything conclusive. I'd say this is pretty conclusive."

"Agreed, but there is protocol—there is procedure. We're supposed to work behind the scenes, always have. It's one of the basic rules."

"It was just a thought, Major. I have lots of them."

She grinned. "Yes you do."

"So you're going to have to stop reading them all."

They entered the café and ate a light breakfast.

Cuthbert met them with the car at exactly nine. He drove onto Tropicana, turned right, and headed north on The Strip to the Las Vegas Metropolitan Police Department's headquarters where they were told about the house on Claremont.

Chapter Fourteen

A rumbling vibration brought Dixie out of a light sleep. She rubbed her eyes and sat up in a hurry, glancing at the unfamiliar furniture in her bedroom. It took her a few moments to realize it wasn't her bedroom, rather the suite at the New York New York Hotel and Casino. Housekeeping carts were being pushed down the endless maze of hallways in search of vacated rooms. She heard the faint sound of doors being knocked on accompanied by a voice calling out, "Housekeeping."

Slowly, like watching a film play backward, the events of the day before rolled through her mind. Names and places revealed themselves: Flynn, Lucy, Bane, and Adam, Sonny Russo and Claremont Drive. Steel.

She raised her head and peered over the edge of the bed at the animal on the carpet. He sat on his haunches, eyes alert, staring straight back at her. His muscles tensed and he stood.

"Stay!"

Steel's lips pulled back, sharp white fangs exposing themselves.

"Steel," she said in the same sing-song, cooing voice she'd used the night before, "that's a good boy. Who's a good boy, huh?"

He growled.

"Okay, baby voice still not working." She rolled over and sat up on the edge of the bed. "Are you thirsty? I'm going to the bathroom and get some water. Stay there."

When her feet touched the carpet, he stepped forward.

"No!" she commanded. She tried to be assertive, just as Adam told her, hoping the dog would obey. "Stay, Steel." So far, so good. After all, she shared the night with a massive wolfhound and hadn't been eaten.

He did not advance, but followed her with his eyes as she trekked to the restroom.

"Good boy," she said over her shoulder as she filled the ice bucket with cold water from the sink. He met her at the threshold, his silent approach startling her. She placed the ice bucket down and put it under his snout, the closest she'd been to the animal. He sniffed at the contents then began to lap at the water in a cadenced slurp-slurp-slurp.

When he finished drinking, he stared up at her, water dripping from his chops onto the carpet. Fur bristled on the back of his neck, and he took a tentative step forward.

"Whoa. Stay. You probably need to go outside." She slid past him and sat on the bed. "What to do," she whispered. "I don't have a collar, a leash, or a…what is it? A poop bag." She stared at him. "Help me out here—can you use the bathroom?" She never owned a dog, or a pet of any kind, and now she knew why. They required a lot of attention.

He sat down.

"Can you hold it?"

A knock on the door elicited a snarl from Steel.

"Housekeeping."

Dixie put a finger to her lips. "Shhh." She stepped lightly toward the door. "Hang in there, Steel; help is on the way." She cracked the door open and peered down at the short maid in a yellow uniform.

"Housekeeping," the maid said.

"I'm so glad you're here. I seem to have misplaced my dog leash. My dog needs to go outside. Can you help?"

"*Si*, the front desk can help. *Uno momento.* Let me call." The maid brought a two-way radio out of her pocket and smiled.

"Thank you so much." Dixie closed the door. "Well, problem solved." She turned back to face Steel. The last few drops of a rather large urine stream aimed at the corner of the bed dribbled out. "You couldn't hold it? Really?"

She ambled to the restroom and closed the door. He growled.

"My turn."

He barked. Dixie opened the door and stuck her head out.

"I need to pee, do you understand?" She shut the door.

He barked again, louder.

"Shhh." She popped her head around the door. "You're gonna wake up the whole casino. I need some privacy, do you mind? You may not think it's a big deal, but I do."

As she pushed the door closed, he snarled.

"Okay, Mr. Bossy Boss, I'll leave it open just a little, like this." She moved the door shut, leaving it ajar a few inches, enough to give her a measure of privacy.

He seemed okay with that.

She flushed, opened the door, and ambled to the bed. Steel found the ice bucket again, bent his head down, and finished the last of the water.

As he drank, Dixie shoved Adam's sketchbook into her back pocket and picked up the telephone.

"KLVA."

"This is Dixie Mulholland, may I speak to Mr. Morrison?"

"Oh, sure thing, hun, I'll put you through."

Hun? Not a good sign.

"Morrison."

"Mr. Morrison, this is Dixie. Thank God, I got you."

"Dammit, Mulholland, you picked a great time to go AWOL. Where have you been? The task force is up to something, and they're keeping us in the dark about it. Freedom of the press, my ass. It's like half of Metro has disappeared. I need to know what's going on, and I need to know now. The ball's in your court. Move."

"Sir, listen to me. I'm the one who made the call to the—"

"I had to get Peggy to cover for you last night, and I had to get Sean to cover for her. Dammit, I thought you wanted anchor. This is not the way to do that. Got it?"

"I do, sir, but—"

"Then shut up and listen. I need to know what Metro's up to. Call your sources and find out what the hell's going on."

"Sir, listen to me: I'm at the New York New York suite with Steel. He's a Giant Irish Wolfhound." Dixie snickered. "Giant doesn't even begin to describe—"

"Dammit, that suite is reserved for the station's VIP guests for the Toretta fight. Didn't you get the e-mail? Oh never mind. The whole damn task force has vanished, and they're not saying one goddamned word about it. Hell, the police have snitches, and so do we, but nobody's saying a frigging thing. I've never seen anything like it. Something big is happening right now, I can feel it."

"Listen to me. Like I said, I'm here with a wolfhound and I think—"

"Shut up about your stupid dog. I need you to find out what's going on. That's what you're being paid for, but not for long if you don't get a story on the air ASAP. Now get your ass out of that damned suite and get to work." The line went dead with a deafening click.

Dixie slid the phone back in its cradle as Steel licked his chops and sat down.

"Listen, Adam…Steel. It's gonna be a long day, so we've got to work together, you and me, like a team. I have to tell Marco—he needs to know about you. He especially needs to know about Sonny Russo. I know you don't want me to go to the police, but Marco's a friend, and the more of those we get on our side, the better. I'll deal with the station later. Sound good?"

Steel held eye contact with her. For the briefest moment, she swore he understood every word she said. Then he stood up, sauntered to the middle of the room and lifted his leg. He directed a steady stream of urine onto the base of the writing table. Dixie shook her head.

A knock shattered the silence.

"Housekeeping."

Dixie stood quickly, a little too fast for Steel. The growl was low and steady, a menacing threat.

"Easy, big fella. Remember, like a team." She trekked to the door and cracked it open a few inches, attempting to hide a full view of the room behind her.

The housekeeper held out a bright red dog leash. It was no more than three feet in length, the kind meant to control a small dog. Dixie took it and studied the loop. She knew the casino's policy of allowing small dogs in the rooms; Steel was way over capacity.

"Is there a collar?"

"No, *senora*, you put one end through the loop then around the dog's neck. *Mira*." The housekeeper demonstrated.

"Oh, I see." Dixie took the leash, bumping the door open in the process.

"*Ay, que grande*." The housekeeper took a half step back. "*Senora*, there is a limit on the dogs. I'm afraid I have to report—"

"Thank you, so much." Dixie shut the door and turned to face Steel.

She held the leash at arm's length and marched forward. Steel stood up and gave her a rumbling growl. He lowered his head.

"Steel! You're gonna have to trust me." She bent over, letting him sniff the leash. "I know trust is gained over time but, guess what, we don't have any." She slipped one end of the leash through the loop and eased it over his massive neck. His lips pulled back, but the growl was absent. The strap barely fit around his neck, leaving her about ten inches of leash to hold onto. "That's it," she cooed, "good boy, you're such a good boy."

Steel shook his head and barked.

"Quiet." She had to stoop down slightly in order to

control the leash. The smell of urine made her wince. “Like it or not this is the way it’s gonna be. I’m in charge and you’re gonna do what I say.”

He tugged at the leash pulling her forward. She lost her balance and let go before she fell forward onto him.

Steel sat down, keeping his eyes glued to her. After a few seconds, he slumped down on the ground and closed his eyes.

“Nice teamwork,” she said, “real smooth, big fella. Like it or not I’m trying to help you. So yeah, piss all over the room. Relax, take a nap and don’t worry about a thing. Let me do everything.” Then, under her breath, she mumbled, “Ungrateful hound.” She shook her head and closed her eyes.

A cold nose nuzzled the back of her hand.

“Sorry.” She patted his head. “We’d better leave before housekeeping reports us.”

****

Detective Ramirez sat on the back deck of an opened van nursing another in an endless line of Styrofoam cups filled with tepid coffee. He’d been at Claremont Drive for twelve hours straight. His head ached and he needed sleep—that wasn’t going to happen.

Evidence was still being gathered, photos and videos taken, and various experts still arrived by the carload. Thank God the press had been kept in the dark. He couldn’t imagine facing their questions. He had enough of his own.

“Why don’t you go home? There’s nothing we can do here,” Special Agent Ed Miller said. “It’s gonna take a few days to process this mess. You look like hell. Let me take some of the load off your shoulders.”

"No thanks."

"Oh, don't trust the black man in charge, huh?"

"What the hell are you taking about?"

"Hey, it's just a joke. Humor's the first thing to go when you're tired, you know. Nothing personal, but you definitely need a break."

"You're right; we could both use a break." Ramirez rubbed at the stubble on his cheek. "Whoa, look who decided to join us."

A black sedan approached and parked in the middle of the street—a cul-de-sac now clogged with dozens of emergency vehicles. Jon Dayton and a shapely dark-haired woman emerged from the backseat. They approached the detective.

Ramirez stood up, tossing the cold coffee out of the cup. "Morning."

"Why weren't we told about this last night? We have a right to know what's going on."

"We?" Ramirez said.

Dayton turned to the woman. "This is agent Jean Ransom from the home office. She arrived last night. What have we got?"

"We?" Miller's turn to ask. He aimed his comments at Dayton. "We have a crime scene. And I still don't know why the NSA is interested in this case."

"Listen, like I said—"

"I hear you, agent," Ransom said, putting her hand on Dayton's wrist. With a broad smile, she said, "It's probably some higher-up in Washington covering his ass. To be honest with you, I'd rather be somewhere else myself, but you know how it is."

Miller blinked. "And you're British, too?"

Ransom nodded. "Special Liaison."

"Right." Miller brought his cell phone out of his pocket.

"Would you give us a minute?" She took Dayton by the elbow and they ambled across the street, speaking in whispers as they walked.

"Ed, will you let it go?" Ramirez said. "This has gone way past jurisdiction. We can use all the help we can get."

Miller moved the phone away from his mouth. "Just gonna check her out, that's all. Besides, I don't like the idea of uninvited help."

"Understood." Ramirez walked across the street, joining Dayton and Ransom.

Dayton's face had gone white. He turned to Ramirez. "How many bodies have you found?"

"Parts of bodies; how did you know?"

"Sheriff Hendrickson briefed us," Ransom said.

"We don't know how many bodies. The lab is gonna have to piece it all together."

"Can we look in the basement?"

Ramirez cocked his head. "Why?"

"Detective," Ransom said, "we're here to help. That's all."

"Of course. Sign in at the tape." Ramirez waved them toward the house then went back to the van and joined Miller. "All at once, I don't like the idea of uninvited help either. They want to look in the basement. They said they were briefed by Hendrickson."

"And?"

"I never told the sheriff about the basement."

Chapter Fifteen

Lighted numbers raced across a stainless steel plate above the elevator doors. Dixie kept her eyes on them, waiting for her number to light up as if it were another casino game. She stood still, anticipating the "ding" announcing the car's arrival. Steel, on the other hand, pranced from side to side, tugging Dixie back and forth, forcing her to tighten her grip on the short red leash.

"Settle down, Steel. Sit."

A family of four joined them at the elevators. A small girl about seven years old stood in front of Steel and smiled. "What a cute doggie. He's so beautiful. He's so big."

The father leaned forward. "Keep your distance, Nicole."

"Is it okay if I pet your dog?"

Dixie grappled with the leash. "I don't think that would be a very good—"

Steel bent forward and slurped his tongue over the little girl's face. She laughed and wiped her sleeve across the spit on her cheek.

"Steel, no. Settle down."

But he wouldn't. Instead, he tugged at the leash, drawing her away from the elevators. She yanked back, getting an earful from him with every pull. He bounced up and wrenched her off balance. "Whoa. Stop," she said. "Where do you think you're going?"

The "ding" sounded. The elevator doors opened, the family boarded the car, and the doors slid shut.

Steel continued his tug-of-war, finally plopping down at the door to the stairwell. He peered up at her.

"No. I'm not hiking down ten flights of stairs with you on the end of this leash."

He wouldn't budge. She pulled at the leash, and he pulled back.

"Okay, I give up. Just keep it slow, okay? I don't want to break my neck."

As if agreeing to her terms, Steel ambled down the stairs at an even, unhurried pace.

By the time they reached the third floor landing, Dixie felt the sticky paste of sweat on her forehead. Her breathing came in labored gasps, and her calves ached. She pulled back on the leash, and Steel sat down as she caught her breath. His tongue flopped out of his mouth and his tail wagged; he seemed to enjoy the exercise.

A noise echoed above their heads—a familiar sound filling Dixie with terror. She glanced up and Steel barked. The sound, a mixture of snarling and growling, grew louder. Whoever, or whatever, the sound belonged to flew down the stairs toward them. Dixie tightened her grip on the leash and tried to run. Steel would not budge. Instead, he labored against her, trying to climb up toward the sound.

"No. Wrong way, Steel. Let's go!"

For the first time since Adam had transformed into a canine, Dixie was convinced he understood her. He backed up, turned, and raced down the stairs pulling her along with him.

"Good boy, two more flights and we're home free." She said this more to convince herself. Thoughts of the Werewolf Killer's victims entered her mind, and she quickened her pace down the stairwell two steps at a time.

Steel jumped at the panic bar, and the door to the parking garage banged open. Desert heat covered them as if they entered an oven. Dixie plunged a hand into her purse in a frantic search for the car keys.

Her heart double-thumped at the sound of growls echoing off the concrete walls and pillars behind them. Steel hesitated for just a moment then picked up his pace. More howls from their pursuers rent the air, each one sounding closer than the last.

They passed dozens of people in the darkened garage. Some were on their phones as Steel pulled her along at a sprint. People held their phones at arm's length, snapping photos and taking videos of the small woman being jerked along by the huge dog.

Dixie finally snagged the keys out of her purse and pressed the unlock button. The familiar "beep-beep" sound directed her to the Hummer. In one motion, she opened the door, jumped behind the steering wheel, and dropped the keys on the ground. Steel jumped over her, and she slammed the door. Panic set in as claws scraped against concrete only inches away.

A heavy thud made her scream. Huge paws banged her window. Two grizzled snouts baring curved white teeth smacked at the side of the Hummer, frenzied paws scratching at the door. Streams of drool splattered the glass. One animal lunged full force against the window, cracking the glass.

Dixie sat frozen in place, shaking, tears blurring her vision. They were trapped inside the Hummer as their assailants pounced against the windows in steady waves. She knew it was only a matter of time before the glass shattered and the two ferocious beasts entered the vehicle, ripping them to pieces; and whether it mattered or not—probably not in the end—it was all her fault.

Steel sat quiet, not at all like him, his snarling and barking muted. Was it possible he blamed her as well? She turned to face him. The least she could do—the last thing she could do—was apologize, to explain she was sorry for being such a klutz and dropping the keys. He'd trusted her all the way down the stairwell, through the parking garage, and into the vehicle, only to let him down by one fumbling act of stupidity.

He held something shiny in his mouth—her key ring. With trembling hands, she plucked the ring out of his jaws, shoved the key in the ignition, and slammed the Hummer into reverse. The two wolfhounds chased the vehicle, continuing to throw themselves against the windows and rear side panels. Steel barked at them now, drool spilling out of his mouth and onto the seat covers. He jumped to his left, putting his weight onto Dixie's legs causing her foot to press down on the accelerator. The Hummer lurched back into the hounds and sent them both to the ground. They were stunned, but not for long. In an instant, their attack continued.

Dixie registered blue and red lights flashing a short distance away as she threw the stick into drive and punched the gas. She swerved right and gunned the gas pedal down hard making the tires scream. Steel jumped into the backseat and continued his verbal assault through the rear window.

A Metro cruiser followed by an animal control truck hurried past Dixie's Hummer in the opposite direction. Two more black and white cruisers raced into the garage as Dixie exited. She made a sharp right onto Tropicana Boulevard and fell in line with the early morning traffic.

She shuddered and noticed her hands in a death grip on the steering wheel. Two shots rang out behind them. In the rearview mirror, she saw more police cars—lights and sirens—rolling into the garage.

"What now?"

****

On hot days, a vision of shimmering water seen miles down the road is created by light shining through a prism. The prism is caused when the asphalt absorbs the heat of the sun making the air just inches above the road hotter than the air a few feet higher. Light shining through this prism creates an illusion known as a mirage.

Dixie raced the Hummer south on the I-15 keeping her gaze alternately glued to the mirage ahead and the stream of traffic in the rearview mirror behind them. Even though she knew it was impossible for anyone, or anything, to have followed them, her definition of impossible had been challenged in the past twenty-four hours.

Steel sat next to her in the passenger's seat, his fur tousled by a stream of cold air blowing from the A/C vents. His eyes were wide and alert; his tongue lapped at his chops. Every so often, he stared up at her as if asking, "What now?"

She didn't have an answer.

As each mile ticked by, the mirage ahead expanded. Dixie now made out three structures blossoming from the desert: Primm, Nevada. The three hotel casinos were located thirty miles from The Strip, but only yards from the California border; a welcomed stop for weary travelers. Business was booming, thanks to the countless visitors heading to Las Vegas for the Sam Toretta comeback fight.

Dixie pulled into the exit lane and sped under an overpass. This led to a combination gas station-fast food restaurant. They parked under the shade of a scraggly pine tree.

She and Steel sat motionless for a few seconds. With the engine off and the air conditioning vents quiet, the silence was deafening.

"Safe at last, huh? Well, Steel," she said, turning to face the animal, "let's get out and stretch our legs. I gotta put this on you again." She let him sniff the red leash before slipping it around his neck. "There's a pet area just over there. I promise I won't watch you do your business. Then I'll fill the tank, grab some burgers, and we'll hit the road. I'm thinking LA might be a good place to disappear for a while. Sound like a plan?"

He gave her a cold stare, as if listening to every word she said, but the words must have been blah-blah-blah-blah.

"Hey, it's not a perfect plan, but it's the best one I can think of. I've got friends in LA." She gave a quick smile. "KTNT With News You Can Use."

Steel yawned.

"I didn't care for that slogan either. Anyway, we can lay low and get our bearings, you know? First things first, though, let's get out."

She drew him out of the Hummer by the small red leash and escorted him to a designated pet area. He towered over the other dogs on the grass and could have made small snacks of them all. The owners of the smaller dogs pulled back on their leashes and cleared a wide path for the Giant Wolfhound being led by the petite blonde.

A small black Schnauzer let out a ferocious growl and a series of angry barks at the sight of the wolfhound. The Schnauzer's owner did her best to pull the dog back. "Sorry, she's not normally like this," the embarrassed owner said. "Quiet Zady, settle down. Stop pulling at your leash." Then, as if in apology, "She's a rescue dog."

Steel turned his massive head toward the little yap trap and let out a booming bark. The Schnauzer yipped, turned around, and jumped into the arms of her owner.

Dixie turned to Steel. "Don't *you* ever do that—you'd break my back."

With a little coaxing, she tucked him back into the Hummer and drove to the gas pump. When the tank was full, she re-parked and rolled his window down halfway. "I'll be back as fast as I can." She raised her hand—palm out—and gave the command, "Stay." He kept his eyes on her as she edged around the vehicle. She checked on him one last time before ducking into the chilly air of the convenience store.

While she waited in line, her eyes found a television mounted from the ceiling. She leaned toward it, keeping her foot in line as a placeholder. On the screen, the familiar face of Peter Hudson—hair dyed black, squinty eyes, lips scrunched up in a perpetual half smile, half snarl—sat behind the KLVA anchor desk. A quick glance at her watch confirmed this was not the regular morning show. It had to be a breaking story. She leaned a little closer to the TV to catch the sound.

"…officers fired their weapons at the two giant dogs. At this time, it is not known how the dogs found their way onto The Strip, or where they are now—nobody has come forward to claim ownership. According to a Metro spokesperson, the officers had no alternative, but to shoot. They have been placed on administrative leave with pay; their names are being withheld pending a full investigation."

Hudson peered into the camera. "Wow, Carol, some pretty dramatic happenings on The Strip for your first day."

"Right you are, Pete." The graphic at the bottom of the screen read Carol Melody. She ran her hand over a strand of bright red hair, moving it away from her face as the wind kicked up, then graced the remote camera with a perfect smile. Her dark blue, sleeveless blouse looked professional and yet, on some level, high school age demographics, sexy and inviting. "Las Vegas is such an exciting city; I'm so glad to be here." *Did she scrunch her nose?*

"Morrison," Dixie said under her breath, "you son of a bitch."

Hudson faced the in-studio camera for a close-up. "And as I mentioned at the top of this bulletin, Metro has announced a news conference scheduled for later this afternoon at two p.m. We've heard rumors about a possible arrest in the Werewolf Killer case. Carol," Hudson pressed on his ear piece, "have you heard anything from the Metro officers there at the scene? Do they know what this news conference may be about? Is it really an arrest?"

"Peter, everyone is keeping tight-lipped," Carol Melody said with another perfect smile. *Did she giggle?* "But all the officers I spoke to were very excited."

"I'll bet they were," Dixie said.

Carol Melody faced the camera and produced a full-fledged smile, probably the one that weasel Morrison fell for at first glance. "We'll know more at two p.m., and I'll be there bringing you all the details, live, as they happen."

"Great," Hudson said, "glad to have you on board, Carol. You certainly are a welcomed addition to our KLVA family."

"Thank you. This is Carol Melody, live at New York New York—back to you, Pete."

"And of course," Hudson smiled at the camera, "the rumors about a possible arrest in the Werewolf Killer case couldn't have been timed better. Thousands of extra visitors are expected to descend upon Las Vegas tonight for the Sam Toretta comeback fight. Virtually every hotel in the city is at full occupancy—"

Dixie turned away from the TV. She winced at the thought of the New York New York hotel room she and Steel had vacated: the station's VIP suite reeking of urine. Still, the nightmare was over. Metro must have apprehended Sonny Russo. She straightened and found the patrons in line had passed her by. She shoved her way to the counter.

"Ma'am," the clerk said, "there are others in line—"

"Damn right," said someone behind her.

She pulled out her credit card. "I was in line, too. In fact, I was ahead of that guy you just helped."

Another angry voice, "Get back in line, lady."

She thrust her credit card out—bullies be damned.

"Six burgers."

The clerk took the card. "Six?"

"You're right, better make it a dozen."

"Twelve burgers?"

Dixie nodded. "Double-doubles."

The clerk ran the card. "Number twenty-two. Wait over there. It'll be a while."

"Please hurry. I've got to get to Vegas as fast as I can."

"I do too, lady," said a man behind her.

"Hey, I know you," another voice said.

Dixie ignored the chatter as she formed a new plan. With Russo in jail, there was nothing to stop her from making that press conference. She was exhausted, would be uninvited, and wasn't camera ready—no makeup and hair—but all that was secondary. Only one thing mattered now: the briefing was sure to be carried by all the major networks, and what better way to introduce Steel to the world? Dixie glanced at her watch. She had just over an hour to get back to Vegas and grab the microphone right out of Carol Melody's greedy little paws.

"Number twenty-two."

She scooped up the bag and raced outside.

"Hey, lady," a voice behind her said. "Dixie."

She stopped at the side of the Hummer and spun around. "Yes?"

A thick man in khaki shorts, turquoise golf shirt, and white tennis shoes approached. "I thought that was you, Dixie Mulholland, right?"

"Yes." Most people she met because of her work were nice, ordinary people, maybe a little star-struck and just wanted to say hi—ask for an autograph or photo, then there was this type of moron.

"Hey, listen Miss Big Shot, just because you're on TV don't give you no right to take cuts in line."

"I'm so sorry, sir, but I'm in an awful hurry—"

"Hey, we all got places to be."

Dixie turned back to the Hummer and reached for the door handle.

"Don't turn away from me, bitch." The man put his hand on her shoulder.

Steel lost control; barking, snarling, and rocking the Hummer as he bounced up and down clawing at the door panel, his head thrust out the window.

"Jesus Christ, what the hell is that?" The man back-peddled, stumbled, and fell on his butt.

"That's my dog." Dixie stared down at the man. "And he's hungry."

She slipped into the Hummer and opened the bag of burgers, unwrapping them and hand feeding Steel. He gobbled them down one after the other.

"That's it, big fella, eat 'em up quick; the networks are waiting for us."

Chapter Sixteen

It soon became clear the location of the news conference would have to be moved from the second floor briefing room to the multi-purpose amphitheater on the first floor. News vans double parked outside the police administrative building. Electricians ran thick cables across streets, down hallways, and into the amphitheater connecting television equipment, satellite feed apparatus, and power generators.

The crowds gathering outside the venue included concerned citizens, victim's families, and the simply curious. The networks tied in to the local feed and were ready to interrupt normal broadcasting the minute the proceedings began.

Field reporters, Internet news correspondents, and print journalists filled the amphitheater to over capacity. Those without a seat stood in the aisles. Still photographers crouched down near the front of the stage while banks of television cameras lined the back wall. Noise from countless conversations buzzed on in an endless drone.

Detective Marco Ramirez and Special Agent Ed Miller positioned themselves out of the limelight, standing against the wall in a side aisle just to the left of the stage. They may as well have been invisible as the crowd's anxious eyes kept constant vigil on the podium on stage, front and center, underneath an enormous

American flag.

"This is bullshit," Miller said.

Detective Ramirez did not say anything; he couldn't. He felt empty inside—even worse, he felt betrayed. From the minute he'd heard Sheriff Hendrickson order the arrest of the old man they'd found at Claremont Drive, he voiced his opposition. Not only did his protests fall on deaf ears, the sheriff made it clear Ramirez should "put a cork in it."

Miller glanced around the auditorium and shook his head. "This is a sideshow. You and I both know that old man's not physically capable of committing murder—not the way those victims were killed."

Ramirez nodded. He scanned the auditorium, his eyes squinting against the harsh glare of television lights. "It's not like Dixie to miss something like this."

"Maybe you're right, maybe she is psychic. She's not here because this isn't news, this is a joke."

A man in a dark suit eased his way behind the podium. "Ladies and Gentlemen," he tapped on the microphone, "please settle down. My name is District Attorney Steven Walters. Thank you for being here. Sheriff Gale Hendrickson has a statement to read."

The sheriff, dressed in full uniform complete with jacket and cap, marched from the wings, stage right, followed by two uniformed captains and four lieutenants. The sheriff stood behind the podium while his men positioned themselves evenly on either side. He took a drink of water. "If I can have your attention, please—can I have your attention?"

An eerie hush covered the room like the uneasy calm in a crowded ballpark during a moment of silence.

"Ladies and gentlemen," the sheriff said. "I have a

brief statement to read. Please hold your questions until I'm finished.

"At approximately 1900 last night, Metro received a call about a disturbance at a residence just south of Las Vegas. A patrol car was dispatched immediately. Upon arrival, my officers noticed indications that a much more serious crime had taken place. The officers reported to their supervisor, and the supervisor called me. From the information I was given, I directed the Special Task Force investigating the recent series of homicides in Las Vegas to report to that location. Evidence was found at the scene linking it to a series of homicides committed by, what the press have termed, the Werewolf Killer." Chatter sprang up from the audience. Sheriff Hendrickson raised his voice. "A suspect was taken into custody at the scene. At this time, the suspect has been charged with four counts of murder—"

Chaos erupted. Reporters stood and shouted questions, each voice louder than the last. Camera shutters clicked and the front row of correspondents edged closer to the stage. Sheriff Hendrickson put his hands out again, as if parting the Red Sea, and waited for his demand to be met before continuing.

As the noise died down, a reporter shouted out, "Is this the Werewolf Killer? Sheriff, do you have the Werewolf Killer in custody?"

A heavy silence gripped the amphitheater. The assembled body of journalists and media personnel waited, breathless, hoping and praying for the words—a sound bite, a headline.

Sheriff Hendrickson took dead aim at the bank of television cameras near the back of the room and announced in a clear voice, "The Werewolf Killer is in custody."

Another explosion of prattle gripped the crowd. Each and every reporter had a question.

The sheriff put his mouth on the microphone, shouting over the pandemonium, "One at a time, please, I'll answer your questions one at a time." Shrill feedback from the amplifier sliced through the air, washing over the assembly in a blanket of white noise. The sheriff straightened, pointed to a reporter, and calmly said, "Question?"

"Sheriff Hendrickson, Hank Delaney, KTLN, Phoenix. Can you give us the name of the suspect in custody?"

"That information is being withheld."

"Why?" Delaney shouted as reporters barked out again. "Why is the suspect's name being withheld?"

"At this time, we're not certain of his identity. As is standard procedure, he's been booked into the county jail as John Doe. Due to the nature of this case, we're doing everything we can to quickly ascertain his identity. Records are being thoroughly researched, and the FBI is cooperating fully with my department. We should have the suspect's name in short order."

"Does that mean you might have the wrong guy?"

"No, not at all. Make no mistake, the Werewolf Killer is off the streets."

"Sheriff," the shouts for attention grew louder. "Sheriff."

Sheriff Hendrickson pointed to another reporter.

"Sheriff Hendrickson, Carol Melody, KLVA Las Vegas. Why are you not revealing the location of the residence?"

"At this time, we have a full team of investigators going over every inch of the property. Our CSI team is being assisted by federal authorities. There is a plethora of evidence still being recorded. As you can imagine, we don't want any of it compromised. The location of the residence will soon be revealed."

"What evidence did you find at the residence?"

"As I mentioned in my statement, the evidence is compelling."

"Can you be more specific?" Carol Melody said.

The sheriff cupped a hand over his mouth and turned to his right.

"Sheriff, can you be more specific?" Carol Melody repeated, her voice carrying surprisingly well over the din.

"Hey," Agent Miller said, nudging Detective Ramirez and pointing to the right side of the stage, "look over there."

Ramirez glanced where Miller pointed. There, postitioned in the shadows of the wings, stood Sonny Russo. Russo nodded and the sheriff nodded back.

"What the hell's going on?" Agent Miller said.

Sheriff Hendrickson turned back to the microphone. He sucked in a drawn-out breath and through a dramatic exhale said, "We found body parts."

Bedlam tore through the amphitheater.

"Shit." Agent Miller pushed off the wall and marched up the side aisle to the exit followed by Ramirez. They slammed through the amphitheater's main double doors in unison.

"He just pulled the pin on this case," Miller said, stopping in the middle of the hallway to face Ramirez. "Is he the dumbest fucking cop in the world? He gave away our hold-back evidence—just threw it away. I'll grant you, John Doe knows something about the murders, hell, he probably even knows who did it, but arresting him doesn't mean the killings are gonna stop. And when did Sonny Russo start calling the shots?" He turned and continued his furious march.

"Where're you going?" Ramirez said.

"I'm gonna go get drunk; this case is closed."

"You're not serious, are you, Ed?"

"What do you mean? Hendrickson invited us in. When the crime's solved, the FBI generally packs up and leaves."

Ramirez put a hand on Miller's shoulder. They stood toe to toe in the empty hallway. "This case is *not* closed, and you know it."

"As far as Hendrickson and Russo are concerned, it is." Miller held out his hand. "Watch your back, Marco. When the shit hits the fan on this, the backwash is gonna be brutal."

Ramirez released the agent's hand. "Backlash."

"What?"

"It's backlash, not backwash."

Miller smiled. "Smart ass. Good luck. I'll be back for the trial if there ever is one—that should be interesting."

"What do you mean if there is a trial?"

"This guy's a patsy. Remember Oswald? They're never gonna let this go to trial."

Sheriff Hendrickson's voice echoed down the hallway over a loud speaker, "Once again, the Werewolf Killer has been arrested. It's all over."

Miller turned and headed for the exit. Ramirez took the stairs back to the task force bull pen. The aroma of cinnamon and roses caught his attention.

****

Dixie made great time out of Primm—for about three miles. That's when she hit a wall of California traffic headed north to Vegas for the big fight weekend. Vehicles lined up in an endless procession ahead of her, disappearing in a shimmering mirage. After pounding on the steering wheel and shouting at the drivers in front of her, she pulled over the white line on the right side of the highway and parked. Countless other drivers did the same, either to save gas or prevent their engines from overheating. She did it to calm down—and to listen to the news conference on the radio.

"Why wouldn't he say it was Russo? Something strange is going on." Something that made her rethink her next move.

Her plan of revealing Adam Steel to the world on live network television had to wait; more than that, it was probably a bad plan to begin with. After all, the presence of a Giant Wolfhound would, in and of itself, mean nothing; the real story—the worldwide exclusive—was the transformation, not the being. And the logistics of that happening would be tricky—mainly because she didn't know the exact moment the change would happen.

But more than the ill-conceived plan bothered her. The nagging voice inside her head, a voice that began as a whisper from the moment she'd found his drawing book, wouldn't let her rest. A voice that said, Adam placed his faith in you; Steel has become protective of you—you're probably the only one he's ever trusted.

Dixie pounded the steering wheel again and turned to face Steel. His ears were cocked, eyes wide, his tongue slipping in and out of his mouth in a rhythmic pant. "Why me? I mean, I'm a reporter and you came to me. Of all the people you could have gone to for help…" Although, she couldn't think of any off the top of her head. "You've only got yourself to blame for whatever happens. I never promised you I'd keep your secret, did I?"

Steel snarled at her hissy-fit, his stare glued to her in almost human scrutiny.

She took some deep breaths, her focus technique, to calm down. It wasn't helping—that nagging word "trust" rolling around in her brain.

She patted him on the back of the head, rubbing her fingers through his coarse gray hair, making gentle fists to grab handfuls of the stuff. He seemed okay with human touch, in fact, he seemed to enjoy it. She smiled. "Nobody's ever been nice to you before, have they? As a dog, I mean. No one's ever petted you." She ran her hand along his back and over his head. "It's okay, big fella. Don't worry. I won't hurt you. Besides, what kind of an owner would I be if I paraded you in front of the cameras?" A mini panic attack shook her—the kind that comes on in a heartbeat and then lingers like a bad smell. "Is that what I am?" she whispered. "For God's sake, am I your owner?"

Adam was a great guy and an extremely protective dog, but owning him? That sounded so wrong. Of course, if he remained a dog—whoops, canine—and never changed back to human, maybe she could keep him. What? He wasn't a lost puppy looking for a home. "I'm a Giant Irish Wolfhound," she imitated Adam's voice. Then, in her own voice, "What the hell am I gonna do with you?"

Steel blinked, opened his mouth wide, and yawned.

"You are so damned cute. Let's go home. We'll figure it out."

Dixie merged back onto the highway and let the miles drift by, her internal dialog continuing between what a reporter would do and the right thing to do. Traffic had thinned out enough to allow them to travel the speed limit. She followed the long ramp to the lanes marked 215 to West Summerlin. Six miles later, she exited, passing by the Red Rock Casino. She turned left onto Charleston at the light and stayed in the left lane, maneuvering the Hummer on auto pilot as she got closer to home.

Steel bounced out of his comfortable position in the passenger seat, bared his teeth and let out a wild series of barks.

"Whoa, what is it? We're almost home, settle down."

Steel's fur stood up on the back of his neck and he howled. He kept up a continuous stream of barking and growling.

"Okay, no joke, Steel, what the hell is it?"

After negotiating a couple of quick rights and lefts, she finally reached the gentle upgrade that led to her gated community. Then she realized the reason behind Steel's strange behavior. A few cars ahead of them, entering the gate opened by the friendly afternoon security guard, drove a yellow van with the words "wash me" spelled out on the rear window. The same vehicle she'd seen in the driveway at the house on Claremont.

Chapter Seventeen

Detective Ramirez sat at his desk in the middle of the now unoccupied task force bull pen, his gaze fixed on the giant map and its colored pins. He scanned the pins, noting how they were all grouped in bunches across the valley—all except one: the red pin at Claremont Drive.

He didn't like things out of place—too messy. In a game of what doesn't belong, the pin on Claremont was the obvious choice. Hundreds of man hours had been spent tracking the various leads phoned into Metro, and one anonymous call had blown the case wide open. It just didn't make any sense. Something was off.

A voice boomed from across the room. "What the hell was that?"

Ramirez swiveled around in his chair and stood up at the sight of Sheriff Hendrickson marching straight toward him.

"Guess what?" the sheriff said. "I was gonna get you up on that stage today to thank you, publicly, for the work you and the task force did on this investigation. That's the kind of thing people kill to get on their resume. But you were gone. You and Miller left me hanging. Why did you just wander off in the middle of my briefing?"

"*Your* briefing?"

"What kind of a message do you think that sends?

We need to show a united front."

"Sheriff, with all due respect, John Doe is not our guy; that old man couldn't kill a lite beer. Don't you get it? This is all gonna blow up in our faces when another victim turns up."

Sheriff Hendrickson hesitated for a moment. "That's not gonna happen, because he *is* our guy. There are body parts all over his property—his prints are all over the house. He's clearly not a victim. He had access to everything. What more do you want?"

"A confession would be nice. So far all we've got is circumstantial."

"We're still building a case, but it looks pretty solid to me. Others have been indicted on much less, and you know it."

"I've known you a long time, Gale. We go way back. We've been through a lot."

Again a short hesitation followed by a booming voice, "Cut the crap. If you've got something to say, spit it out."

Ramirez paused, but only for a moment. "If you're so sure that old man is our guy, why didn't you release a photo of him? Why did you keep the address a secret? Hell, why didn't you even give the task force a heads up before you booked him? I tried talking to him—I don't even know what language he's speaking. He's feeble, weak. There's no way this is our guy."

"That's your opinion. When those body parts start getting matched up to the victims—"

"That's another thing. You haven't even gotten the lab results back yet on the body parts. Sheriff, why the rush to judgment?"

"Because Las Vegas needs to be done with this

Werewolf Killer business. The city of Las Vegas needs closure."

Ramirez took a moment. "This is bad police work, Gale. It's too soon to—"

"That's enough, Detective."

"I know you're under a lot of pressure to close this case—"

"Watch what you're saying."

Another cold stare between the men. "You sent me to talk to Sonny Russo and I did. It was against my better judgment, but I went. He had a ridiculous idea to help us with the investigation so this whole thing would just go away. He seemed to think it would be better for the City of Las Vegas if this thing just disappeared."

"What are you implying?"

"Look," Ramirez said, deciding to change tact. He approached the map and pointed to the pin at Claremont Drive. "I've been trying to get this clear in my head. Why is this pin, the one that broke the case wide open, way out here, miles away from all the rest? The other pins are grouped." He waved his hand across the map. "In clusters from downtown, south to The Strip, west to Summerlin, and north to Aliante; four distinct groups on the map with a few connectors in between. That red pin at Claremont is out of place—a rogue—with nothing around it, but miles of empty desert. There's nothing, not one single pin, anywhere near it. Not one lead, not one rumor—nothing. Then, suddenly, out of the blue, we get an anonymous call about this place. I don't buy it, any of it."

The sheriff narrowed his eyes. "It's not uncommon for a serial killer to commit his crimes miles away from where he lives."

"We found that old man sitting in the living room smoking a cigarette. He didn't try to run—hell, he could hardly walk. There's no way—"

"That's enough, Detective."

"But the evidence doesn't—"

"Go home. It's over."

Ramirez grabbed his coat from the back of the chair and slipped it on. He told himself to keep his mouth shut, just walk away. He couldn't. "Because Sonny Russo says it's over?"

Sheriff Hendrickson's face burned scarlet. In a faltering voice, "Get out."

Ramirez drove home in a trance, his mind too cluttered, his body too tired to bother with the mechanics of driving. After fifteen years of the same commute, his car knew the way.

He parked in the garage, entered through the kitchen, and cracked open a beer. It tasted bitter. He reached for the bottle of Jack Daniels he kept on the counter and poured a shot. It tasted better. The gears in his mind whirled: the damned red pin on Claremont did not belong.

A knock at the front door stopped the gears in his mind from turning. He didn't budge from the kitchen table. Instead, he closed his eyes, took another shot of whiskey, and tried to concentrate on that damned red pin at Claremont.

If it was important, they'd knock again. They did.

****

Dixie Mulholland attempted a weak smile when the door opened. "Marco—" She listed to the left, then right, then back again as if she were on a fishing boat in the high seas. "Marco, we need your help."

"What the hell is that?" Ramirez stared at the big gray dog on the end of the short red leash. "When did you get a dog, and when did they start breeding them with horses?"

"Please," Dixie moaned, "can we come in?"

Ramirez stood aside and held the door open. Dixie coaxed Steel inside by pulling on the leash and telling him everything would be okay. When the animal trotted past Ramirez, it sniffed and snorted at his pants, the floor, and his shoes.

"Hey, I'm clean—no bombs or drugs, promise." He closed the door and turned to Dixie. "Go ahead and put him in the backyard, okay? It is a him, isn't it?"

Dixie nodded. "His name is Steel, but he's got to stay inside."

"Absolutely not. Dogs belong outside the house—at least in my house they do."

"I can't let him outside; someone's chasing us."

Ramirez's tone changed, officious and detailed. "Did you call Metro?"

"No." She jerked a thumb toward Steel. "He wouldn't let me."

"The *dog* wouldn't let you call?"

She nodded and held fast to the leash as Steel sat down. "I hoped you'd help us—you know off the books—like before?"

"That was a speeding ticket, no big deal. What is it now? Who's chasing you?"

"I don't know exactly."

Ramirez reached into his pocket for his cell. "I'll get a black and white over here just in case, they can take a look around and let me know if—"

"No." The loud and sudden cry from Dixie brought

Steel to his feet. He glanced at her then turned his head to Ramirez. His lips pulled back in a snarl.

Her voice softened with an almost embarrassed explanation. “Settle down, Steel. Everything’s okay.” She turned to Ramirez. “There’s something I need to tell you first...please?”

“Sure, okay.” He put the phone back in his pocket. “How about putting the dog in the spare room, that be all right?”

She smiled and relaxed, like a burden had been eased off her shoulders.

“Good, you take care of the dog and I’ll get some beers, looks like you need one.”

“Thanks. Have I got a story to tell you.” She guided Steel down the hallway and called out over her shoulder, “You still keep that bottle of Jack in the kitchen?”

“Sure. By the way, I hope your dog’s empty; I just cleaned that room.” He grabbed two beers from the fridge, two glasses, the bottle of whiskey, two shot glasses, and juggled it all back into the living room. After placing dry-stone coasters on the marble-top coffee table, he eased the glassware down, arranging the drinks in an even line across the table, nudging a couple of coasters until he was satisfied with the arrangement. He heard Dixie speak in a soothing and reassuring tone from the spare room.

Ramirez followed the sound, not exactly tip-toeing, but not being obvious either. He peeked around the open door.

The spare room was spotless, the walls painted in a sterile, icy cold bone-white. Wood paneled louvered doors closed off the closet.

Ramirez checked his breathing and listened.

"I'll be right back," Dixie said, kneeling in front of the dog, her hands cradling its giant head. "I need to explain everything to the detective. He can help us, I know he can, but you've got to trust me. And don't make a mess—he's a neat freak. After we're done talking, I'll come back and let you know what's going on, okay?"

Neat freak? Who talks to a dog that way? Ramirez stepped lightly back into the living room and sat on the couch, easing back into the soft tan leather.

"You weren't at the news conference today," he said when she entered the room. He handed her a shot glass three quarters full; they air toasted and drank. "I never thought you'd miss the grand finale. Where've you been the last couple of days?"

"It's a long story, but I listened to it on the radio."

"It was something, wasn't it? The sheriff single-handedly solved the Werewolf Killer case." Ramirez took another quick sip from his glass.

"Why didn't the sheriff mention Russo?"

"Russo?" He placed his glass on the coaster. "What do you mean?"

"What do you mean what do I mean? Hendrickson kept saying the suspect, the suspect. Why didn't he just say Sonny Russo?"

"Russo's not a suspect."

"What? Then who the hell's been arrested?"

"Slow down. Why should Sonny Russo be a suspect?"

"I don't understand. You have a suspect in jail, and it's not Sonny Russo?"

Ramirez shook his head. "Take a drink and tell me

what's going on."

After a shaky sip and a steadying breath, she said, "Where to begin?"

"From the beginning, how about that?"

She nodded. "Okay, what I'm about to tell you is…pretty weird. I'm just trying to figure out *how* to tell you, I can hardly believe it myself. But you've got to promise you'll listen with an open mind, okay? Do you promise?"

He nodded and spun the top off his bottle of beer.

"Okay…here goes. You know I'm not crazy, right? I mean not insane crazy." She cleared her throat. "That dog in there is a very unique breed; in fact, he's not really a dog at all. He's a person." She waited for a reaction. There was none. "That dog can change into a human; his name is Adam when he's human, and when he's a canine—"

"Dixie, please. Tonight's not a very good night for practical jokes. I've been up for two straight days. I have no idea what you're talking about, but—"

"Well, then shut up and listen." She banged her shot glass hard on the table.

He waited a beat then eased the glass up and placed it dead center on a coaster. "Calm down. You said you needed my help, that someone's chasing you. Why don't you start there?"

"That's right." Her volume increased. "I was on my way home when I saw a yellow van with the words 'wash me' on the rear window driving into my neighborhood ahead of me. The guard at the gate let it right in. Can you believe that?"

"So *you* were chasing someone, not the other way around?"

"No, no this is coming out all wrong." She put a hand to her forehead and giggled, but it wasn't a giggle, more of a sad and pitiful snort. "Great, I go on camera every night and tell thousands of people the news, but I can't even tell you one simple story."

He put a hand on her shoulder. "Take a breath." He smiled. "And just talk to me. I'll listen—I won't interrupt—just tell me your story nice and slow, okay?"

She did as he suggested, a slow and easy breath, in a calm voice. "That dog in your spare room can transform into a human—" She held up a hand when he opened his mouth. "Just listen, okay? I don't know how it happens and I don't know why, but I saw it with my own eyes. And I know it sounds insane. Hell, I thought so too when he explained it to me—"

"It's a talking dog?"

"No," she barked, "he's not a talking dog. He talks when he's human."

Ramirez folded his arms and melted back into the couch. He didn't know how much she'd had to drink before coming over, but he decided not to pour her anymore. He'd let her ramble on, then sleep it off.

"He told me, *when he was human,* he thought he was the Werewolf Killer, but he's not," Dixie said. "We don't know exactly who it is, but we think it's one of his pack. One of his siblings. Listen, he came to me for help a couple of days ago. He told me he was from the Department of Wildlife and he worked with the task force. He sounded so believable, you know?"

"Uh-huh." Ramirez nodded, his eyelids drooping.

"When I drove to his house, I saw his brothers. They're nothing like him—they're mean and vicious—except his sister, Lucy, who helped us escape. We jumped into my car, and we barely got away. Bane, that's one of his brothers, chased us right down the hill; Giant Wolfhounds are so fast."

"Giant Wolfhounds?" Ramirez raised an eyebrow. "The two dogs Metro shot at were Giant Wolfhounds."

"That's right, they were. They chased us all the way from his house to the New York New York."

"That's where the shooting happened."

"That's what I'm saying. They tracked us for like ten miles all the way from Adam's house. What normal dog can do that?"

Ramirez shook his head in an attempt to clear the whiskey-colored cobwebs. "They followed you for ten miles? Where does Adam live?"

"Just south of Vegas, on top of a hill off a gravel road: Claremont Drive."

Ramirez sat up straight, his mouth hanging open like a cartoon character. "That address was never released to the public." He bolted off the couch, ran down the hall to the spare room, and flung open the door. The room was empty save for what appeared to be a pile of fur and flesh on the ground.

The window was wide open.

Chapter Eighteen

The suite at the MGM was cool, almost chilly, in sharp contrast to the world on fire outside. Major Jean Ransom spoke with purpose—a passion Colonel Dayton appreciated. "I have some type of connection with the reporter. She was at the house on Claremont. She's with him."

Dayton plopped down on the edge of the bed, holding a cold plastic bottle of water to his forehead. He kept silent, knowing his thoughts would speak as loudly as his words to her.

"Do you hear me?"

"Yeah, I hear you, can't you tell? What do you mean by a connection to the reporter?"

"When we were in the basement, next to those cages, I got inside her head, or she got inside mine, I couldn't tell. It's as if she's trying to communicate with me, or…"

"Or what? You're going to have to be a little more direct with me. After all, I don't possess your gift."

"Very funny, Jon. I'll do my best to explain. It was as if someone was trying to contact her through me." Ransom opened a bottle of cold water and sipped at it as she paced the room. "As if somebody wants to find her as much—maybe more—than we do."

"How is that even possible?"

"I have no idea. You know I've always had the

gift—this ‘mind-reading’ thing as you call it, for as long as I can remember. But it’s more than that. When I was recruited by UNPAD, they tested me for all sorts of special abilities. They said I was some kind of Empath: someone who can feel the emotions of other people. You must think I’m some sort of freak.”

“Would you stop it? You know what I’m thinking, and freak is not even in the equation. Now, suppose you just take a breath, calm down, and tell me what’s going on in that beautiful mind of yours?”

Major Ransom smiled. “Well, remember this morning, over there?” She pointed toward the window. “I saw a red leash and felt truly panicked. I think Dixie Mulholland was there, at the New York New York and she was in some sort of danger. But she wasn’t alone.”

“The red leash?”

“Exactly. She was with someone—or something—that needed her help, needed her guidance.” Ransom finished the bottle of water and joined Dayton on the edge of the bed. “I had that same feeling at Claremont, only it came from someone else; someone trying to find her like we are.”

“Why didn’t you say anything then, when we were there?”

A slight blush crawled across her face. “To be honest, I didn’t recognize what was happening. That sort of feeling has never happened to me before. It’s taken me a while to process the information.”

“So basically you have the ability to become someone else.”

Ransom shook her head. “No, not become someone else, not the way you think. But acquire the feelings of someone else; to know what they think, what they want."

He pursed his lips and tried a weak smile. "Listen, you said earlier she was with someone, or something. Any guess as to whom?"

Major Ransom closed her eyes and rubbed her temples. "It's not a werewolf. It's much more complex than that. Whatever this thing is doesn't change into an animal. It *is* an animal that transforms into a human." She opened her eyes. "And Dixie is with it—she's helping it."

"Helping it?" Dayton stood up. "Why would anyone want to help it kill people?"

"Because it's not killing people. It's trying to stop the killing."

"You know I trust you, Jean. Of course you do, you know exactly what I'm thinking. But just so it's perfectly clear, I have no idea what you're talking about. You say the reporter is with something—an animal that can change into a human—and they're trying to stop the killings. Forgive my skepticism, but—"

"There's more."

Dayton stared down at her, almost afraid to ask. "More?"

"The person trying to contact Dixie is her aunt. She's trying to find Dixie through me."

"Why doesn't this aunt contact Dixie directly?"

"She's tried, but she can't get through. Dixie's not an empath. She's not like me. Apparently, the aunt can sense I'm looking for her niece, and so she's using me like a sort of tracking device to find her. She's very powerful—Dixie, not so much."

"And what do you think the aunt wants with her?"

Major Ransom hesitated before answering. “Like I said, her aunt is very powerful, almost otherworldly. I think she’s trying to warn her niece about something terrible coming.”

Dayton sat down next to Ransom. “Something more terrible than that thing on the end of the red leash Dixie’s wandering the city with?”

Ransom nodded.

****

The clothes I find in the closet after transforming are definitely not made for me; the fabric is soft, but the fit is tight, rubbing me wrong in so many places. It’s a black cotton sweat suit so there’s at least a little wiggle room where it counts, but not much. I’ll never fit into any of the shoes lined up in pairs on a shelf, so I’ll just have to go barefoot. I’m used to the feel of almost any type of surface on my padded canine paws, but human feet are tender and always beg for mercy. It’s odd that humans refer to their feet as “dogs.” So ironic.

One glance around my surroundings tells me I’m not in Dixie’s house. It’s too neatly organized, too clean. With only a quick glimpse of her place yesterday, it’s clear this can’t be her home. No way.

This is the most bizarre part of my existence: transforming from canine to human. Since I have only vague memories of my life as a canine, the first few minutes after changing back to human is always surprising—sometimes frightening. It takes a minute or two to get my bearings.

Muffled voices come from somewhere in the house, so I crack the door open a bit and sneak a listen. The words echo down a short hallway; two people are talking and one of them is Dixie. The other person sounds familiar, although I can't put a name to the voice. I'm guessing he's not only the homeowner, he also owns the clothes I'm wearing.

Dixie sounds confused and afraid. Thanks to me her reality's been altered. I back away from the door and try to remember what happened during my last interim as a canine. The transformation occurred in a room at the New York New York Hotel, this is a clear recollection. Dixie and I had to have spent some time together—time I can't fully recall.

I remember being chased by wolfhounds through a dark, concrete structure: a parking garage? That's all that comes to mind. Try as I might, everything else is lost in shadows.

Dixie's voice gets louder, barreling down the hallway. "I was on my way home tonight when I saw a yellow van with the words 'wash me' on the rear window driving into my neighborhood in front of us. The guard at the gate let it right in."

I can only assume whoever she's talking about must be looking for Flynn—or me. In any case, Dixie's home is in danger and I have to act on instinct. And it has to be now.

The window slides open easily and it takes little effort to jump outside. My hope is to make it to her house before the sun goes down. There's only one little problem: I don't know where I am. As soon as my feet hit the ground, I scan the terrain looking for landmarks: buildings, mountains, anything that can help me.

The sun is still up, but just barely. It's settling in for the night behind Red Rock Canyon which doesn't look too far away. The top of the Red Rock Hotel and Casino is easy to see above the flat sweep of surrounding houses and shops. It's plain that I'm on the west side of town just a few miles from Dixie's house.

I run, jog, and walk down sidewalks, across streets, and through parks toward my goal. My "dogs" start to ache, but I can't let that slow me down. I keep up a steady pace, covering about three miles in short order, even with my human limitations. The sun is just a memory when I arrive at her gated community.

A truck drives through the gate giving me solid cover, allowing me to slip into the neighborhood without being seen by the security guard. I run the remaining mile to her house, crouching behind the sparse shrubbery. The yellow van is parked in front of her house. Darkness is my friend and the black sweat suit helps.

Wolfhounds possess an uncanny ability to see clearly at night. In fact, our sight is somewhat better than our sense of smell, and that's saying something for a canine. But I'm not a canine now. In my human form, I have to muddle along as best I can. I run the risk of being caught off guard in the dark.

Somehow, I'm aware of movement on her property. I squint my eyes, as if that helps, and wait for anything that might stir in the shadows.

In a moment, from around the right side of her house a figure slides into view. The shape is formless at first, just an outline. A motion sensor light flicks on and a human silhouette freezes, no doubt startled by the sudden illumination. He's wearing blue jeans, dark tennis shoes, and a green polo shirt; I'm too far away to get a good look at his face. He hops back out of the light and disappears into the shadows on the side of the garage.

I formulate a plan of attack: overpower him and get information. My odds of taking him are good for two reasons—we're both equals in the dark with poor human eyesight, and he has no idea I'm here.

"Adam," a deep voice calls from the other side of the house and shocks the hell out of me. Green Shirt is not alone. "Don't do anything stupid, we knew you were coming from a mile away." It sounds like he's decided to stay where he is, and that's a good thing. It fits in nicely with my brand new plan of attack.

They might have known I was coming from a mile away, but Green Shirt will have no idea I'll charge at him from a few feet out. I rush forward through the darkness and crash into his body, sight unseen. We tumble to the ground, me on top. It's so dark, like fighting with a blindfold on. He puts his hands behind my neck and head butts me. It feels like a brick smashing into my noodle. Even though my eyes are now starting to adjust to the darkness, it doesn't help much: I'm seeing double.

I thrust my knee up and know I've hit pay dirt, so to speak. It feels like I smashed into a couple of ripe peaches. His squeal and sudden paralysis lets me know it's much more painful than smashed peaches. He shudders and gasps for breath; I roll off him and stand up.

He slithers toward the driveway on his stomach. It's a curious crawl—a mix between a crab and a snake. The security light clicks on again so there's really no excuse for me not seeing his leg whip out and kick me in the calf giving me an instant Charlie-horse. I answer his kick with a kick of my own to the back of his head. He's out cold.

Gravel crunches to my right as Green Shirt's crony approaches. He speaks in a calm voice, "Adam, tell me what happened to Flynn."

He enters the light. It's Mikael.

"How do you know anything happened to Flynn?"

He smiles. "She told me."

She? My calf muscle cramps up where Green Shirt kicked me. It tightens and sends me kneeling to the ground.

Mikael bares his teeth in a down-turned grin. Long strands of greasy black hair above his dark eyes give him a wild, untamed look. "You always did enjoy being human, didn't you?" He unbuttons his white shirt, slips it off, and lets it float to the ground. "She warned us about you; you and that nosy reporter friend of yours. She wants me to take care of you."

"Who does? Who are you talking about?"

He kicks off his shoes and stands barefoot in the driveway, then unclasps his belt. His pants slide down around his ankles. He's naked. His body is toned, a weightlifter's torso standing six feet tall. "She wants you dead, Adam, but we're brothers, and I won't let that happen—not until you apologize for killing Flynn." His human face shows no emotion.

It takes me a few sickening moments to realize what he's doing, but it doesn't take too long to catch on. He strips the flesh from his body—transforming into a canine right before my eyes. It's effortless, as if he's simply removing skin as he would a set of clothes. Showing neither emotion nor pain, he emerges from his human cocoon faster than I could ever have imagined possible.

When his transformation is complete, he glares at

me through cold eyes. His muscles are even more pronounced as a wolfhound than they were as a human. The fur on the back of his neck bristles. His human teeth have been replaced by large canine razors.

A thought enters my mind, the kind of thought that grips my heart, but in the grand scheme of things is meaningless. Humans have a name for this kind of thought: regret. I should have left Las Vegas after the first murder. How far away would I have been by now?

Chapter Nineteen

The high beams of a vehicle, changing night into day, catch us dead on. I shade my eyes from the glare and turn away.

At the sound of a car door opening, Mikael growls. I glance back and see him pad toward the vehicle. A loud "pop" rings out, and the air reeks of gunpowder. Mikael veers away from the noise, sprinting off so fast it's as if he was never there.

Two human silhouettes stand in front of the headlights, but I can't make out their faces.

"Adam, are you okay?" Dixie runs up to me.

A familiar voice shouts out, "Hey, is he wearing my sweats?"

Neither of them says anything about Green Shirt lying in a crumpled mess near the driveway, nor do they seem to notice Mikael's remains.

"Marco, this is Adam. Adam, this is Detective Marco Ramirez."

Ramirez leans over and studies my face. "Looks like somebody hit you pretty hard. You might have a concussion."

"That would explain my double vision."

Dixie shrieks and staggers back. "Who the hell is that?"

We gather around Green Shirt and watch as he rolls onto his back in slow motion, like an animated creature waking up from a nap. Light washes over his face.

"It's Bane." Thoughts of Lucy race through my head. I want to kick him, stomp on his face, and end his life. Instead, I know he has information I need. "We have to tie him up before he changes."

"Changes?" Ramirez cocks his head. "Would somebody tell me what the hell's going on? Dixie, you know I trust you, but—"

"You know what he's talking about," Dixie says, "the transformation from human to canine like I told you."

Ramirez shoves his revolver into his holster and leans forward. "This I gotta see."

"No, you don't, Detective. It might be the last thing you ever see." I turn to Dixie. "We need to restrain him. He only needs a few seconds to transform."

Ramirez straightens up. "I've got a pair of handcuffs in the car."

"No, those won't do any good; his paws might slip right out."

"Paws?"

Dixie scampers to the garage door and presses a few buttons on a keypad. With an awful screeching sound, forcing a wince from myself and Detective Ramirez, the door rolls up.

"I've got some rope," Dixie says, "be right back." After some banging around against some boxes, garbage cans, and a bicycle, she emerges holding a roll of twine.

"Good girl." I prop Bane up into a sitting position and wrap the twine around his upper body as fast as I can, then pluck it like a guitar string. I nod. "That should hold him."

"Steel," Bane calls out my canine name. He grimaces and starts to struggle like a magician in a straitjacket. The more he fights against the twine the more frantic his expression becomes. "Steel, what are you doing? Let me go, cut me loose."

I latch onto his elbow and glance at the detective. "Help me get him inside."

"Not until somebody tells me what the hell's going on."

"There isn't time right now," Dixie says. She points at Bane. "That's who chased us out of Adam's house yesterday. He killed Adam's sister."

"So, you made that anonymous 911 call—a murder at Claremont Estates?"

She nods and puts a hand on the detective's shoulder. "I'll explain everything when we're inside, promise. But right now it's important that we get inside. Please."

Ramirez takes hold of Bane's other elbow and we haul him through the courtyard, passing Flynn's human remains from yesterday. I notice the detective looking straight at the curious mound of dirty clothes and strips of flesh. Even though the smell is nauseating, the detective says nothing about it. I don't think he has any idea what he's looking at. He hasn't yet grasped the full idea of transformation.

He stops in his tracks. "Why's the front door open?"

Dixie steps inside first. "It's a long story."

Bane struggles at the threshold. "You're making a mistake. Steel, there's more happening than you can even imagine. You'll both be sorry."

Ramirez snarls back, "Shut up and keep moving."

Bane lunges at the detective, using his shoulder to try and knock us both off balance. Ramirez rewards him with a fist to the nose. Our prisoner goes limp, and we drag him inside.

I just met Ramirez, but already I like his attitude.

We stumble down the hallway, past the stacks of newspapers and magazines and dump Bane into a wooden rocking chair in the living room. Dixie wraps row after row of twine around him and the chair. When he wakes up, he won't be going anywhere.

"I need to go outside and park my car," Ramirez says. "The engine's still on and it's sticking out in the street. I'll call this in to the station when I'm out there."

"Wait." I stop him at the door. "Mikael's still outside."

"Who's Mikael?"

"The wolfhound you took a shot at."

With a snicker, "I was just trying to scare it away. If I meant to hit him, I would've. He's probably in the next county by now. Besides, it looked like a coyote to me."

Maybe the detective's attitude, the one I admired so much earlier, needs a little adjusting. "That was no coyote. His name is Mikael. He came here tonight with one purpose in mind: to kill. And he won't leave until he does just that."

Even though it's warm in the house, muggy and humid, Dixie shivers. "Why does he want to kill you?"

"Not only me." I stare at her, a little too long. My bad.

"Are you serious? Why would he want to kill me?"

"That's one of the things I need to ask Bane."

On cue, Bane moves his head from side to side,

moans, and opens his eyes. "You're dead, Steel. You're all dead."

I cup his chin in my hand and yank his head back.

"Hold on." Ramirez stiff-arms me away from Bane. "This is a police matter now. When Metro arrives, we'll—"

"No!" Dixie flat-out yells. "Please don't call the station—not yet. Adam's right, we've got to find out what he knows."

Ramirez peers at both of us. If I'm reading him right, he's being more curious than cautious. Either way, I can't wait while he decides whether or not he's going to let me ask Bane some questions—so I don't. "Tell me about The Convergence."

"How do you know about that? You were always on the outside. You act so human, you might as well be." He says the word human as if it tastes bad in his mouth.

"Lucy told me about it. She told me about the packs from all over the country coming to Vegas. She called The Convergence something terrible for humans."

Bane formed an odd smile and spit on the floor. "The bitch."

Whether he's using the accepted human term for a female canine or not, the word strikes me as just plain heartless. I hit him so hard he's out again.

"Get away from that man." Ramirez shoves me back. "If he's committed a murder, then he's under arrest. I'll take him downtown and book him—"

"You don't understand," Dixie says. "You can't arrest him; he's not even a man."

Her words cut through me. Is that what she thinks

of him—of me? Is the hate I feel toward Bane an exclusive human emotion, or is it the canine in me that wants to strike out and kill him? It's time to choose.

In as calm a voice as I can muster, "I'm sorry, Detective; I apologize. I need to ask him some questions. It's very important. I promise, just a few questions, that's all."

Dixie puts a hand on Ramirez's shoulder. "Please, Marco. After everything I've told you—after everything you've seen tonight—let Adam ask him a few questions."

"But I haven't seen anything. You keep telling me about dog-people, transformations, and changes; so far I've seen a coyote, an open front door, and some piles of clothes. I wish I could believe you—"

"Just ten minutes," I say, "that's all I'm asking for."

He sighs, a long, drawn out breath. "I must be crazy. Okay, ten minutes—under my supervision. I need to move my car first." He glances back at Bane. "Besides, he's in no condition to go anywhere right now."

"Thank you, Detective." I join him at the door.

"Where do you think you're going? I can move my own car."

"Mikael might still be—"

"Oh right, Mikael might be outside, yeah, I forgot. The big, bad wolf. C'mon, then."

We step out into the night.

****

"Sir, this road is closed. You have to turn around." The officer aimed his flashlight straight at the face of the middle-aged man behind the wheel of the SUV.

"Is there a problem, Officer?"

"Turn your vehicle around and go back the way you came." With a no-nonsense expression, he motioned back to the highway.

The driver—gray hair, beard, and glasses—shielded his eyes against the glare of the flashlight. He squinted up at the young Metro officer. "I'm almost out of gas, Officer. I'm running on fumes. I told the wife to fill it up but, of course, it slipped her mind."

"Didn't you see the sign? Police Closure. That means this road is closed. Turn around and go back the way you came, otherwise you will be cited. Do you understand?"

"I'm sorry, Officer, I don't want a ticket. I just need some gas, that's all."

"There's no gas station down this road. Turn around and go back to the highway. Head north, and take the first exit."

The engine died. "Shit." The driver slapped the steering wheel. "It's totally dry. I told you I was running on fumes. Now what the hell am I supposed to do?"

"Stay inside your vehicle. I'll radio for a tow truck."

"Thank you, Officer. I got an AAA card; I think they're supposed to bring out a couple of gallons of gas, right?"

"Wait here." The police officer strode back to his black and white. It was parked across the road blocking traffic in either direction—red lights flashing. Two more uniformed Metro officers joined him. They all kept their eyes on the SUV. "The guy's out of gas," the young officer called out, "I'm gonna radio in for a tow."

The middle-aged man opened his door.

The young officer barked out an order. "Get back in your vehicle."

The driver sat still for a moment. Then he swiveled in his seat and cracked open the rear door.

"Sir, keep all doors closed, I'm not gonna tell you again."

The rear door flew open. Two Giant Wolfhounds jumped out of the SUV and darted toward the police officers. There was no time to draw weapons, call for help, or run. Muffled screams filled the night as the hounds tore through uniforms and ripped into human flesh.

In a few moments, the wolfhounds sat on their haunches, licking their chops. Blood and viscera dripped in sticky clots from their panting mouths.

"Hurry now," the middle-aged man said as he stepped out of the SUV. "Move the police car out of the way. Police closure, my ass. This road is open."

The canines lifted their hind legs and scratched at their shoulders in a frenzied pace. They bit at the fur around their front paws. Hair fell to the ground, in little tufts at first, then in large sections exposing human shoulders, arms, and hands. Once the hands were free, they tore off large sheets of skin. Their canine teeth fell to the ground in streams of blood. In short order, two men appeared, naked, standing in piles of the fur and flesh they'd worn as wolfhounds. They both turned and faced the middle-aged man.

"Good." He smiled. "Now push the police car off to the side. Hurry, there are plenty more snacks at the top of the hill." He jumped back in the SUV and started the engine while the two men pushed the black and white off the road.

A motor home pulled up behind the SUV, followed by a truck, then a van. Soon there were dozens of vehicles lined up on the road that had once been blocked by the Metro cruiser. Still more vehicles pulled off the I-15 from the north and southbound lanes, their headlights slicing a narrow path through the night. They formed a single column—a convoy—and began snaking their way up the hill toward Claremont Estates.

Glowing mists of various colors descended from the sky, dancing in the wind and settling onto the ground.

An onyx Bentley Mulsanne pulled aside and parked. Sonny Russo stepped out.

A blue mist broke away from the other colors and hovered over the ground near the black sedan. The fog swirled in the hot Vegas wind, touched the ground, dissipated, and then dissolved altogether. Translucent shadows appeared in the remnants of the blue fog. The shadows took a solid form.

Gorgeous emerged from the form and scanned the procession of vehicles. Her smile—the mask—glowed brighter than normal. Flowing strands of her blonde hair, caught by the breeze, whipped around her face, dancing like golden flames. Her blue eyes shimmered in cool radiance, her feet hovering just above the ground. Sonny Russo shook at the sight.

Gorgeous smiled at him through the unwavering mask. "You know me, Sonny. I don't like to brag, but the sheriff was an excellent last minute substitution for the detective. The city has its guard down now, thanks to the marvelous police work of Metro's finest."

"And Carl."

She frowned at him. "Yes, poor Carl. Who would have ever thought a sweet old man like Carl capable of such unspeakable acts?" She laughed.

Russo flinched. He knew she could have just as well used him as her patsy. "Are you gonna let the sheriff's wife and kid go?" He didn't know why he asked, he'd already guessed the answer. He wanted to hear it anyway, just to be certain.

Her smile grew. "Of course I am, Sonny. Of course I am." She stroked his face with an icy finger, her gaze shifting to the vehicles advancing on the hill. "Go on and join them, Sonny. Make me proud."

Russo rubbed at the blisters on the back of his hand and turned to the sedan. He glanced at Gorgeous one last time before driving away.

Two words crossed her lips, dripping from her mouth like a dark poison, "It begins."

Chapter Twenty

Colors faded then sparked. Men in machines and four legged beasts crawled through the shadows. Screams and squeals flew through the night. Shots rang out; bullets finding homes in fur and flesh. The smell of death. A shrill cackle:

Long ago, in times before men
The garden was tended by Daemon.
With magic and spells, death and disease—
Soon it was clear, God was not pleased.
He created man with dominion over all
And banished the Daemon;
Tis known as The Fall.

~*~

From then until now, Daemon have sworn:
Use any means to regain the throne.
Pledging apostasy, they wage a war—
Fire, flood, and plague, their great herald.
Heed me well, the plot is rife with vengeance
With nature's imperfection;
Tis known as Convergence.

Major Jean Ransom sat straight up in bed, her breath sticking somewhere deep in her throat. After a painful gasp, she inhaled a deep lungful of air and cried out.

Jon Dayton rolled over and flipped on the light. "What is it? What's the matter?" He reached for her, but she pulled away.

It took a few moments for her to realize where she was. She scanned the suite in wide-eyed terror, her breaths coming in irregular gasps, more like panting than anything else. After examining the room, she turned her gaze to Dayton, studying him as if he were a stranger. Like a picture coming into focus, she recognized him; she knew where she was. Slowly, the scenes of terror that jolted her from sleep faded into hazy, dreamlike memories. She closed her eyes, trying to bring them back.

"Are you okay?"

Using the headboard for support, she sat back and put her hands in her lap. "I had a dream. No, it was more than a dream. It was a warning."

"What are you talking about?"

"I don't know. I've never experienced anything like it before."

Dayton scrambled to the restroom and came back with a glass of water. "Here, drink this."

The water cooled her lips, and her breathing returned to a steady rhythm. "It was all there, the Daemon, the plan to regain control of the earth from humans—"

"Whoa, slow down. It really sounds more like a nightmare than anything else. You'll be okay in a little while, just try and relax." Dayton put the glass on the nightstand and cozied up next to her.

"No. It wasn't a nightmare."

"Did you have a vision again? Something about Dixie's aunt?"

"Yes, but it wasn't *about* her, I think it was *from* her."

"What do you mean? Like she sent you a message?"

"Yes. She's at her home right now. She wants me to collect her niece and take her to her house. She wants me to make sure Dixie is safe."

"Safe from what?"

"This is gonna sound crazy…safe from the end of the world." She held up a hand. "Don't say anything. Her aunt told me the whole story, in a poem. Her aunt is a Daemon."

"A Daemon? You mean like a devil or something?"

"No, it's not like that." Ransom rubbed at her eyes. "I wish you could read *my* mind."

"You said it was called telepathy—"

"Oh, for God's sake would you just shut up and listen? It was very clear in the dream—or, rather, the message. Daemons were once angels. God created them and gave them rule over the world. He gave them freewill and they soon became corrupt, obsessed with power. Over centuries, the angels became Daemons. This went on until God's wrath pushed them out of the Garden and sent them to all corners of the earth. God started over and created Man, putting him in charge of the Garden. Well, you know what happened with that. But there's some really bad Daemons still pissed at God for putting humans in charge of the world. They're using these half human, half animals to destroy—"

"Stop right there. Put the brakes on, Major. Okay, I'll buy that you've had a bad dream. I'll even concede you think it's a message from God, but—"

"You're not listening. It's a message from Dixie's Aunt. She's a Daemon—one of the good Daemons. Her message was very clear: The Convergence is starting. Not only that, she told me where her niece lives. We've got to go and take her to her aunt's house."

"Jean, just calm down. I'll get you some more water."

Ransom scowled and jumped for the phone on the nightstand table. She dialed 999. Realizing her mistake, she slammed the receiver down, scooped it up again and re-dialed 911.

"What are you doing? It was just a dream," Dayton said. "Why don't you—"

"No, it wasn't just a dream, or a nightmare, or anything of the kind. Hello, yes, this is Major Jean Ransom. I'm working as special liaison to the Werewolf Killer task force. Something dreadful is happening at Claremont Drive. Yes, this is an emergency. What do you mean you'll get…?" Ransom stared at Dayton and deadpanned, "She's getting her supervisor."

"Jean, you're not making any sense."

"No, it all makes perfect sense. I'm just saying it all wrong."

"Take a deep breath and tell me again."

"In my dream—vision, message, whatever—there was a blue fog at the base of the hill, you know, Claremont Estates, just where the road begins. A line of cars, dozens of them, drove through the fog to the top of the hill. The people up there—the technicians, police, and detectives, all of them—are being hunted by packs of wolfhounds and slaughtered." Ransom's voice grew shaky and weak. "Hundreds of animals, beasts, are being driven to the top of the hill and killing everyone. And it's happening at this very moment." She squeezed the receiver with a death grip and shouted, "Hello?"

Dayton scrambled into his clothes and dragged a hand through his hair. "And you say they're not werewolves?"

"Yes—no, how should I know?" She yelled into the phone, "Hello? Listen to me: you've got to dispatch someone to Claremont Drive. People are being killed—butchered—as we speak. This is Major Jean Ransom of the UN."

Dayton put a hand on her arm, but she slapped it off.

"Yes, the United Nations. You need to secure Claremont Drive. No, you don't have time for me to come in. What?" She turned to face Dayton and spoke in a whisper. "I'm on hold."

"Jean, you told him you were from the UN."

"Did I? And so what if I did?"

"You've got to slow down, get a hold of yourself. This morning you didn't want me to tell Detective Ramirez about us. Remember? You reminded me about protocol, procedure—"

"Dammit, Jon, this has gone way past protocol. Can't you understand what I'm saying? This is bigger than our mission—this is genocide." She slammed the phone down. "This idiot is taking too long. Call the admiral. He'll pull some strings."

Dayton did not move.

"Am I speaking a foreign language?" She raced to the nightstand and grabbed her cell phone with shaking hands. "We'll need to hire a taxi, or nick a car, there's no time to wait for Cutty to collect us."

"Don't let a dream trick you into making a bad

decision. Your career could—"

"Career? Bad decision? This isn't about a werewolf. It never was. This is a war. A war between those things and us."

"Us?"

"Humans."

****

Detective Ramirez un-holstered his weapon and motioned for Adam to stay behind him as they stepped into the courtyard. They approached the fountain.

"What's this?" He pointed to the pile of skin and clothes surrounded by a dark sticky pool of dried blood.

"That was my brother. He changed into a canine. He transformed yesterday."

Ramirez used his foot to slide a piece of fabric off the top of the pile and jumped back as a shriveled face, resembling a rubbery Halloween mask, stared back at him. "Jesus! For the love of all that's holy."

"Detective, that's what's left of my brother, Flynn, after he transformed."

"Are you serious?"

"Dixie witnessed the transformation."

"Stop it. This," he motioned to the remains with his gun, "is impossible. People don't just change into dogs. Once Metro gets out here and we analyze this mess—"

"You promised me ten minutes with Bane first."

Ramirez held Adam's gaze. "Ten minutes."

They continued through the courtyard to the driveway. The security light clicked on bathing them in a bright white beam.

The detective's sedan sat half in the road and half on the driveway, lights on, and engine running. Ramirez knew if anything were going to attack them this would be the perfect spot for an ambush. Unseen crickets chirped in the bushes, a good sign nothing lurked in the vicinity.

"Go park the car, and I'll cover you." Ramirez held out the car keys.

"No. Give me your gun, and I'll cover you."

"Never gonna happen. C'mon, hurry up."

"I don't know how to drive."

"You're joking. Who doesn't know how to drive?" With a huff, he said, "Follow me and we'll both go, okay?"

Ramirez parked the car and they were back inside the house in less than a minute.

"Are you two okay?" Dixie met them at the door, an iPad in her hands.

"Like I said, whatever it was must have turned tail and run," Ramirez said. "It's not coming back. As for this change thing, Dixie we gotta have a talk."

"No, Marco." She thrust the iPad at him. "Take a look at this first."

"What the hell is it?"

"This is the footage of the security cam in the courtyard from yesterday. Take a good look, maybe then we'll be on the same page."

Ramirez stared at the black and white image on the screen: two men fighting; Dixie opening the door and shooting one man with a Taser; she dragged the other man inside.

"Well done, Dixie. Looks like that Taser training paid off—"

"Would you shut up and keep watching?"

He turned his eyes back to the screen. The man who had been tased lay still for a moment, then stood up, staggered toward the fountain, and began to take off his clothes—and his skin. In rapid succession, strips of flesh were thrown to the ground. A snout emerged and a tail appeared. The image was not blurred. In sharp focus, the human became a canine.

"What the hell?" He let the device slip from his hands and drop to the ground.

Dixie said, "Do you believe me now?"

Ramirez trundled into the living room and plopped down on the sofa. "How is that even possible? What the hell is going on? I've never seen anything like that in my life."

Dixie knelt down and stared into his eyes. "It is possible. It does happen. Adam can change into a canine. He's the wolfhound I brought to your house tonight. How else would he be wearing your clothes? And Sonny Russo is involved. He controls Adam's pack. He's what they call The Alpha."

"So all this time," he said, staring straight ahead as if in a trance, "we've been after real live werewolves? Like Adam?"

"No, not werewolves. And certainly not me," Adam said at once. Then with a wave at Bane, Adam said, "Maybe him. Certainly Mikael. Maybe others from my pack. That's what I'm hoping to find out. My sister told me about something called The Convergence." He took a step toward Bane. "We need to find out as much as we can about that from him. Ten minutes, Detective?"

Ramirez nodded in slow motion.

"Hey." Adam patted Bane's cheeks. "Wake up. That's right, open your eyes."

Bane shook his head. Again he struggled, trying to

break the restraints.

"I've got some questions for you." He got in Bane's face. "I suggest you answer them or the detective here is going to have to put a bullet in your worthless head."

Bane spat on the floor again. "I'm not afraid to die."

"I'd be willing to bet you are." Adam put a thumb on Bane's throat and pressed. Bane gagged. Ramirez watched, but didn't move.

Adam lightened the pressure on Bane's throat. "When does The Convergence begin?" He waited while Bane recovered with a series of loud coughs. "When and where." With no answer, he pressed his thumb down on Bane's windpipe again. After several seconds, he eased off and allowed Bane another chance to answer. "Tell me when and where." He placed his thumb on Bane's throat again.

"Wait. It's starting tonight," Bane said.

"Where?" No answer. Another press on the throat.

"At our house. Claremont. The Alpha owns the entire hill. All the packs are meeting there tonight."

There was a banging on the front door. Ramirez pulled his gun and released the safety. He took aim at the door. Another loud thud.

Adam whispered, "Be careful, it could be Mikael."

"Adam, he's changing," Dixie shouted. All eyes turned to Bane. His elongated snout opened wide revealing large yellow fangs. All of his human skin drooped, sliding onto the floor from under his clothes. A pool of blood formed at the base of the rocking chair. His claws sliced the twine around his torso like knives cutting through licorice ropes.

"Stop," Ramirez said, aiming the gun at Bane.

Bane growled and jumped out of the chair. Detective Ramirez fired once, bringing down the wolfhound.

The front door crashed open.

Chapter Twenty-One

Detective Ramirez faced Colonel Dayton, each man aiming his weapon at the other. The front door lay between them in splinters on the floor.

"Detective Ramirez, don't shoot," Major Ransom said. "Please, lower your sidearm."

He complied, as did Colonel Dayton. Both men holstered their weapons.

Dixie stormed forward. "You broke down my door. Who the hell are you?"

"Sorry, ma'am, I heard a shot." Dayton took a cautious step over the threshold.

Ramirez motioned at Bane's carcass. "That thing was about to attack. I had to kill it."

Major Ransom and Colonel Dayton approached the dead wolfhound with tentative steps. The colonel leaned over and studied not only the animal, but the pile of human remains beside it. "Oh my Lord." He turned to the major. "Is this what you saw in your dream?"

She nodded. "They can change from animal to human, and back again. A sort of werewolf, but without need of the moon."

"Without need of a wolf, either." Adam spoke up. "I don't know who you are, but that's not a wolf lying there. He's a canine—a Giant Irish Wolfhound to be exact. One of the largest breed of canine in the world."

"Adam," Dixie said with a smile, "maybe we

should know who we're talking to, don't you?"

"Dixie," Ramirez said, "meet Colonel Jon Dayton and Major Jean Ransom of the NSA. They're working with us on the task force." He turned to face them. "But I don't understand why you're here?"

Dayton moved forward and tightened his lips.

"It's okay, Jon," said Ransom, "go ahead and tell them."

"Major Ransom possesses certain abilities that prove quite useful to the NSA in these types of investigations." Colonel Dayton smiled, seeming pleased with his explanation. "She had some type of a vision tonight—hallucination, actually—isn't that right, Major? And, well, we thought—"

"Stop, Jon, that's enough." Ransom approached the detective. "We're actually from the United Nations." She held a hand up as both Ramirez and Colonel Dayton opened their mouths. "We work for, what you might call, an off-the-books department—extremely hush-hush. No, we don't usually hunt werewolves, and yes, I do have certain abilities. I'm called an Empath. I'm able to focus on visualizations that appear to me."

"Like a medium," Dixie offered.

"That's right, very much like that. Some people," she gave Dayton a quick glance, "call it mind-reading, but it's more involved than that. I can also collect thoughts—ideas, visions—from those with a particular need." She turned to Ramirez. "Those in distress. That's why we're here."

"You're a little too late," Ramirez said, eyeing Bane. "The distress has been put down."

"One of them has. There are others—hundreds, in fact."

Ramirez cocked his head. He felt the other foot about to drop.

"In my vision, I saw Claremont Estates. It's under attack, right now, by these beasts."

"We're not beasts," Adam said.

Colonel Dayton reached for his firearm.

Dixie stepped between Adam and Dayton. "Oh no you don't. Adam isn't a threat."

"She's right," Major Ransom said, "he's trying to stop what's happening."

Dayton removed his hand from his gun and relaxed, but still kept a watchful eye on Adam.

Ramirez faced Ransom. "What do you mean 'under attack'?"

"Call your office," Ransom said, "I've already called mine. The National Guard should have a perimeter set up around Claremont Estates by now."

Ramirez pulled out his cell phone and dialed Metro. "This is Detective Marco Ramirez, I want to speak to Sheriff Hendrickson. What? Oh my God, when?" He hung up and faced Major Ransom. He spoke in a halting, slow whisper, "The National Guard has sealed off the roads. Several distress calls were made from our units onsite. It's a massacre. Sheriff Hendrickson is dead."

Dixie put a hand on his shoulder. "I'm so sorry, Marco."

He turned to the major. "But how could you have known…"

"My vision. I called our home office and set up the response." She turned to Dixie. "The message I received tonight came to me from someone very close to you—your aunt."

"Aunt Rose?" Dixie's eyes widened. "What has she got to do with all of this?"

"Everything. She needs to see you now—right now."

****

The drive to Aunt Rose's house is a bit awkward to say the least. Detective Ramirez is driving with Dixie, in tears, beside him. Major Ransom, Colonel Dayton, and I sit cramped together in the backseat, squeezed together like pickles in a jar.

The drive gives me time to think, to reflect on all that has passed between Dixie and I—between myself and the pack. I wonder what kind of future I might expect. I've heard people say, "Be careful what you wish for, you just might get it." I hope so. I want, more than anything, to live in the human world. I want to get to know people, to have friends. I want to grow old and look at my drawings, memories of my life as a human. Most of all, I want to be at peace—to know I did what's best, that I made the right choices.

"Don't worry, Adam," Major Ransom says. "I understand what you're going through."

When I first heard the major possessed a special gift, I thought it was some sort of trick.

"It's not a trick," she says.

I stare over Colonel Dayton at her. She reaches across the colonel and puts her hand on my knee.

I'm acutely aware of Colonel Dayton eyeing the major's hand and almost expect him to growl as he lifts it up like he owns it, holding it tightly in his.

"Don't worry," she says, her eyes still on me. "Just relax."

That's the last thing I can do. I look out the

window and concentrate on the passing desert. I force myself to think about Bane and Mikael and The Convergence—I keep my mind occupied with anything other than her rummaging through my thoughts like items at a garage sale. I think about Lucy.

"I'm so sorry for your loss."

"Stop it. I don't appreciate you being in my head."

"Stop right here," Dixie says.

Ramirez parks at the curb, and we pile out.

Aunt Rose opens the door and greets Dixie with an ear to ear smile—then she sees me. "Come in, my boy, come in." When I enter her house, I smell the rich aroma of baking bread. I love it.

"Aunt Rose, this is Adam." With a quick glance at Ramirez, she says, "Remember, the one I told you about the other day?"

"So this is Adam? You have no idea how glad I am to meet you, my boy—no idea at all."

"I'm sorry it's so late," Dixie says. "I don't know exactly why we're here. This is Major Ransom from the United Nations. She said you were in some sort of trouble."

"Oh yes, I sent for you," Aunt Rose says in a matter of fact tone. "Where's the conduit? Ah, there she is, and who is that with her? Oh well, never mind, introductions can wait; come in, come in. Marco, so good to see you again." She holds the door open and ushers everyone inside. "Dixie, why don't you ever answer your phone? I've been calling for hours."

"It's a long story."

We follow Aunt Rose into the living room. She guides Ramirez and Dixie onto the couch, and she gives me a wink and a pat on the back.

Her familiarity is a bit disturbing. "Do I know you?"

"No, my boy, but you will. Are you hungry?"

"No, ma'am."

"Well, you should eat all the same. I've got some nice hamburger in the fridge. Follow me." She clutches my hand and rushes me into the kitchen. Her surprisingly strong hands hook over my shoulders and sit me at the table. "Here you are, Adam." A plate of raw hamburger materializes in front of me. "Eat up."

"Aunt Rose, what are you doing?" Dixie comes into the kitchen.

"What am I doing? Oh my sweet Dixie, where to begin?"

Major Ransom squeezes into the small kitchen. "I can tell her if you'd like."

"No, my dear. Thank you for coming, but she should hear it from me."

"Hear what, Aunt Rose?"

A voice booms from the living room. Detective Ramirez and Colonel Dayton have gotten into a heated argument. Dixie and Major Ransom rush out of the kitchen.

"That should keep them busy for a while," Aunt Rose says with a grin. She sits next to me and holds both my hands. "My name is Rosalyn. I know all about you, but I had no idea you're the one my Dixie is sweet on."

Dixie's "sweet" on me? The message makes me feel warm—the messenger, however, leaves me cold. I'm still uneasy about Detective Ramirez knowing my secret, Major Ransom rummaging through my mind, and Colonel Dayton giving me the stink eye. Now I'm having a private chat with Dixie's aunt who says she knows all about me. This particular group of humans gives me the creeps.

"Oh, I'm far from human, my boy."

"What the…you're a mind reader, too?"

"I'm not as in tune as the conduit out there, but I have my moments. I couldn't contact my Dixie, but the conduit was easy to communicate with, and through her—well, here you all are."

Shouts come from the living room. Detective Ramirez and Colonel Dayton yell back and forth. Dixie and Major Ransom join in, trying to calm them down. The noise serves as background to my discussion with Aunt Rose.

"I wanted Dixie with me tonight, to keep her out of harm's way, but then she arrives with you. Sometimes things work out in just the right way, at just the right time. I believe your presence here tonight is more than mere coincidence—it might even be providence."

"I don't understand."

"You, and only you, will be able to blend in with the packs. You, my boy, just might be able to stop The Convergence."

I'm stunned. "Who are you again?"

With a sad smile, she says, "I'm a Daemon, not a bad Daemon, a good one." She says this as if I'm supposed to be happy. I'm just more confused. "They call for The Convergence tonight."

"They? What do you mean?"

"There are some who would destroy humanity. But there are others, like me, who would not. Their numbers are small, but their powers are great. I wanted Dixie with me tonight, to protect her as best I can. And then you," her smile grows, "you are here and I have a plan."

"But there's supposed to be hundreds of wolfhounds. How can I kill—"

"But you don't have to kill the wolfhounds. You only have to stop the Alphas. Without the Alphas, the packs are as disorganized as a collection of homeless coyotes. The Daemon control the Alphas. The Alphas control the packs. And the Alphas are only human, after all."

I hear what she's saying, but I don't think she's hearing me. "How many Alphas?"

"Oh, I would assume no more than twenty, maybe thirty."

"Is that all?"

"Yes, maybe a few more, forty or so."

She didn't catch my sarcasm.

"Yes, I'd say no more than fifty. You see, there are hundreds of wolfhounds and they are controlled by their Alphas. The Alphas are controlled by their Daemons. So, by my math, seven to eight hundred wolfhounds means seventy to eighty Alphas, controlled by six or seven Daemons. That's all."

I don't think more sarcasm would help.

"Now, my boy, in order to blend with the packs, you'll have to strengthen your powers. And there's only one way to do that." She stares at the plate of meat.

My stomach gurgles, and I shake my head.

"Honestly, killing humans is simple—and the Alphas won't expect your attack. It should be easy. Go for the throat—it's the most humane. Now eat."

Again, I shake my head.

"Do you understand? You may be the only hope Dixie has of survival. I don't know if I can protect her. I have no guarantees of safety should events go terribly wrong for the humans tonight. I knew at once what you were when you arrived on my front porch. More than that, I knew exactly why you were here."

I hear her, but I don't want to. She's starting to make sense.

"Now you need to eat. You have to be able to change at will. You need the capabilities of the other wolfhounds. If you don't meet them on their level, with their powers, you're as good as dead." That last word is followed by a smile. *What?*

"But, what if I kill you?" I point to the living room. "What if I kill all of them?"

"The creation spell was said to be flawed. The wolfhounds were tested, sent out to kill. Some, like you exhibited freewill. I know what you are, and I know what you're not. Hurry now, time is our enemy. Eat."

It's as if a light turns on. She's right. Lucy told me about the connection between red meat and controlling the transformation. That's why Mikael, Bane, and Flynn were able to change so quickly and without the pain. That's why they're all so strong, and how they're able to easily keep track of me.

The light that switched on in my head—the light I know Aunt Rose turned on, makes more and more sense. The Convergence won't stop itself. I have to be the wolfhound I was bred to be: a killer.

Chapter Twenty-Two

Blood-stained pavement. Body parts half covered in shadows. The battle for the house at the top of the hill was over; The Convergence had begun.

Sounds of occasional gunfire, screams, and mournful howls carried through the pine grove on the incessant wind. Dark clouds, illuminated by the three-quarter moon, drifted overhead—unsympathetic observers of the bloodshed below. A light rain began to spray down from the heavens.

Sonny Russo never signed up for this, not really. True, he hadn't complained about the money and power in exchange for his services. Also true, Gorgeous never kept the plan a secret. But now that The Convergence was a reality, it was time to get real. There was nothing for him here anymore. After all, exterminating the entire human race would put a serious dent in the casino industry.

He used to get depressed when he thought about the end of his empire. He hit the bottle pretty hard, hell, he hit everything pretty hard. But booze and violence didn't do the trick anymore, not like it did in the past when he was just another thug on the streets. This was different; this was Daemons and killer wolfhounds and end of the world crap.

He knew only one thing would help, the only thing that ever cheered him up: revenge. He began skimming the regular skim at the casino about a year ago and put together a getaway bag. The duffel bag crammed with credit cards, a passport, and enough cash to last him the rest of his life waited at the penthouse. That was true revenge—living a life of luxury on some little island a million miles away from the wolfhounds, The Convergence, and especially Gorgeous.

Somehow he'd managed to keep his little plan of survival a secret from her. Maybe she never thought he'd try anything as smart as that, who knew? Maybe she knew all about his plan, but never thought he had the guts to carry it out. Wrong.

From what he could tell, the other Alphas had also been well rewarded for their services but, for whatever reason, they seemed to accept their role as middlemen between the wolfhounds and the Daemons as part of the deal. They actually fought alongside their packs against the police. What a bunch of losers. Didn't they understand who the real enemy was in all this? Maybe their Daemons, or devils, or whatever the fuck they called themselves, kept a tighter rein on them than Gorgeous did him. Maybe.

In any case, he knew hanging around this war zone was out of the question. He'd had a good run; lived the good life, but it was time to get back to the penthouse, grab the bag, and hit the road.

He crouched behind a pine tree, concealed by shadows. Alphas and wolfhounds raced back and forth in a dizzying blur, but he kept still and out of sight. If anyone saw him, he'd use Plan A: feign injury and ask for help. After all, a lot of people were injured in the fight, he could hear them crying out for help in the distance. If that failed, he'd fall back on Plan B: the pistol tucked in his belt.

Another scream echoed through the pines. The few humans that were alive, those who'd managed to escape the house on top of the hill, were being hunted. A shotgun blast cracked. Another howl. Another scream.

He stood up, but stumbled right back down. "What the fuck?" He wasn't feigning injury; he'd actually taken a bullet in his leg. He took off his jacket, tore the sleeve, and wrapped it around the wound. Even though the blood was already clotted, gunshot wounds were tricky, a lesson learned from his life on the streets in Chicago.

He stood up again, slower this time, and glanced around. Claremont Road was empty, but he still heard footsteps, two legged and four, scampering through the pines. Gunshots were few and far between now, unlike the initial assault when bullets exploded like firecrackers on Chinese New Year. The New Year was here now—the new age—one that held no future for him if he stayed on this hill. But right now, the chances of escape looked bad. In casino speak: odds against.

He took a few steps, his head on a swivel. Gunpowder filled the air, mixed with the unusual colored mists hovering overhead, making visibility poor. With each step, he kept a wary eye on his surroundings. Each rustling in the woods, distant movement, or flash of gunfire made him shiver. The road started to dip down, slanting toward the bottom of the hill. He picked up his pace, the mêlée receding into the background. For the most part, the battle was behind him.

An unexpected grin crawled across his face. He was going to make it back to Vegas. The farther he scampered down the hill, the wider the grin became until soon, it was a genuine smile. His odds of escape looked better: even money now.

Two yellow eyes and a set of gleaming fangs materialized out of the fog ahead of him. There may have been more gunfire in the distance, but the low and steady growl from the wolfhound was all he heard. Reaching for his gun would do little good, the animal was too close. He fell to his knees and put his hands on the sides of his head. The joy of escape vanished, replaced by the fear of death in one agonizing heartbeat. He'd seen other humans ripped to shreds by the wolfhounds—and now, so close to freedom, it was his turn.

"Why do you kneel?" a woman's voice said.

He glanced up to see Nina, a member of his pack. She stood before him, naked, in human form, a quizzical look etched on her face.

"Where do you go?"

Sonny got up off his knees, expelling a genuine sigh. "I've been shot." He pointed to his leg. "I need a doctor. Come with me." All the authority, the power, of an Alpha resonated in his voice. "Help me."

Nina bowed her head, an acknowledgment of the command.

His spirits flew. With her by his side, riding shotgun, the odds of making it off the hill were now in his favor. Nina was a warrior—a little slow on the uptake but, for her role in his escape that was perfect.

Twenty minutes later, they reached the bottom of the hill. He saw a small group of Alphas and wolfhounds through the pine trees. They mingled near abandoned police vehicles at the crossroads. The wolfhounds lifted their snouts toward him and sniffed the air.

Sonny stopped, putting a hand on Nina's shoulder. "Let's go that way," he whispered, pointing to the right, away from the Alphas.

"But they will help you. Your leg needs tending."

"Quiet. I said go to the right."

They continued their march off the road which ran just parallel to them. They moved away from the group of Alphas. He kept the road in sight, looking for a deserted vehicle—a car, motorcycle, anything to take him away from this mess. He spotted a dark sedan, its driver's side door left open, parked thirty feet ahead. His spirits soared. He was so focused on the sedan that Nina's hand on his chest, pushing him back and stopping him in his tracks, surprised him.

A light gray wolfhound stared at them a few yards ahead. It blocked their path, the fur on the back of its neck bristling.

Sonny moved behind Nina. "Kill him," he whispered.

She did not move.

"Kill him now."

Nina transformed in an instant and pounced at the animal. In just a few seconds, she'd ripped the light gray wolfhound to shreds.

She hovered over the animal's carcass for a moment, then turned back to face Sonny. A shot pierced the night and she crumpled to the ground with a yelp, blood oozing from her thigh. Sonny tucked the pistol back under his belt and sprinted to the sedan. The keys were in the ignition.

He'd done it—he'd beaten the odds. Time to head

back to Vegas and cash in.

****

"I told you before, we're wasting our time here," Colonel Dayton said, his voice booming across the living room.

Detective Ramirez jammed a finger into Dayton's chest. "Listen, I don't care what you say. This is the way it's gonna be—"

"Terminum!"

Everybody turned to face Aunt Rose. A hush fell over the room as they realized the little old lady was the source of the great big noise. The fire in the hearth crackled, the only sound in the living room.

Colonel Dayton and Detective Ramirez stared at each other, both wearing faces that made it clear they wondered what they'd been shouting about only moments ago.

"Dixie, may I speak to you alone?" Aunt Rose held a hand out.

Dixie hesitated before taking her aunt's hand and following her into the hallway. As they passed the kitchen, she glanced in at Adam. Another man sat at the kitchen table next to him. He was about Adam's age, with a similar build. She couldn't help but notice a certain similarity in their eyes, not only in color, but intensity—passion?

Aunt Rose tugged at her hand and pulled her along.

Dixie entered her aunt's bedroom and sat down on the edge of the large queen-sized bed.

"My Dixie," Aunt Rose said, "where do I begin? There's so much to tell you, and so little time."

"Who was that man in the kitchen with Adam?"

"Oh, that was Ivan. I managed to summon him

here. He is in tune with our needs."

Dixie stood up, but was settled back onto the bed with a gentle push.

"Who's Ivan?"

"I'll tell you as much as I can, and then we must form a plan. All is not lost; the bridges have not yet been crossed."

"You're rhyming. Why are you rhyming?"

"Yes, I do that." A small chuckle. "We all tend to do that now and again."

"We, who?"

Aunt Rose told her about the Daemon, about The Convergence, and what led them all to be at her house tonight. Dixie sat quietly, enthralled by the story, not once questioning its veracity—Adam's very existence proved it was true. She remained silent well after her aunt finished.

"Did my parents know about you, I mean, what you are?" The question came all at once, and with tears.

"Oh, my little one, your parents were incredible; they were my dearest friends; we were inseparable. Have I ever told you that your mother could have been your twin? The same color hair, eyes—and your laugh: identical. When I close my eyes and you laugh, I almost think she's in the room with us. Did you know she majored in journalism?"

Dixie nodded.

"Honestly, every time I look at you…" It was Aunt Rose's turn to wipe away a tear. "Did I ever tell you she and I played tennis every chance we got? Can you believe it? She had the meanest serve, wicked fast with a lively spin. And cards. And bowling. And hiking—"

Dixie laughed and Aunt Rose closed her eyes.

“It’s as if we fed off each other’s energy. She was more of a sister to me than a friend. If we thought about something, we’d do it. Dancing, and roller skating, and golf—”

“And my father?”

“And your father. He was over the moon for you; you were the diamond in his eyes. He told me one night, ‘Rosalyn, I only want three things for Dixie, just three things.’ ‘And what would that be?’ I asked. ‘I want her to go to the finest school, I want her to have a remarkable career, but most of all I want her to be happy.’” Her voice trailed off and she stared at the floor. “Not long after he told me his three wishes for you, when you were just four years old, they died in that terrible fire. If only I could have seen it coming. But, of course, no one can see into the future, not even Daemons.”

“Sometimes, in the back of my mind, I think I remember that night. I have dreams about it, about the fire. I want to tell the world my house is burning down—I want to shout it out. But I can’t. I can’t open my mouth. I’m not even able to tell Mom and Dad to get out of the house. It’s as if, I don’t know, as if—”

“As if you were under a spell. And you were, sweetie, you were. The Daemon killed your parents. They started the fire.”

“What? Why did they kill my parents?”

Aunt Rose sighed, a heavy burden kept for years. “The battle between good and evil is always at work. An evil Daemon, one known as Gorgeous, killed your parents. She is the driving force behind The Convergence. Your parents stopped The Convergence years ago. Your parents were killed because of it.”

"But The Convergence is happening again. That means they died for nothing."

"Nonsense. Don't ever think that. Without their sacrifice, who knows what would have happened. It's up to us to stop The Convergence now. And with your friend Adam, I think we just might be able to do it."

Dixie sat on the bed, trying to digest everything Aunt Rose said. "So, my parents were Daemons? Does that mean I'm a—"

Aunt Rose held Dixie's hand and smiled. "Of course. I adopted you. I couldn't have gone on living without you. I wouldn't want to. And you *did* go to one of the finest schools in the country."

Dixie nodded. "Harvard."

"And you *have* begun a remarkable career."

With a quick laugh, she said, "I have indeed."

"But, are you happy?"

"What?"

"A simple question, my dear. Your father's final wish: are you happy?"

"I'll tell you tomorrow, if there is a tomorrow."

Aunt Rose stood, drawing Dixie up with her. "Oh, tomorrow will come. You'll see. Have a little faith. It will come."

Dixie blushed. "I hope you're right but, you said so yourself, no one can see into the future. And that's okay with me. I don't know how many more surprises I can take."

"What do you mean?"

"Well, let's see: I find out my parents, *and* me, are something called Daemons; that the end of the world is scheduled for tonight, and the man I love is a dog—enough surprises for one night, wouldn't you say?"

"Canine," Adam said from the hallway with a grin. "I'm not a dog, I'm a canine."

Aunt Rose gave Dixie a hug. "I'll leave you two alone, but only for a moment or two. All too soon we'll have much to do."

Dixie smiled and sat down on the bed. "You're rhyming again."

Adam shuffled into the room, past Aunt Rose, and sat next to Dixie. "Did I hear the word love?"

"I must be crazy, but you heard it because I said it."

Adam smiled. He kissed her lightly on the cheek. "You know, I still have so much to learn about the human world. But one good thing about canines is we tend to give love unconditionally."

Chapter Twenty-Three

"Well now," Aunt Rose said to the gathering in the living room, "I think it's time we put our heads together and discuss our plan."

"Our plan?" Colonel Dayton said, glancing away from the TV. Aerial shots of Claremont Estates from a news helicopter delivered scenes of soldiers spreading out and shooting into the night. A reporter's voice in the background sounded nervous giving a hesitant description of events half seen by the camera. "The only plan that makes any sense is to call in an air strike."

"Oh that would have been an excellent idea," Aunt Rose said, "about three hours ago."

Colonel Dayton turned red in the face. "What the hell are you talking about?"

"I have it on good authority that the perimeter established by the National Guard has been breached. The wolfhounds are now advancing on the city."

"And how the hell would you know that?"

"Hey, that's my aunt," Dixie said, "and this is her house. Show a little respect."

Aunt Rose put her hand on Dixie's shoulder. "Thank you, sweetie. But I think I can handle this one on my own."

Dayton leaned forward. "What the hell do you mean by that?"

With a snap of her fingers, Colonel Dayton sat down and closed his mouth. A smile planted itself across his face. Major Ransom crouched down and stared into his eyes.

"Oh, don't worry about him," Aunt Rose said as if describing a medical condition, "he's in a happy place."

"Set him free," Major Ransom said.

Aunt Rose approached Colonel Dayton. "If he promises to listen more and speak less, then the spell will be removed—and stop cussing, young man. I don't like that kind of language in my house."

Colonel Dayton, still smiling and staring forward, nodded.

Aunt Rose snapped her fingers. "Good. Now time is growing old. Adam and Ivan will infiltrate the wolfhound packs. That will be easy for them. The hard part is for you, Marco."

"Me? What's my role?"

"An essential role: You will be their Alpha."

"You can't be serious."

"Oh yes, very much so. The two of them would be under immediate suspicion from the other packs if they appeared to have no tie to an Alpha." She held up a hand as both Dixie and Ramirez began to speak. "It's how they know who to trust. Those without an Alpha are suspect, seen as interlopers, and cast out."

Dixie shook her head. "Cast out?"

Aunt Rose steadied her gaze on her niece. "Killed. But we needn't dwell on that. I will form the bond. It's a simple matter." She closed her eyes and placed her right hand on Adam's head, then on Ivan's, then Detective Ramirez's. "There," she said with a laugh, "it's done." She glanced at Colonel Dayton who held his hand up in the air.

"Yes, do you have a question? A civil question with no cussing?"

"I do, ma'am. I understand what they'll be doing out there, but what about us?" He motioned to Major Ransom.

"As little as possible. You two wouldn't stand a chance, being humans. And that goes for you, too, Dixie."

"But Aunt Rose, I'm not—"

"Enough. My mind is made up about that, young lady. Major Ransom will inform us as to what's going on. She'll be able to communicate with Marco. Colonel Dayton will secure the house. You and I will sit tight. Any other question?"

"You said you have a source. Somebody who told you the wolfhounds had broken through the lines. Who is it?"

"One of my kind. That's all you need to know."

Detective Ramirez cleared his throat and wiped his forehead. "Where do we begin? I mean, what do I even do?"

Aunt Rose closed her eyes and tilted her head, as if listening to a distant voice. "The packs are venturing up Las Vegas Boulevard, just south of Silverado Ranch. The freeway has been shut down by the police. Evacuation of the hotels has begun. I suggest you three make your way south on Las Vegas Boulevard to Blue Diamond Road. That would be a good place to slip into the battle, lots of room there." She opened her eyes and stared at Ivan and Adam. "Remember, you won't have to kill the wolfhounds. Concentrate on removing the Alphas. Without the Alphas, the packs won't fight—

they'll have no will, no direction."

"And how do we recognize the Alphas?" Ramirez said.

"We'll know who they are," Ivan said. "They'll be easy to spot."

"One last question." Ramirez stood up. He hesitated before speaking. "How do we recognize a Daemon? More importantly, how do we kill it?"

Aunt Rose wavered a bit, then. "Each Daemon has its own color, its own essence. There are as many Daemons in the world as there are colors. Also, they have their own aroma."

"Like cinnamon and roses?"

Aunt Rose frowned. "No need to worry about all that. If you find yourself close enough to a Daemon, you'll probably be dead."

Dixie jumped up and hugged Adam. "You don't have to do this."

Adam wrapped his arms around her. "Yes. I do."

"It is important to know a Daemon can take many forms, any form it desires. You may be able to feel the power it emits, but that may be too late."

Colonel Dayton snickered. Aunt Rose turned to him. He cowered in his chair, a film of sweat covering his face.

She smiled at him. "You felt that, didn't you? I wasn't even trying."

"Humor me, Rose," Ramirez said. "How do we kill a Daemon?"

Aunt Rose deadpanned: "Disembowelment. Beheading. Fire."

"Which one?"

"All three."

****

I sit in the living room and listen to Aunt Rose along with the rest of them. I'm sure on the outside my appearance is calm and cool. On the inside—that's an entirely different story. In the back of my mind—as a distraction—I tell myself Dixie loves me; a human woman is actually in love with me. That doesn't help. Ivan, Detective Ramirez, and myself are about to venture into the wilds of Las Vegas and face packs of killer wolfhounds. I don't know much about warfare strategy, only what I've seen on TV and in movies, but what we are about to do seems like a suicide mission. I can't keep that thought to myself.

"Aunt Rose, I have just one question."

"Yes, Adam? What is it?"

I almost say "when," but I change that word at the last second. "If we're killed, what happens to you, to Dixie?"

"You won't be killed."

"How do you know? Why don't you get out of here while you can and head north? You've got to leave Las Vegas. Wouldn't that be the right decision?"

She brushes my concerns aside. "You said you had just one question. That's at least three. Besides, we have Colonel Dayton and Major Ransom here to protect us. Everything will be just fine, my boy. You'll see."

I wish I shared her optimism. My stomach gurgles. Is it all the meat I crammed in my gut, or is it my fear? Maybe both.

"Remember all the crap we had to put up with?" Ivan says. "The Alpha treating us like dogs? Carl taking us out on those night kills? We fight against all that. We fight for ourselves, for the humans, and for Lucy."

"For the Gipper?"

"Who?"

Ivan had embraced his human side, but not as much as I had. My reference was not in his scope of understanding. I smile at him, a grim, stiff-upper-lip type smile. "For Lucy."

He pats my shoulder. "We would not kill then, when that was what they wanted. But they will not stop us now."

His confidence is infectious. And that's just what I need. I need to think about Lucy. I need to remember what I want for my life. I give him a "follow-me" nod. "We'll be right back. C'mon, Detective. If we're going to be a pack, we need to practice."

Detective Ramirez hesitates. "What are we gonna to do?"

"Let's go out to the backyard and try a few transformations. I've never caused it on my own before, not without a world of pain."

Ivan grins. "You can do it, Adam. There's nothing to it, just follow my lead."

We race out the back door with Detective Ramirez in tow. I keep my eyes on Ivan. The three-quarter moon gives us a little light, enough to stumble over a couple of lawn chairs. In a few seconds, Ivan is out of his clothes and his wolfhound is pushing through his human skin. His snout elongates, and his paws form. I hear the cracking of his bones, but he isn't in any pain—not that's apparent to me, anyway. It takes about half a minute for his transformation to be complete. He stands before the detective and me as a Giant Irish Wolfhound, and howls.

Fear of the pain—of the unknown—stops me. I

take off my shirt in slow motion. Ivan barks, urging me on. Lucy's words echo in my head, "You have to really, really want to change." With a last look at Ramirez, I drop my pants and concentrate on the change. The first thing I notice is my skin slipping off me like a heavy sheet blowing in the wind. My feet slide out of my shoes as my paws form. I hear my bones crack and reform as well, but it doesn't bother me. I'm standing on all fours. I've transformed in a few seconds. There is no pain. I howl.

"Oh my God," Detective Ramirez says.

I *hear* him say this; I understand the words coming out of his mouth. Ivan brushes up against me, and we tear around the yard. For the first time in my life, the first time I can ever remember, I know what it is to be a canine. I'm free.

Ivan and I sit on our haunches, just in front of Detective Ramirez. The connection Aunt Rose has woven between the three of us is something I've never felt before. Even though I know he's not my true Alpha, he's the Alpha I want. I'd do anything for this man. The feeling isn't forced, it's natural. This is a bond, not bondage.

I sense Detective Ramirez getting a little flustered. I'm sure he's never been in this position before, and he's at a loss for what to do. I take it upon myself to help him out. With a nudge at Ivan, I convince my brother to back up a few paces. He follows me around to the side of the house, out of the detective's sight. Ramirez needs to call for us so we can give him the confidence of being in charge.

We wait around the corner. Nothing. What the heck is the detective doing? I glance around the corner and see him. Ramirez stands with his back to the door, doing nothing. He looks confused. He notices me and just stares. I back around the corner again and wait for him to call. He needs to call Ivan and me so we can respond—do what he commands, but he's got to command first. Nothing.

Training humans proves to be more difficult than I'd imagined.

Ivan prances straight to the detective, rises up on his hind legs, and leans forward putting his full weight on the man. Ramirez extends his arms and yells, "Get off!" Ivan complies immediately, sitting perfectly still at the detective's feet. Or is he *on* the detective's feet?

"Back off." Ramirez starts to get it. "Come here, Adam."

Ivan scampers back about a yard, sits down, and glances up at Ramirez. His tail is wagging. What more does Ramirez need to see that he's in charge? I follow Ivan's lead and jump up, leaning onto Ramirez's chest. Again, "Down. Move back." I comply as quickly as I can.

I must admit, I enjoy the feel of the wind running through my fur, the freedom to dash around the yard as I please, and the security of knowing the Alpha has got my back. For a brief moment, I think about what my life would have been like if I'd had a devoted Alpha, one with my best interests at heart. Maybe my longing for the human world would not have been so strong. It's hard to tell. After all, this is the first time in my life I've ever enjoyed being a canine.

Then I remember the bond formed between Detective Ramirez, Ivan, and myself is false. Aunt Rose invoked a spell to make it so.

I also can’t stop thinking about the reason behind the bond. To go to war. To kill.

Chapter Twenty Four

"C'mon, let's get out of here," Colonel Dayton whispered to Major Ransom. Aunt Rose and Dixie hurried into the kitchen to watch the goings on in the backyard from the window. He'd held the major back in the living room. "We'll get some backup and—"

"What? No. Didn't you just hear Aunt Rose explain the plan?"

"The plan? Are you out of your mind?"

"No, but I'm in yours and what you're thinking is out of the question. There's no way I'll ever be a part of that."

Dayton studied her face. She was serious. She'd forgotten why they were here.

"I haven't forgotten anything. You have no right to harm these people, let alone kill them. That's not why we're here."

"Those two—outside—those aren't *people*. The UN needs one of those hounds."

"Why? Proof of werewolves? Proof of a plot to end humanity? Do you think all this madness will end because we have proof? No, we've got to do exactly what Aunt Rose says to stop this attack."

"The military will stop this attack, not some old lady."

"She's more than an old lady, Jon. Didn't you see her eyes when she spoke? And the fire flare when she entered the room? That old lady is probably humanity's only hope."

"Okay, listen to me, I'll try and make this real simple. We have an opportunity here—a chance to verify the existence of unexplained paranormal activity. That's why this unit was created. That's why the admiral sent us here. That's our job." Dayton's brow gleamed with sweat. His voice rose with each word until he was shouting at her. "Now let's get the hell out of here and—"

A shadow moved across the major's face. Dayton turned, throwing a punch on instinct. He caught Aunt Rose square in the stomach. The old woman doubled over, wheezing and gasping, unable to catch her breath. Dayton jumped up and grabbed Ransom's hand. "Let's go while we can."

She wriggled free of his hold. "No, I'm not leaving."

He stared at her for just a moment before dashing out the front door.

The neighborhood was alive with activity. Cars sped up and down the street, probably in a wild race to get out of the neighborhood. Shouts of: "Oh, leave that behind, let's just go," and "Hurry up, the werewolves are coming," echoed across the block. Children cried and dogs barked. Palm trees lined the street, bowing in the furious wind. The smell of a recent downpour filled his nose with the grit and grime of the street.

Dayton had no intention of leaving Major Ransom behind, but she'd given him little choice. She didn't understand the opportunity that presented itself: the chance to capture an actual werewolf. And once the military destroyed all the others, the UN would have the only living specimen in existence.

He glanced inside the detective's car. No keys. The front door of the house opened so he crouched down behind the sedan.

Aunt Rose's voice carried on the breeze. "Colonel Dayton, come back inside. It's much too dangerous out there. Come inside where you'll be safe. Don't be so reckless."

"Yeah, right," he mumbled, "safe inside a Daemon's house."

He waited until he heard the door shut then jumped up and sprinted across the street. He turned north on the sidewalk, still running as fast as he could. Most of the houses he passed had the lights on; no doubt their doors were locked as they watched the horrors of the attack on live television. This neighborhood was miles away from the main action and these people were safe—for now.

Dayton reached into his coat pocket searching for his cell phone. It wasn't there; more than likely it fell out when he bolted from the house. He was certain Aunt Rose would send the two werewolves after him. He sprinted a few more blocks, flying up one street and down another until he felt it was safe. He needed a phone.

He climbed the steps to the front porch of a house in the middle of the block and banged on the door. It creaked open a few inches, a wary eye staring at him from inside.

"What you want?"

"I need to use your telephone. It's an emergency."

"Go way."

The door would have slammed shut, but Dayton

kept his foot wedged in the threshold.

"Please." He thrust his NSA badge up. "I need a phone."

"You'll need a doctor when I shoot you." The homeowner shoved the barrel of a pistol through the crack. "Go way now."

Dayton backed up and stumbled down the steps into the front lawn as the door slammed shut. People were frightened—he heard it in their voices as they evacuated the neighborhood. They might need more persuasion than a fake NSA badge to be of assistance. He eased his own pistol out of its holster.

A door flew open across the street and three people ran out of the dark brown stucco house. They scrambled into a sedan and it raced out of the driveway, burning rubber as it headed for the end of the block. It narrowly missed another car backing into the street.

Dayton ran toward the house. With one kick, he broke an opening through the door, reached inside, and unlocked the deadbolt. The house was vacant. He flipped on a light switch and found the telephone in the kitchen.

"Admiral Garrison, this is Dayton."

"Thank God, Colonel. Are you all right?"

"Yes, for now. Hundreds of werewolves are attacking the city. They've broken through the military lines and are headed for downtown Las Vegas."

"Yes, we've been following the news from here. Las Vegas seems to be the city hit hardest so far."

"The hardest hit? What do you mean?"

"Other cities are under attack: New York, San Francisco, Paris—"

"Listen to me, sir. Listen to me. These are not

werewolves—well, not in the traditional sense. They were created…" He swallowed hard and shook his head before he said it, "With a spell cast by Daemons."

Silence on the other end of the line.

"The dogs are able to transform from wolfhounds into humans as they please. They mean to kill every real human that crosses their path."

"How do you know all this?"

"I managed to hear it all from a Daemon. Major Ransom and I came face to face with it tonight. The plan is to destroy humanity. They're calling it The Convergence."

"Who's calling it that?"

"The Daemons. According to them it's the beginning of the end."

"Well, the U.S. military is forming a plan of attack as we speak. It may be a bit dicey at the moment, but they'll soon set it right, there's little doubt of that. In the meantime, I need to know your status."

"I'm on my own, sir. Major Ransom is being held by the Daemon, and I have no idea where Cuthbert is."

"Oh my lord. Is the major alive?"

"Yes, the last time I saw her. In any case, sir, I have a plan. I'm going to capture one of the creatures, and I'll need an exit plan."

"No, Colonel. The council has changed its mind about—"

"Sir, we've got to study the beast, find out what makes it tick. You said yourself other cities are under attack. This may be our best chance of knowing how to stop them."

Another stretch of silence. "I'll put together a plan and call you back."

"No good, sir. I have no phone. Just have a team waiting for me at McCarran. I've got to go." He hung up and checked his watch. He knew an extraction team could be scrambled and ready in less than two hours. Time was critical now.

He raced out of the house and down the street looking for just the right opportunity. A white Volvo with its engine running sat in a driveway a few houses down.

"C'mon Julie, hurry up. Them dogs are coming. Nobody cares if you're in your nightgown." A man stood in the doorway, his back to the street.

Dayton slipped behind the wheel of their vehicle and drove away. He saw the man running after him in the rearview mirror. "Tell Julie I'm sorry," Dayton whispered, "the greater good, and all that."

He drove in circles for a few minutes until he found his way back to Aunt Rose's house. Detective Ramirez's car was gone. He parked the Volvo across the street and jumped out. The front door of the house opened, and he ducked down. A garage door opened; the hinges were so loud they could have raised the dead. Lifting his head for a look-see, he observed Major Ransom, Dixie, and the Daemon enter the garage.

The sound of a footstep behind him froze his blood. He turned and looked up.

"Hello, sir," said Cutty.

"Get down, out of sight." He tugged on Cutty's shirt and dragged him down to the ground.

"Whoa, what the—"

"Quiet. How did you ever manage to find me?"

"GPS in your phone. You been outta touch for a while so I figured I'd find out what you and Major

Ransom were up to, you know, if you needed any assistance. All hell's broke loose in Vegas tonight, I couldn't just sit around and do nothing." Cutty gave Dayton a toothy grin.

Dayton shook his head. Would Cutty's presence complicate matters? "Where did you park?"

Cutty pointed to the black sedan halfway down the block. The car would stand out far less than the white Volvo.

"Let's go. I want you to follow the car that's about to pull out of this garage."

"I don't understand."

"Good."

****

Detective Ramirez drives around the neighborhood for a few minutes, searching for Colonel Dayton. He can't believe the man punched Aunt Rose. I can't either.

That's not all that confuses me. Before we piled into the car, Dixie put her hands around my neck, pulled me down, and kissed me—right in front of Detective Ramirez, Major Ransom, Aunt Rose, and Ivan. It took me by surprise and still lingers in my mind as we head south on Las Vegas Boulevard. Was it a kiss for luck? I've seen that in a movie called *Star Wars*. I need time to think about what it meant, but there isn't any. We're headed into the war zone.

Our side of The Strip is almost empty, just a few cars darting across our path then turning onto side streets. The opposite side of the road, the side heading away from the battle, is bumper to bumper—a line of headlights as far as I can see. Ramirez floors the gas pedal, and we scream down the boulevard. We zoom past The Grotto, across Sahara Avenue, and come to the major hotels on Las Vegas Boulevard. Vehicles are crowding over onto our side of the street. The hotels are being evacuated and emergency vehicles, their blue and red lights flashing, seem to be everywhere.

Ramirez slows down, but keeps heading due south. He steps on the brakes as people dart out in front of the car. It's slow going through the throngs of people rushing past us.

"We may have to get out soon," Ramirez says. "It's a long way to Blue Diamond from here. You two can probably make it by foot in a few minutes."

"Aunt Rose wants us to stick together," I say. "Besides, if we transform right here it would only cause more panic."

"The freeway's no good, it's blocked off."

"Why don't you try Paradise?" Ivan says.

Ramirez makes a hard left and bolts toward Paradise Road. He's braking, accelerating, turning and cursing, but still manages to pull his cell phone from his pocket and dial.

"Ed, this is Marco. I know. Can you believe this shit? Listen, I need a favor. Can you get to The Grotto? Find that son of a bitch Russo and arrest him. He's behind all this. That's right, Sonny Russo. Trust me, I'll explain later. I'll do my best to meet you there as quick as I can. Yeah, the whole world's gone nuts. Thanks."

The car skids through a few intersections and suddenly we're past the airport and driving through a tunnel. There's a car on fire in the opposite lane, blocking traffic for miles. Hundreds of people are on foot running north through the tunnel.

"We'll be there in about five minutes," Ramirez

shouts.

"Ivan!" I have to yell to get his attention. He's focused on the human drama playing out through the window. "Ivan, how do I spot an Alpha?"

"Easy, nothing to worry about—wow, did you see that?"

He seems mesmerized by the events around us. But he's not at all a passive observer. His eyes are wide and he's shifting around in his seat, turning back and forth to get the best view. His excitement reminds me of a human's pet dog riding in a car for the first time. He's literally bouncing up and down in his seat.

"Ivan. Tell me, how do I know which human is Alpha, and which are not? It's important."

He doesn't bother looking at me as he answers, "The Alphas have a power you can feel, like a magnet—a magnet that grabs your soul."

"My soul? What does that even mean?"

"Haven't you ever felt that pull from our Alpha? It's something you just feel. Like when he comes into a room—you don't have to see him to know he's there. You just know."

"I haven't spent as much time around him as—"

"Wow! Did you see that car? It just flipped off the overpass!"

Ivan's too excited to talk right now, and I'm afraid it will only become worse the closer we get to the front lines.

Ramirez jams on the accelerator and flies down the 215. "Couple more minutes."

Traffic is thinning out, only a few desperate drivers on the highway, most racing away from the conflict.

"Get ready you two. It's time to get ready."

Ramirez reminds me of a pilot in an old World War II film telling the troops it's time to jump into the battle. And maybe he is.

Ivan stares at me and gives me a wink. It surprises me. He's so animated—electrified—by the upcoming fight. I wish I had one tenth of his enthusiasm.

He starts to transform. His snout elongates, but a few human words still slip past his wagging tongue, "Wow! Look at the—woof—" The words stop. He's changed.

I do the same, stripping off my human skin and piling it on the car seat next to me. We're both in our furry battle gear now. It's time to jump into the fray.

Ramirez jams on the brakes and opens the doors for us. "Let's go." He leaps out and we huddle together, ducking low and out of sight, shielded by the car.

We're in the middle of a few dozen humans. They're running for their lives. Two policemen run with them, shooting back into a pack of wolfhounds chasing after them. Ivan darts away from us and jumps past the wolfhounds. He tackles a man in a black suit. The man screams and sprawls on the street as Ivan rips out his throat. The wolfhounds chasing the group of people stop and stare at each other. They scamper off into the desert. Taking the Alpha down has removed them from the fight—just as Aunt Rose promised.

"One down," Ramirez says. "Let's find another pack."

Ivan made it look so easy. He eliminated the Alpha with no problem. I'm hoping I can do the same when the time comes. Dixie's kiss may have been for luck, but I'll need more than that to get through the night. Besides, did the luck move to the wolfhound when I transformed, or am I reading too much into it?

Oh, what's the use, maybe, as the song says, a kiss is just a kiss.

Chapter Twenty-Five

Sometimes adrenaline can be your best friend. Sometimes it can get you into trouble. I'm sure what makes me pick out a pack of wolfhounds and run past them toward their Alpha is adrenaline. I'm just not sure if it's the best friend kind or the trouble kind. The wolfhounds I run past send menacing stares and vicious growls. Are they wondering why I'm running in the opposite direction, or trying to figure out who I am? A few of them snap their jaws at me. As far as I can tell, it's just reflex, a warning to keep clear or lose a limb, nothing personal. I count five of them hunting down a group of teenagers who wound up in the wrong place at the wrong time.

The wolfhounds work as a team, flank the kids on either side, and herd them up against the side of a block wall. Nowhere to run.

Ivan is right, I sense their Alpha. He's a man positioned behind the pack—enjoying the anonymity and safety of the shadows. He's walking slowly, almost as if it's just a stroll in the park. There's a crooked smile edging its way across his face, as if he's anticipating the coming massacre of the teens. I sense he likes the power, the control he has over his pack—over life and death.

I gallop toward the man and leap into the air. Just before I land on the Alpha and put my full weight on him, his smile vanishes, replaced by shock; he's opening his mouth to say something. I'll never know what it was he wanted to tell the world. His throat is in my mouth—I taste the iron in his blood. His body goes limp under me. It's over in just a few seconds. My first kill.

I turn back and stare at the wolfhounds surrounding the teenagers. There is no attack. The canines back away and seem confused, disinterested in their prey. A helicopter flies overhead and a searchlight illuminates the scene. The wolfhounds scatter. The teenagers run away.

"Way to go," Ramirez yells. He points to his left toward another pack of wolfhounds on the run.

Woof. Ivan races past me and through the advancing pack of wolfhounds. He dives at the Alpha, ripping the man apart. The wolfhounds slow down, turn, and scurry off into the desert. One of the members of the now disbanded pack of wolfhounds, a particularly oversized male with a long scruff of gray beard comes back into view and jogs toward me. Killing humans is easy; fighting a fully grown Giant Wolfhound will be another matter entirely. I steady myself and prepare for the worst.

Ivan is at my side at once. He's noticed the gray beard wolfhound zeroing in on me. Ivan is covered in the blood of his kills, he's been fighting hard and is exhausted, but it's still good to know he's got my back.

Graybeard approaches us, his large eyes focusing on me. The closer he gets, the more purposeful his stride becomes. In just a few steps, he's standing nose to nose with me. Just then, I realize what he's up to. Aunt Rose said not all of the wolfhounds trained to kill passed the test. Some, like me, exhibited freewill. Graybeard wants to help us in our fight. I can not only sense this, I feel it in my bones. We have an ally.

Ivan catches on as well. He nudges graybeard with his snout. He's pushing him toward the next pack. Graybeard sprints past an advancing pack and tears into the Alpha behind them. The kill is quick and ruthless. The pack disperses and wanders away.

Hopefully, Graybeard is the first of many allies we'll pick up as we go along. My spirits are lifted until I lift my head and look around. As far as I can see there are waves of advancing wolfhounds galloping straight at us. They won't attack us unless they know what we're doing. As far as they're concerned, we're just another pack searching for humans to kill. And they're right, as long as those humans are Alphas, but they have no way of knowing that.

Ramirez appears and takes up a position a few feet from us. He plays the role of Alpha well, motioning with his hands, pointing out targets. Little do the real Alphas realize, as they're pointing out human targets to their packs, Ramirez is pointing them out to us. And we respond—Ivan, me, and our new recruit. Ivan takes down the next Alpha Ramirez motions to. I kill the one after that and Graybeard dispatches the next. But not without incident.

Aunt Rose had formed the bond of a pack between Ivan, me, and Detective Ramirez using a magic touch, or spell, or charm—whatever she did, the other packs believe it. They know we're a pack, they can sense it, and leave us alone. Not true for Graybeard. He has no pack, his Alpha is dead. The wolfhounds that pass us by begin to slow down and sniff at Graybeard. He's a loner, a canine without a purpose. As far as they know, he has no business being here. If we don't do something soon, he'll be torn to shreds.

It takes only a few seconds for Graybeard to be surrounded by a pack of four wolfhounds. They ignore their human prey long enough to size up this perceived threat to their war. Ivan barks and Detective Ramirez pulls out his handgun. It all happens in an instant. Ivan attacks first, taking down a wolfhound in one vicious bite. Graybeard engages another, and I tear into a third. Ramirez shoots, and before I can catch my breath I realize what we've just done: we killed four wolfhounds in as many seconds.

"C'mon," Detective Ramirez says, "we gotta get back to the car before the rest of them catch on to what we're doing."

He's right, of course. There are too many eyes on us now, both wolfhounds and Alphas. We may have gotten lucky taking down the four canines, but we'll need more than luck to stop the hundreds more behind them. Ramirez sprints to the car and dives in. He opens the passenger side door and the back door. Graybeard follows Ivan into the backseat, and I jump in next to Ramirez. Our tongues hang out of our mouths. We're all panting so hard, the windows fog up in a few seconds.

Ramirez turns the key, fiddles with a few of the controls, and the condensation evaporates. Dozens of yellow eyes surround the car accompanied by menacing growls and salivating mouths. Ramirez throws the car into drive and the engine shudders. The car is dead.

****

"Aunt Rose," Dixie said, "do we know what's

happening? Is everything all right?"

Aunt Rose put her hand up for silence. She closed her eyes and breathed in a deep lungful of air. The fire flourished, crackling to life. "I don't hear anything, either good or bad. This is disturbing. My source has gone quiet."

"Who is your source?" Major Ransom said.

Aunt Rose opened her eyes. "A trusted friend, one of my kind. In fact, many of my kind are here tonight to help, but something is wrong."

Dixie shook her head. "We can't just sit here while Adam, Ivan, and Marco are out there risking their lives. We've got to do something. I just don't know what that something is."

"Maybe it's me," Aunt Rose said, putting her hand on her stomach. "Maybe your colonel punched me harder than I thought. Let me try again, shall I?" She closed her eyes and the fire ignited into a dazzling array of blinding light. It changed into a greenish color, and finally fluttered down to an even flame. Aunt Rose shook her head. "No, it's not me. It must be my source. I'm afraid something is very wrong indeed."

"C'mon, Major," Dixie said, "we've got to get out of here and do something."

Aunt Rose sighed. "No, Dixie, you've never been to war. You've never fought a battle against creatures such as these."

"Yes, I have. I killed a wolfhound—hit it with my car—they're not so tough."

"And what are you proposing? To run over them all?"

"If I have to."

"You're not thinking straight, my dear. No, you

must stay here. I'm keeping you out of harm's way. There's an old saying: they also serve who sit and wait."

"I've got a new saying: I don't want to sit and wait."

Major Ransom put a hand on Dixie's arm. "I'm with you, Dixie. There's another old saying, Aunt Rose: it's time to break our duck."

Aunt Rose cocked her head. "Dogs?"

"Ducks. It's an English saying. It means there's a first time for everything. I've never been to battle either, and yet here I am, a major in the Royal Marines. It's time we stop sitting and waiting and do something. What do you say, Dixie? Shall we venture out?"

Dixie grinned. "Let's go break some ducks."

"I forbid it," Aunt Rose said.

"I'm a little too old to be forbidden." Dixie tried to open the door, but it would not budge. "Aunt Rose! Open the door this very instant."

"No, it's just too dangerous. They aren't ducks; they're Giant Wolfhounds hell bent on destroying humanity."

"Then come with us," Major Ransom said, "we could use your special skills."

Aunt Rose blushed, turned, and then snickered. "It's been a long time since I've been to war. A very, very long time. It's an awful thing, you know—meeting the enemy on the field of battle. Taking a life."

Dixie hugged her aunt. "I know. And right now Adam, Ivan, and Marco are doing that very thing. And they're alone. We can't cower back here while they take all the risks. We should do everything we can to help them."

The door flew open as if caught by the wind. "You are the most headstrong woman I've ever known."

Dixie smiled. "I'm my mother's child."

Aunt Rose stopped Dixie from racing out the door. "No. Your mother would never rush blindly into anything. She always had a plan. She was very careful."

"Uh, didn't you mention skydiving?"

"Yes, well, she was careful in a reckless sort of way. What I mean is she and I tackled danger together. We always watched out for each other."

"And you'll watch out for me."

"For us," Major Ransom said.

Aunt Rose nodded and put her hands on their shoulders. "Yes, I'll be with both of you. And I'll do my very best to keep both of you safe. Now you do have a plan, don't you, my dear?"

"I do indeed."

Aunt Rose raised her palm in the air as they scampered out of the house. The garage door rolled open, screaming into the night on rusted rollers and hinges. "I rarely drive it, only now and then." She pointed at the 1957 green and white Chevrolet Impala. "It's in great condition. The engine purrs like a kitten."

"You're full of surprises tonight, aren't you? I never knew you owned a car."

"It's not a car, sweetie. It's a classic."

They hopped into the sedan, Dixie behind the wheel, Aunt Rose beside her, and Major Ransom in the backseat.

"Now, about that plan," Aunt Rose said.

Dixie turned the key and the engine did, indeed, purr like a kitten. She hit the gas pedal a couple of times, and the sound changed to the roar of a tiger. She pulled the knob on the dashboard for the lights and rolled down the driveway into the street. "I think we should pay Mr. Sonny Russo a visit."

"Russo? Why is that name familiar?" Major Ransom said.

"He's the most powerful man in Vegas. The main man on The Strip." She shifted into first and stomped on the accelerator. The Chevy raced down the street.

"Why him?"

"He's the one who raised Adam's pack. He should be able to give us some information."

"All we're after is information?"

"Hey, information is power. It's what I do. Trust me." She ran through the gears until they were flying down Las Vegas Boulevard.

Aunt Rose smiled. "That's my girl."

Dixie glanced at her aunt. The smile wasn't quite a smile. It was more of a grimace. "Is there something I should know, Aunt Rose?"

"I know who created Adam. I knew it when we met, but it didn't make any sense. I can see into Adam's heart, and I know his motives are pure. But still, I also know the Daemon who controls Sonny Russo—her picture's been in the newspapers, standing in the shadows behind him." Aunt Rose chuckled.

"What is it?"

Under her breath, but loud enough to be heard, "Has Gorgeous devised her own demise?"

Chapter Twenty-Six

Detective Ramirez tries the ignition key again. This time the engine roars to life; the sound aggravates the wolfhounds surrounding us. They paw and scratch at the sides of the car, the hood, and the trunk. Some of them leap past the windows and onto the roof. They pad around, clawing at the sheet metal. The steady drone of barking and growling increases as more of them bunch around our sedan.

Graybeard is going crazy in the back. He's foaming at the mouth, snarling, and howling at the wolfhounds outside. His ruthless intensity and gung-ho attitude was more than welcomed when he first joined our little pack, but now it's just plain annoying. If I were in human form, I'd tell him to "put a cork in it." Instead, in my current state, being more canine than human, I join in and bark as loud as I can. Barking, like yawning, is contagious to us.

Ramirez steps on the gas, cranks the steering wheel, and makes the car skid around in tight little circles. Wolfhounds fly off the roof, landing in heaps several feet away. There's a thud-thud-thud as the vehicle strikes several of them. When the mob of wolfhounds is somewhat cleared, Ramirez lets off the gas, straightens out the wheel, and then hits the accelerator again. We slam into more than a few canines as we drive away. I glance through the rear window and see some of them chase after us. Ramirez is doing about sixty, and we leave them in the dust.

"I'm going to go around the block and sneak up behind them. If we're lucky, they won't hear us. We can go after the Alphas again."

Even though I appreciate his enthusiasm, I'm not looking forward to round two. We've already faced swarms of killer wolfhounds, taken down several Alphas, and picked up an ally, but the odds of surviving another battle seem stacked against us. Ramirez doesn't consult me. He doesn't have to, he's in charge.

Graybeard has calmed down, but still seems jittery. We make a series of rights around the block and swing in behind the mass of canines who had just surrounded us. Wolfhound carcasses are strewn about the parking lot in willy-nilly fashion.

My thoughts linger on Dixie, on what might have been, but now seems so far out of reach. I force those thoughts away as Ramirez flips off the headlights and cuts the engine. The car rolls forward to a slow and noiseless stop. He reaches back and pops open the rear door. Ivan and Graybeard slip out of the vehicle like ghosts. When Ramirez opens the passenger side door, I jump out and watch Graybeard sprint toward the enemy.

"No!" Ramirez shouts. "Come back." But Graybeard doesn't obey, Ramirez is not his Alpha.

The element of surprise is gone. Hundreds of yellow eyes are on us at once.

"Get back in the car."

But it's too late. Graybeard charges full speed toward the wolfhounds. Ivan and I exchange a quick glance. It would be suicide to go after Graybeard and try to stop him. I'm not even sure we *can* stop him if we catch him. He's hell-bent on confrontation.

Without warning, Ivan takes off in pursuit. Against my better judgment, I do the same idiotic thing—three lone wolfhounds against one hundred. For whatever reason, thoughts of Dixie fill my mind once again. This time, I make no conscious effort to force them out.

Ivan catches up to Graybeard and paws at his hind quarters. This slows him down just enough for me to catch up. The fastest of the oncoming packs are on us. I'm knocked to the ground, but manage to roll and jump right back up. A wolfhound is on me and Ivan lunges at it, sending it to the blacktop. He bites the hound, it yelps, and staggers away. I tear into the flesh of an attacking wolfhound, blood spurts across my snout as the canine drops to the ground. Graybeard brushes past me. Two wolfhounds are latched onto his flesh. He yelps. They chew into him; a violent shaking of their heads sends blood spurting everywhere. His struggle is over. Graybeard is dead.

More wolfhounds arrive. Ivan is, by far, quicker and deadlier than most of our attackers. He dispatches several wolfhounds and keeps them off of me as best he can. Ivan is a true warrior. Although I do my best to keep up, I'm tiring. There's just too many of them.

My vision is blurry; my eyes are covered with blood. The smell of it permeates the air. As more enemy combatants arrive, I give in to the fact that it's almost over. We're horribly outnumbered. It feels like everything is moving in slow motion. I begin to anticipate the fatal bite that will end my life.

Three gunshots blast through the night in rapid succession. Ivan, me, and our attackers freeze in place for a moment. Three more shots. Bullets zip past my head and wolfhounds begin to fall. Detective Ramirez has driven up to us and stands outside the car, firing his pistol into the fray. The passenger's side door is open.

"Get in!" Ramirez yells as he fires more rounds.

I try to move, but feel the heavy claws of a wolfhound rip into my hind quarters. I fall to the ground and look up behind me. It's Mikael. His face is covered in blood. He pounces at me, opening his jaws as he goes for my throat. I roll away, and he falls flat on the pavement. A bullet whizzes past his head, followed by my paws tearing into his left ear. If he were human, I'd say the look he gave me was one of shocked-surprise. Since he's a wolfhound, the look is fear.

Mikael had come to Dixie's house to kill both me and her. I open my jaws and bite into the fleshy part of his shoulder. He yelps and tries to stand up. He can't. His neck is exposed and just waiting for my bite. It comes quick. His blood fills my mouth. Mikael lies motionless on the ground, his eyes open, staring at the clouds.

Three large grays tumble to the ground in front of me. Ivan runs past me, a wolfhound right behind him. Ramirez fires at it, but misses. The wolfhound bites Ivan. He yelps.

"C'mon, Adam, get in the car." Ramirez aims at the wolfhound on Ivan and picks him off with a clean shot.

I bite into the throat of an attacker, hack the blood from my mouth, and scamper to the car. Ivan joins me. He's bleeding badly. A wolfhound jumps at him, but is brought down quickly by another shot from Ramirez. Our attackers are treading with caution now. They see the danger of a direct assault and scurry around, trying to flank both sides of the vehicle.

"We gotta go, Adam." Ramirez jumps in behind the wheel and revs the engine.

Ivan lunges at me and I stumble backward, landing half inside the car. I try to stand up and get out, but Ivan presses me into the car. Ramirez grabs me by the scruff of my neck and yanks me fully into the front seat. I nip at his hand, canine instinct.

The sound of helicopters above us fills my ears. Bright lights and bullets rain down from the sky. A few bullets penetrate the roof of the car and bury themselves in the backseat. Dozens of wolfhounds fall dead around us. The rest scatter, fleeing into the shadows of the black desert.

I turn and look for Ivan only to see him being dragged away by two huge wolfhounds. When Ramirez hits the gas, the car door slams shut. We race away as the two wolfhounds tear into my brother's flesh. His cries of pain fade away fast—my memory of his heroism never will. If he hadn't prodded me into the car, I would have been ripped apart.

I'm exhausted. It takes me a couple of minutes to fully change back into human form; the process drains any energy I have left. I lay back in the seat, covered in a bloody coat of torn fur.

Neither Ramirez nor I speak.

Finally, he looks at the bite on his hand. "Am I going to become a wolfhound?"

I shake my head. "I'm not a vampire." I sit up and take a deep breath. "I'm a Giant Irish Wolfhound." And proud of it.

****

Sonny Russo heard the military helicopters overhead. At least he thought they were military, who the fuck knew? It took him over two hours to make the normally twenty-minute drive from Claremont to The Grotto. The car he'd stolen was a piece of shit Hyundai and the route he chose, staying off The Strip, took him through areas of Vegas he'd never seen before.

Hundreds of people were out in the streets, some looting, some evacuating, and some just out. It was early in the morning—two or three a.m.—and a heavy blanket of rain and heat hung in the air.

The scene in front of The Grotto reminded him of the Chicago riots of the sixties. People milled about, darting across the street, and generally just getting in his way. And the expression on their faces gave him the creeps: they were angry. Angry at being booted from their rooms; they were pissed at the world. He palmed the sweat off his face with one hand and banged on the horn with the other. People who had been happy campers just a few hours earlier—playing nickel slots, taking a dip in the pool, chowing down at the buffet—now banged on the hood of his car, flipping him off, and screaming at him.

"To hell with this." He stopped the car in the middle of the street and got out. Someone brushed past him, jumped into the driver's seat, and drove off, hitting several pedestrians. More screams, more panic.

Sonny began to think it might have been a bad move to come back here. Even though his getaway bag lay stashed in the penthouse, how would he ever get away with it? Somebody crashed into him from behind. He turned around and threw a punch at the hapless old man. The old man fell to the ground, his hands on his bloody nose. Nobody came to the man's rescue, nobody offered assistance—no one said a word.

Under any other circumstance, this would have been the world Sonny preferred: survival of the strongest. Fuck the weak. But things were different now. The world had changed in just a few short hours. With killer wolfhounds and Daemons, he was on the side of the weak—a side he'd never experienced.

He turned and surveyed The Strip. Above and to the south, helicopters flew in formation, lighting up the sky with gunfire. Some of the familiar hotel signs—The Mirage, The Venetian, The Wynn—were dark. And then there was the sound. The sickening roar of humanity—screaming, crying, yelling, shouting. It sounded like the fans at a freaking football game echoing through the canyon of casinos.

He raced into the lobby of The Grotto and another sound assaulted his ears: silence. Not a staff member in sight—no security personnel, no cashiers, not even a bell hop. Garbage was strewn everywhere, including half packed bags discarded near the elevators. Food and clothing dirtied the hallways of his hotel. He wanted to throw another punch at someone, at anyone. This was *his* hotel, his baby. People were fucking pigs.

Sonny kicked through the trash and stopped at his private elevator. He slammed the call button, an elevator normally guarded by one of his rather large security thugs. An unexpected smile appeared. Forty flights up, forty flights down and he'd be gone. Screw Vegas. Screw The Grotto and screw Gorgeous.

Ding.

The doors slid open and Sonny's eyes widened. The barrel of a pistol pointed at his forehead. He froze in place.

"Who the fuck are you?"

"FBI. C'mon in, Sonny, I've been waiting for you. Let's take a ride up to your place. The view is amazing."

"Fuck you, you can't—"

The hammer of the gun cocked. "Shut up and get in. Oh and slip that pistol out of your belt and throw it behind you, nice and slow."

Sonny complied with the order and entered the elevator.

"Let's go." The FBI agent eased around him into the car. "There's only one button."

Sonny pressed the button and the doors closed. He faced the front of the car, hands at his side. "Who are you?"

"Agent Miller."

"What do you want with me?"

"A friend of yours, Detective Ramirez, asked me to drop by and babysit."

The high speed elevator whisked them up to the fortieth floor. An express trip, the private car made no other stops.

Ding.

The doors slid open to Sonny's luxury penthouse. He hesitated before stepping out. The thought of Gorgeous waiting for him played in his mind like a horror flick, looping over and over, since he'd planned his escape from Claremont.

He glanced around the suite. No sound, no movement. It was empty.

Both men stepped off the elevator, and the doors shut behind them.

"Over there on the couch," Miller said, waving to the white settee. "Have a seat. Ramirez should be here soon."

"What's this about, anyway? Why the fuck are you here?"

"Ramirez told me some interesting things about what's going on out there…and your connection to it."

"Me? That's ridiculous, I'm legit. I even offered to help the detective find the Werewolf Killer. Just ask him, he'll tell you. Listen, this whole city is going to hell, and I gotta get outta here before it does. See them choppers over there?" Sonny stood up and pointed out the windows to the south. Helicopters, seven blocks away over The Bellagio, were nearly in line with his finger. "One of them could make a mistake, you know, shoot the wrong way, and we'd be toast. I'm telling you we gotta—"

"Shut up and sit down." Miller took aim at Sonny's head. "That's all you gotta do."

Sonny complied and eased back into the settee. "Okay, okay, just watch it with that gun, boy."

Miller cocked his head. "What did you call me?"

"Nothing, sir. I'm from the south, that's just the way we talk. Don't mean nothing."

"You're from the south all right. South Chicago. I know everything about you, tough guy. What I don't know is how the gaming control board ever let you set one foot in Las Vegas. Why don't you tell me who you paid to make *that* little miracle happen?"

Sonny grinned. "I got myself a guardian angel. I've always been lucky that way."

"Just a lucky guy, huh?"

He had to think of a way to get rid of this G-man.

He peered past the agent and out the window again. The helicopters were slowly moving north toward The Grotto. A bright flash appeared from one of the gunships. The nose of the chopper see-sawed up and down. A smile spread across Sonny's face.

"What are you smiling for?" Miller lowered the gun. "Is there something funny about this situation? If there is, please tell me, 'cause I just don't get it."

A helicopter started spinning in the sky, guns blazing. Sonny followed the line of tracers arcing through the air.

"Oh, you're about to." He slid off the couch, covered his head, and landed prone on the marble tile.

"What the hell are you—" Miller hit the floor at the first sound.

Glass sprayed everywhere as bullets buried themselves in the walls of the penthouse. A blast of hot air flew into the suite through the gaping remains of the shattered window. The wind knocked over statues and dislodged paintings from the walls. Sonny felt as though he'd been trapped inside a wind tunnel.

The FBI agent lay still on the ground. He no longer held his gun—that was the good news. The bad news: the gun was nowhere in sight. Sonny stood up and kicked the agent's head. A quiet moan and Sonny knew the man was out. Kicking the agent felt good. So good, in fact, he kicked him again, harder this time.

"You come into my fucking house and hold a gun on me?" He kicked at the agent's head again, then again. A pool of dark blood oozed across the white marble tile. Sonny brushed glass from his coat sleeves and spit on the agent's back. Wind churned through his hair and ruffled his suit. He shouted, "Not in my house, boy. I'm Sonny Russo, you fuck, the luckiest man in Vegas."

Chapter Twenty-Seven

Rules of the road no longer applied. Whatever the color of the stoplight, the order of the day called for full speed ahead. Dixie kept her foot pressed hard on the accelerator ever since leaving Aunt Rose's house. Major Ransom rode shotgun and Aunt Rose sat in the backseat, leaning over with every high speed turn.

For the most part, Dixie applied the brakes only when necessary: to avoid pedestrians, abandoned vehicles, and oncoming traffic using her side of the road. Many streetlights, and some rather large neon signs, had gone dark.

"Someone's following us," Dixie said as she stepped on the brakes, swerved to the right, then punched the gas.

"How can you possibly tell?" Aunt Rose turned her head and peered through the rear window. "There're at least a hundred cars behind us. As far as I can tell, they're *all* following us."

"Well, one of those cars has been with us since we left your house."

"How do you know that?"

"The brights are on and one is way brighter than the other. It's so annoying." She made a hard left. "See, it made the turn right behind us."

Aunt Rose straightened up. "Give me a little warning next time, dear."

"It's Jon," Major Ransom said. "I guess he's decided to join us after all."

Dixie shrugged her shoulders. "Why would he do that? Honestly, I have no idea why he bolted in the first place. Do you?"

"No, he wouldn't say."

"No, not in so many words," Aunt Rose said. "But we both know why he's here now, don't we, Major?"

"Hold on, we're here." Dixie hit the brakes and slid to a stop just outside The Grotto. "This is where Russo lives. He has a penthouse on the top floor. If he's here at all, that's where he'll be."

Major Ransom waited for a group of people to stagger past the car before she hopped out. Dixie joined her, then turned and craned her neck, making eye contact with Aunt Rose who sat still in the backseat.

"Let's go, Aunt Rose. We're here. I'm going to need your help—we both are."

"You two go on ahead. I'll park the car."

"What are you talking about? We won't get a ticket for parking in the street if that's what you're worried about. Tonight is self-park anywhere you want."

"Dixie," Aunt Rose gave her niece "the look." "I love my car and I will not leave it in the middle of the street. I'm going to park it properly in the parking garage. Now run along, I'll be with you in a few minutes."

"But Aunt Rose, we've got to hurry."

"Hurry on then."

"We've got to stick together, you said so yourself."

Aunt Rose's eyes sparkled for just a moment, a bright green twinkle. "I insist. You go along. I'll catch up."

"Be careful." Dixie turned and waved to Major Ransom. "C'mon, let's go."

They ran into the eerie silence of the lobby, the only illumination provided by emergency lighting. It was apparent the hotel had been evacuated long ago, but one employee still manned the front desk.

"Excuse me," Dixie approached the counter. "Can you tell me—"

"Shit. Let's get outta here."

Another man popped up from behind the desk. Both men jumped over the marble counter and ran into the depths of the darkened casino.

"Looters," said Major Ransom. "What are you looking for?"

"Russo's private elevator. It's gotta be here somewhere."

"Over there." Major Ransom pointed to a small alcove just to the right of the main bank of elevators. The emergency lights flickered for a few seconds then came back on.

They rushed into the alcove and Dixie slammed on the call button. "Do you have a weapon?"

Ransom shook her head. "No. Do you have a plan—in case he's here, I mean?"

"No."

The doors slid open. Dixie entered followed by Ransom. The doors closed and the whirring of motors, cables, and gears sounded, lifting them up forty floors. They were both out of breath and leaned against the walls of the car. Dixie closed her eyes and used her focus technique to regain a semblance of calm. Her heartbeat evened out.

"What happened to your aunt?"

"She had to park the car."

"What? You left her down there to park the car?"

"I didn't mean to…I didn't want to, but she insisted. It made sense at the time."

"She insisted? What the hell does that mean?"

Ding.

The doors slid open. A warm gust of air hit their faces. A loud whistling rang out as the breeze rushed through the broken windows. The penthouse appeared empty. They scampered into the suite as the doors slid closed behind them.

"Agent Miller." Ransom darted across the marble tile and crouched down beside him. She felt for a pulse. "He's lost a lot of blood, but he's alive."

"My mistake." The voice came from down the hallway. Sonny Russo stepped into the living room holding a duffel bag in one hand and a butcher knife in the other. "I guess I'm a little rusty at the physical stuff. Back in the day, I woulda killed him with one punch."

"Sonny Russo," the name slid from Dixie's lips.

"Well, if it isn't Dixie Mulholland. I watch you every night."

"Thank you—er, I mean, tell me about your connection to the attack. Do you realize I saw you yesterday at—"

"Sorry, but you know how I hate interviews. I'm a little busy right now. If you'll excuse me, ladies." He marched to the elevator and hit the call button, waving Dixie to the middle of the room with the knife. "Must be a big night for you, darling; lots of things to report on. I hear reputations are made on nights like this. Too bad you won't have the chance."

Ding.

The business end of a gun pressed against the back of Russo's head. "Drop the knife, Sonny."

Russo let the knife clatter onto the tile and set the duffel bag down as his hands went up. "Detective Ramirez."

"Get going, slowly, to the middle of the room."

"Marco." Dixie rushed back to the elevator. "Adam."

"The mutt's here, too? What a surprise." Russo ambled to the settee.

Adam moved out of the elevator and into Dixie's arms. The elevator doors slid shut.

"What the hell happened?" Ramirez said. "Is Agent Miller okay?"

"He's alive." Ransom stood up. "But he needs medical attention."

"You son of a bitch." Ramirez marched toward Russo.

"Marco, wait," Dixie pleaded. "We need to get information from him."

Ransom raced for the phone. "I'll call the paramedics."

"It won't do any good," Ramirez said, "they won't respond. We'll have to drive him to UMC and hope they let us in."

"What do you mean?"

"If protocol is being followed, the city's in disaster mode: hospitals are locked-down, no response from emergency units—Vegas is under Martial Law."

Ding.

The elevator doors opened.

****

I don't know what Ramirez wants with Russo. He

doesn't talk much on the way. I keep pretty quiet as well. I'd just seen my brother, Ivan, murdered right after he saved my life. My mind is on auto-pilot as I put my clothes on. I've never been through anything like that before.

I stare at my hands. They're shaking. Then I realize I'm shaking all over. Every time I close my eyes, all I see is Ivan being dragged away from the car. He stared at me—straight into my eyes as if he wanted to say something. But, of course, he couldn't speak. Still, I felt some sort of a connection to him before the battle and during, but especially after. As he realized his next breath might be his last, I swear he said something to me, I know he did. Even if it was less than a whisper—more of a thought—I heard it. I caught it in my mind.

One word: accept.

I don't know what he meant by it. Accept what? All the possibilities race through my mind: accept the fact he would die? Accept the world and what it's become? Accept myself as I am? Or, accept all of it?

I may never understand what he meant by it, but I'll always know one thing for sure: I know he died at peace with himself, knowing he did everything he could to stop the madness.

And that's what it is: madness. More than half my pack is dead. Lucy, Ivan, Flynn, and Bane. And Mikael. And for what? A plan devised by something called Daemons to rule the world? How is that even possible?

"We're almost there," Ramirez says, bringing me out of my thoughts.

I struggle to put my clothes on in the car. "Where?"

"The Grotto. A member of the task force is there, and hopefully he's got Sonny Russo under arrest."

"Russo? What do you want with him?"

"Dixie told me he was your Alpha. I'll start there. I've got to find out what he knows about their plans."

"Aunt Rose said they plan to destroy humanity."

"Yup."

"Then what do you need him for?"

"It's a start."

He drives on the sidewalk when the road is blocked. He drives on the road when the sidewalks are blocked. The drive north is so slow. Too many people, too many cars in our path. Accidents clog The Strip—fender benders, T-bones, and roll overs. Crowds of wandering tourists, searching for a way out of the hell they found themselves in, whirl around us like plastic bags caught in the wind. Ramirez hits the brakes whenever someone darts out in front of us. When he mashes the accelerator down, my head jerks back. After an hour of this stop and go nonsense, I have a good idea what "car sick" means.

He skids to a stop in front of The Grotto and tells me to stay put. That isn't going to happen. Despite the heavy winds and light drops of rain, I still catch her scent. It's stronger in the lobby of the deserted hotel. Stronger still in the elevator. Dixie is here.

"Keep alert and stay behind me," Ramirez says, as he draws his weapon and flicks off the safety. We enter the elevator together. "Agent Miller is good, but that son of a bitch Russo is tricky."

The first thing I see when the doors open is Dixie. She looks helpless; she looks frightened. I want to run to her and put my arms around her, but someone blocks my way: The Alpha.

"Drop the knife, Sonny." Ramirez has his gun

trained on the back of The Alpha's head.

The Alpha drops the knife on the floor. He sets down a black bag and raises his hands. "Detective Ramirez."

"Get going, slowly, to the middle of the room."

My eyes are still on Dixie. She runs toward the elevator. "Marco." Then her gaze falls on me. "Adam."

"The mutt's here, too?" Russo says. "What a surprise."

When I get out of the elevator car, Dixie hugs me. Even though I'm covered in blood, I wrap my arms around her and squeeze her with all the strength I have left. I've lost so much tonight—I'm not about to lose her as well.

Chapter Twenty Eight

The sound of helicopter blades and gunfire is deafening. The packs have fought their way up The Strip to The Grotto and the battle rages on forty floors below. Choppers circle the building in a tight formation. The wolfhounds and their Alphas kill as many people as they can. This war is far from over. Spotlights shine through the windows of the penthouse, panning back and forth along the walls and floor. The gunfire sounds like cannons in the sky. It makes all of us shake when heavy rounds are fired toward the ground.

"What's the plan, Sonny?" Ramirez says, aiming his gun at The Alpha. "What's next on the agenda? We've got to end this now, and you're going to help us."

"Do you think she'd tell me what the fucking plan is? I did whatever stuff she told me to do, but now I'm out. That bitch is crazy—wacko—and I'm done."

"Who? Who told you to do stuff?"

Even though the gunfire pounds in my chest and makes my ears feel like they're filled with cotton, I hear the tap-tap-tap on the marble tile as a woman walks into the room. She's accompanied by a brilliant blue light. I have to shield my eyes against it. After a few seconds, it fades away. The smell of cinnamon and roses fills my nose.

"Detective Ramirez, how nice to see you again." The woman is dressed in all white and glides across the floor to the window. She sticks her head through the broken glass wall and surveys the battle below. Her hair and dress are tousled by the wind, but she keeps smiling, seemingly unafraid of the height. "It looks like my darlings are putting up quite a fight. Is it really fair to use military gunships against them?" She snaps her fingers and two helicopters collide, bursting into a ball of fire and whirl to the ground. She giggles. "That's better."

Ramirez trains his gun on her. "Gorgeous."

"You remembered my name," she turns to him, "how thoughtful, Detective."

"You're behind this—part of the Daemons Aunt Rose told us about."

"Rosalyn? She's still playing her part as the good little human? I wonder what side she'll be on when there are no more humans."

Detective Ramirez fires his weapon at her. The bullet slows in mid-air, hovers, then falls to the ground with a "clink." Gorgeous waves her hand at him. He winces and drops the gun. Steam rises from it as it lies on the tile.

She smiles. "How brave of you, Detective. I think I'll save you for dessert. But first, as an appetizer—Sonny. The bitch? Wacko? Really?"

The Alpha falls to his knees and starts crying. I've never seen anything so strange. This man held such power over me—over my entire pack—and now he's on the floor, begging for mercy.

"I didn't mean anything by it. I was stalling, trying to buy time until you came and rescued me. Please, sweetie, you know I'm a standup guy. I'd do anything for you."

"From what I hear, you've done quite enough." Gorgeous turns toward the hallway and nods her head. "C'mon girl, time for your entrance."

Nina is in human form. Her blonde hair cascades over her naked shoulders. She limps into the room, dried blood caked on her leg from her hip to her toes. She glares at The Alpha.

"Nina," he says, standing up on shaky legs. "There you are. What happened to you? I lost you. Thank God you're okay."

"Why did you shoot me?"

"What do you mean shoot you? What are you talking about? She's lying, Gorgeous." The Alpha tries a smile, but fails at it. "I don't know what the hell she means; you know I would never dream of hurting one of your hounds."

Gorgeous stares right at me. "I can see that. You look well, Steel. A little worse for wear, but well."

I can only guess by her tone that she expected The Alpha to kill me when he had me locked up in the basement. If that was the case, Dixie rescued me just in time.

"It's too bad you and your human plaything won't witness the dawn of the new age. An age without war, without suffering," she turned to The Alpha, "without weakness."

The Alpha backs away as Nina limps toward him.

"I know how this might look, Gorgeous." He's trembling, tears streaming down his face. "You've got to believe me. I'm on your side." He holds a hand straight out, palm up, but keeps retreating to the broken window. “Stop, Nina. Stop right there.”

Nina doesn’t stop; she staggers forward, her eyes fixed on The Alpha. She pauses next to Detective Ramirez and draws in a deep breath. Ramirez scampers away from her as if she’s contagious. She begins to scratch at her skin, slowly at first, and then with more purpose. Her snout elongates and her claws develop. It takes her no time at all to transform. Major Ransom hurries next to Ramirez, putting her arms around him.

“Okay, okay, Gorgeous,” The Alpha says, “if she was shot it was an accident, honest. You’ve got to believe me. Look, look at this, I was shot, too.” The Alpha attempts another feeble smile, but he missed the mark. He has nowhere to go; he’s backed up to the edge of the broken window. He takes a quick glance behind him then holds both hands out to regain his balance.

“Another one of your accidents?” Gorgeous shakes her head. “Look at you, Sonny. When I found you, you had nothing—a two-bit hood in a one room dump. I saw the potential in you and gave you everything: money, power, everything you ever wanted. All I asked was that you be loyal. Now you’re right back where you started.” She laughs. “You probably shot yourself.”

The Alpha is whimpering, big dramatic sobs. “I did everything you asked. You can still trust me. Why won’t you believe me? I’m as solid as they come.”

“No, Sonny. You gave it all up—and for what? Money?” Gorgeous points at the duffel bag and it rises in the air. “Is that all you want? Take it.” She flicks her finger, and the bag flies across the room at The Alpha. He clutches the bag to his chest with one hand while his other does little circles in the air to steady himself.

The wind rushing in through the broken window

fans his hair and his suit flutters like a sheet on a clothesline. Helicopters are right outside the window firing their weapons to the ground. The Alpha has nowhere to go.

The noise is overwhelming, and he yells over it, "I can make it right. Okay, so I ran and I'm sorry. Please, give me another chance."

"No more chances, Sonny." Gorgeous shouts over the noise, her smile still present. "There will still be room in our world for humans—mundane tasks and such—but there'll never be a place for anyone as pathetic as you. So here it is: you needn't be scared of me anymore, my sweet." She glances at Nina. "You have more immediate concerns at hand."

Nina creeps closer to him. The hair on the back of her neck bristles, her fangs bared in a snarl. The Alpha's choice is clear: have his throat ripped out, or jump. He backs just an inch and drops the duffel bag. A high-pitched scream fills the room. It fades away, covered by the sound of bullets, helicopter blades, and Nina's howling.

I'll never know if he decided to jump, or if he lost his footing and fell. In any case, The Alpha is gone and I feel a weight lifted off my shoulders. I have only one Alpha now; a true and honest Alpha I would do anything for.

Gorgeous glides back to the window and kicks the duffel bag over the edge. "Don't forget the money, you've earned it."

Nina stares up at Gorgeous.

"You must be famished." She twirls around and waves a hand across the room. "Why don't you grab a bite to eat before we go?"

****

Nina jumps for the nearest human—Major Ransom. Before I can transform, the major is splayed on the floor, blood spilling from every bite Nina has inflicted. Gorgeous laughs, a wicked, sarcastic cackle that drowns out all other sounds.

In rapid succession, Detective Ramirez seizes Gorgeous by the neck, the elevator door opens, and Nina slinks toward Dixie. I transform in an instant and pounce at Nina. My jaws latch around her neck and she crumbles to the floor. She yelps, claws at my snout, and buries her teeth into my shoulder; my turn to yelp. I'm stunned for just a second, enough time to realize she's going after her original prey: Dixie.

With a flick of Gorgeous' finger, Detective Ramirez flies across the room, crashing against the wall next to the elevator. He lays motionless on the floor. I scramble to regain my footing, ignoring the burning pain of Nina's bite.

Colonel Dayton emerges from the elevator, his gun drawn. As Nina jumps at Dixie, he shoots her in midair. Her carcass falls onto Dixie.

Gorgeous dissipates into a dazzling blue light. The light fills the room, illuminating everyone and everything. Colonel Dayton falls to his knees, his hands on his head. The pain that grips him also tears through me, contorting my face and bending my spine. Gorgeous is sucking the life out of us. Dixie screams, her body going into convulsions.

The sounds of war pierce my ears—gunshots, helicopters, and screams. The last thing I see before I pass out is a brilliant green light filling the room. I smell the warm aroma of baking bread reminding me of a sweet old woman welcoming me into her house.

With a booming crash, the room becomes nothing but white light. My head spins into darkness.

When I open my eyes, an angel hovers over me. Her tears fall on my face. She cradles my head in her lap.

"Adam, I thought you were gone." Dixie is crying.

"What happened?" I try to look around the room, but she holds my head steady in her hands. The sounds of helicopters and gunfire are gone. "The green light. What—"

"Shhh." She puts a finger on my lips, then replaces the finger with her lips. It's warm and quick, a kiss that takes me by surprise.

I put a hand on the back of her neck—a human hand—and kiss her back. Dull pain still rattles through my body, but it's a pain I can deal with. I try to sit up, but can't find the strength. "The green light. What was it?"

Dixie smiles. "Aunt Rose. She overpowered Gorgeous in a brilliant white light."

I manage to sit up with Dixie's help and glance out the window. Dozens of sparkling white lights explode like fireworks over The Strip. Streaks of various colors dart across the skyline, disappearing into the desert. "The Daemons are leaving."

"It's over." Dixie tightens her arms around me.

I turn my gaze to the penthouse. The first thing I see is Detective Ramirez lying prone on the floor. His eyes are shut, but his chest is moving—he's alive. Nina is sprawled out next to him, a pool of blood around her body. On the opposite side of the room, Major Ransom is lifeless; her body ripped apart by a beast. Agent

Miller is still breathing.

"Where's Aunt Rose?"

"I don't know." Dixie sobs and I hug her.

My face is nuzzled on her shoulder when I hear the thud and her body goes limp. My eyes shoot open; I see the business end of a pistol inches from my face. Dixie rolls away from me and crumbles to the floor. She's bleeding.

"Don't move you son-of-a-bitch." Colonel Dayton, his eyes red and raw, his jaw trembling, stands over me.

Rage is the only thing I feel. I narrow my eyes and hope I can transform as fast as Nina. Already I feel my incisors growing.

"Don't even think about it." Colonel Dayton whips the gun away from my face and points it at the back of Dixie's head. "Can you change into a dog faster than I can pull this trigger? Are you ready to take that chance?"

I freeze. Pain still ripples through my body. "What are you doing?"

"Don't be an idiot. I own you, mutt. You're coming with me."

"I don't understand. Why would you want me to come with you?"

"Believe me, mutt, if it were up to me I'd kill you where you are, just like you killed her." He nods at Major Ransom.

"But I didn't kill her." I point at my sister. "Nina did."

"What's the difference? She was murdered—torn apart—by a rabid dog. You or her, it doesn't matter. Get up slowly and get in that elevator or I'll shoot Dixie, then I'll shoot you." He cocks the hammer.

"Don't test me." His gaze darts over my shoulder, and I know he's staring at Major Ransom. "Believe me, I'd like nothing better than to put you down."

I get on my knees, then fight the pain and stand up. My head pounds.

Colonel Dayton nods to the elevator. "Don't even think about escape. We can make things real easy for Miss Mulholland. Or we can end her. It's your choice."

"We?"

I look back at Dixie. A man with scraggily red hair holds a pistol to Dixie's head.

Colonel Dayton barks an order to the man. "Keep her covered until you hear from me, Cutty. Understood?" The red-haired man nods.

I shuffle toward the elevator. "What do you mean make things easy for her?"

"Keep her alive. My people can make that happen, all they want is you. If you cooperate with us, she's safe. If you cause trouble, she dies. Simple. Now move."

We climb into the elevator and the doors begin to slide shut. The last thing I see is Detective Ramirez crawling on his hands and knees to Dixie. The man with red hair backs up and holds them both in his sights.

Chapter Twenty-Nine

"Good evening and welcome to Nightly News, your trusted source for information. Tonight's top story: The Las Vegas Disaster—what really happened? When we return."

The floor manager held his finger up, watching a small monitor on a metal stand, then yelled "And…out. That was great, Dixie, really terrific."

"C'mon, Terry, you say that every night."

"And I always mean it."

"Well then, keep saying it."

Makeup and hair rushed to the anchor desk and went to work on Dixie as if she were coming in for a pit stop at the Daytona 500. She let them have their way, realizing long ago they would anyway.

"Say, listen Dixie, I took a look at your copy," Terry said, leaning over, his hands resting on the front of the desk. "Are they okay with it upstairs? Nothing's in the teleprompter."

"Of course they are. You think I'd go on without approval? And don't worry about the teleprompter, I'll read from my copy, okay?"

"Wow. This is one hell of a story." He shook his head and moved back into position.

As the hair spray dissipated, she listened for the familiar buzz, then turned her eyes back to the floor manager.

"Four…three," he air counted to one then pointed at her.

"Welcome back. Tonight we take an in-depth look at what has become known as the Las Vegas Disaster. It's been six months since the Purdue Commission released its findings. The commission, appointed by the president and authorized by a joint resolution of Congress was given a mandate to investigate the events surrounding the horrible night when one thousand three hundred and twenty-two people lost their lives on the streets of Las Vegas, Nevada.

"The commission subpoenaed a total of seven hundred and twenty-three witnesses. They reviewed documents submitted by the FBI, NSA, CIA, Department of State, and the Attorney General of Nevada. They also scrutinized the records of the Las Vegas Metropolitan Police Department, the Department of Justice, the United States Air Force, and the Atomic Energy Commission—to name just a few."

"The commission also traveled to Las Vegas to visit the scene of the tragedy. After ten months of investigation, The Purdue Commission presented its final report to the president. Each of the nine members concurred with its findings. The final report, its related documents, and all pertinent information now reside in the National Archives, a permanent record depicting an American tragedy.

"But what did the Commission conclude? Allow me to quote, verbatim, from the official summary of the report:

"The Commission to investigate the Las Vegas Disaster, having completed its assignment in accordance with an Executive Order by The President

of The United States finds no single cause for the disaster. Rather, several factors combined to form a singular anomaly. These factors included: unseasonable weather conditions in the Sierra-Nevada Mountain Range, untracked and unchecked migrations of wolves and coyotes along the California-Nevada border, and a 6.5 earthquake four miles below the surface of the Spring Mountains in Nevada. In addition, other factors contributing to this disaster included: residual effects from above ground nuclear testing conducted over the course of several years north of Las Vegas, the general effects of global warming, and an extreme solar flare detected at approximately 6:05pm the night of the disaster. The cause of these combined elements, while tragic in its final outcome, in no way indicates the possibility of a future recurrence of an event of this magnitude. Therefore—"

Dixie leveled her gaze on the camera. "Please. The U.S. government spends millions of tax-payer dollars, including thousands of billable hours by the best attorneys in the business, speaks to hundreds of expert and eyewitnesses, and this is the best they can come up with? Basically calling the tragedy an Act of God? Well, this reporter isn't buying it." She saw the producer, out of the corner of her eye, running toward the set, his arms waving in the air. "Adam, I know you're out there," she said. "Don't lose hope. I promise to—"

"Commercial! Go to commercial," the producer shouted.

"And…out."

The cadre of makeup and hair artists descended on Dixie, only to be shooed away by the producer. He leaned on the desk and whispered in her ear, "What in the hell do you think you're doing? I got a hold of your copy, don't ask me how, but it was no thanks to you. You're not gonna read another fucking word of this shit on my show." He turned to the floor manager. "Get Bob in here, now."

Dixie put a hand on the producer's arm. "You can't do that."

"Listen to me, Dixie, and listen good, you got this job because of your link to the Las Vegas Disaster. The public connected with you, I don't know, felt sorry for you. Somebody upstairs gave the go ahead, and here you are. But just because you don't agree with the findings of the commission—"

"You call this bullshit findings? Solar flares? Weather conditions?"

"Are you insane? You're not going on the air with any crap about Daemons, talking dogs, or a UN conspiracy. What's the matter with you? We're credible news not Jerry Springer."

"But you said if I can prove—"

He turned away. "Get Bob over here, now! Get out of that chair, Dixie. Terry, go to black."

Dixie did not move.

"Get out of that chair or so help me security will haul your ass out. Bob, get ready. Carry on with the next story. Terry, countdown."

"Four…three…" Terry pointed at Bob who slid behind the desk as soon as Dixie stood up.

He fussed with the microphone and ran a hand over his hair. "Good evening once again. We continue tonight with a train derailment in Montana."

Dixie stormed off the set, unwilling to make eye

contact with anyone. She held the copy crumpled in her hands. Her cell phone rang.

"Aunt Rose. Can you believe they—"

"Of course they took you off the air. What happened to being subtle?"

"I can't do subtle anymore."

"Dixie, we talked about this. You have to play by their rules until you get in a position to make your own rules."

"That'll take too long. Adam and I don't have the time. You may live forever, but we won't. It's been more than a year now; I know Adam's out there somewhere."

"And we'll find him, I promise. We'll figure it out."

Dixie sat down and closed her eyes. Deja vu swept over her. She felt like her house was on fire again, someone she loved was in danger. But just as before, no one could hear her scream.

****

I don't know where they're keeping me. When Colonel Dayton threatened to hurt Dixie, I went with him; I would have done anything to keep Dixie from harm. But it's been six months now, and I haven't heard from Dixie, or Aunt Rose, or Detective Ramirez. Nor has anyone let me know how she is. All I can do is hope Colonel Dayton kept his word: Dixie's safe and well. As long as I keep that hope alive, I don't care what they do to me.

Sometimes, when I'm sitting in my cell, which has a lot more room than the little cages in the basement of the house on Claremont Street, I like to think of Dixie reading the news at one of the big network stations.

That's all she ever wanted, and I'm glad if I helped her get there in some way.

As for my daily routine: I give my captors almost everything they want. They've taken samples of my blood, urine, hair, saliva, tissue, spinal fluid, to name just a few. I hear the medical technicians talking about me—they speak to each other as if I'm a piece of furniture and am not listening—and how they're determined to "get to the bottom of my problem." Of course, I don't have a problem, except for their infuriating poking and prodding.

My cell is actually quite comfortable. I have a soft bed, a toilet and sink tucked behind a screen—there are four cameras in the ceiling hidden behind little globes of smoked glass—a writing table where they encourage me to write anything that comes into my mind. Of course, instead of writing I draw—pictures of Dixie usually, and scenes of Las Vegas, the way it was before. It's all from memory, and I think they're quite good, but who's to say?

They've also given me a large flat screen television, and I can watch it anytime I want. Sometimes the TV goes black. I can only assume a program is on they don't want me to see—something about what they now call The Las Vegas Disaster, or something about werewolves, or something about Dixie. So I watch movies mainly. It's funny, as a human, I can see everything in color, but my favorite movies are the old black and whites. Maybe because they tend to have more story—more emotion instead of relying on flashy computer graphics and technology. Give me *Casablanca* any day of the week. It's my all-time favorite.

I sometimes pretend I'm Rick and I'm being held in Casablanca (my cell) and because of an unselfish act, Ilsa (Dixie) can now live a normal life. I know it sounds childish, but it makes me happy and, after all, what else have I got except my own emotions?

I've only seen Colonel Dayton twice in the past few months. Both times, he's come to the little window in the door and looked in on me. He didn't say anything, just stared at me as if I were an animal in a zoo and then walked away. I'll never forget how he referred to me as a "mutt." I assume it made him feel superior to me in some way. Maybe he was angry at me because of the way Major Ransom died. I guess I'll never know.

At least once a week, I'm escorted from my cell, down a long hallway, and into a large white room. Inside are an MRI tube, a CAT scan machine, X-ray equipment, and other devices they use to examine my body. I don't know if they've found what they're looking for, and I don't care. At least this room is a change of scenery for me.

Once, I heard one technician talk to another technician about "the strangest DNA sequencing he'd ever seen." But that meant nothing to me. Like I said, the lab technicians tend to talk around me, and so it's not as if I had any say in the matter whatsoever. It's not as if I were in the hospital hanging on every word the doctors said about my cancer, or brain tumor, or anything I want cured. I'm not sick, and I don't need to be cured. So they run their tests and write their reports, and I suppose they'll keep on examining me until the day I die.

On a happier note, they feed me well. The food is

amazing: all sorts of international cuisine prepared especially for me. They let me request anything I fancy. I assume they're trying different combinations of food to see if that will stimulate a change.

It won't. I always make sure to order meat.

I know what they want from me, what they've been hoping for all these months, but I'll never give them the satisfaction. Lucy, Aunt Rose, and Ivan have taught me well. I know the more meat I consume, the more control I have over the transformation. And my captors give me plenty of meat dishes. I guess they think this will encourage a transformation. Little do they realize, it only gives me more self-control.

But in the end, Dixie taught me more than anyone else. She taught me about knowing what I want, and being who I am; she taught me how to change stripes.

Whoever it is keeping me prisoner will never get what they want from me for two reasons: one, because I will never give them the satisfaction of seeing the wolfhound—never. And two, because I've finally decided who I am and what I am: a human being.

A word about the author…

Richard Arthur Newberry lives in Las Vegas, Nevada. He considers himself a person who "cannot not write" and regards Las Vegas as a unique setting for his short stories and novels.

He has been published in The Writer's Block, an anthology, and placed second in the 2014 Las Vegas Flash Fiction competition.

Mr. Newberry, his wife, Betty, and their son, Samuel, share their home with Zady and Schnoodles, two loving rescue dogs who provided a world of inspiration for his latest novel, *Sin City Wolfhound*.

http://richardarthurnewberry.com

www.ingramcontent.com/pod-product-compliance
Lightning Source LLC
Chambersburg PA
CBHW060522260626
47161CB00003B/725

* 9 7 8 1 5 0 9 2 0 3 6 0 4 *